MW00528537

*To Zachary Lukas
Welcome to the
world of Midgard!*

CAUGHT
⟢—⟤ BY ⟢—⟤
DEMONS

LAILA OF MIDGARD
❖ BOOK 1 ❖

KATHRYN BLANCHE

First published in the United States of America in October 2018 by Kathryn Blanche

Library of Congress Control Number: 2018909455

ISBN: 978-1-7326651-1-8 (Hardcover Edition)

Also available:

ISBN: 978-1-7326651-0-1 (Paperback Edition)
ISBN: 978-1-7326651-2-5 (Electronic Edition)

The characters and events in this book are fictitious. Any similarity to real persons, living or dead, is coincidental and not intended by the author.

Editing by The Crimson Quill
Cover Art by: Damonza.com

Printed and bound in the United States of America
First printing October 2018

Distributed by Ingram
www.ingramcontent.com

Printed by Lightning Source

Visit www.kathrynblanche.com

ACKNOWLEDGMENTS

There are so many amazing and supportive people in my life, but there are a few in particular that I need to mention. A special thank you to Cindy, Brittnie, Eric, Rene, and Liz for always listening and helping me grow as a writer, and to my parents who are always there for me and continue to encourage me throughout this process.

CAUGHT
BY
DEMONS

PROLOGUE

Most people knew that the planet was overdue for a catastrophic event, but whether it would involve nuclear war, disease, or a natural disaster, nobody could foresee.

Most people lived their lives paying little attention to predictions of an apocalypse. Such predictions were merely stories meant to encourage them to live a good life, or to recycle.

Some people imagined that a Zombie apocalypse would occur from a disease that would reanimate the dead and turn them into mindless killing machines. Some were so fixated on this idea that they even began to create elaborate Zombie survival plans. Yet when it actually came, no one was prepared for the horror that would unfold.

This Zombie apocalypse, or The Event as it is now called, began in India and China and eventually spread to the rest of the world. Wars and politics were abandoned. Leading scientists rushed to find out what was causing long-dead remains to animate, and more importantly to find out how they could be stopped.

They found nothing.

These Zombies could not be killed and would slowly

reassemble themselves if someone managed to remove a limb or a head. Fire could reduce them to ashes, but even the ashes could regenerate.

They were totally unstoppable. And the worst part was that they would kill by whatever means possible, whether it was by eating you alive, slowly ripping you apart piece by piece, or even suffocating you. Once your heart stopped and all brain activity ceased, you would become one of them.

People prayed for salvation out of fear that they had offended their Gods, for that could be the only explanation for this apocalypse. Or so they thought.

The truth of the matter would turn all of human belief upside down.

As the remaining heads of state met for what they thought would be the last time, a strange group of people entered the hall. A woman, more beautiful than any mortal, with raven hair and purple eyes, followed by two men. One with a grim countenance and blood-red eyes who was pale as bleached bone, the other tall and strong with shoulder length brown hair and the brightest blue eyes they had ever seen. He was wearing a heavy gold necklace in the shape of a dragon curled around a large diamond. They each exuded an air of authority and claimed to know the cause of the apocalypse.

They asserted that the Zombies were created by a group of Necromancers—that is, Sorcerers who practiced magic of the dead and undead. What was more, they had an idea of where the Necromancers were hiding.

Naturally, the heads of state were unconvinced and asked for some sort of evidence to support such an outrageous claim. The three reluctantly revealed themselves as the Fae queen, an ancient Vampire, and a Dragon. They explained that they came from different realms or dimensions that were interconnected with Earth but had remained separate from the human world for millennia.

After demonstrations of magic and superhuman ability,

the trio eventually convinced the humans to send their few remaining soldiers along with their own people to hunt down the Necromancers.

The combined forces were successful and found the Necromancers in a remote cave in the Himalayas and destroyed them, putting an end to the Zombies that plagued the human race.

However, this aid came at a price.

By helping the humans, the Fae, Vampires, and Dragons violated an ancient treaty that had been created to keep the realm of the humans separated from the other realms. This had protected the humans, who were generally weak in super-natural abilities, from the wars between other realms. Now that this treaty had been broken, Earth was fair game for whoever, and whatever, arrived through the inter-realm gates. Every creature from fairytales and nightmares appeared practically overnight. Thus began the race to control Earth.

CHAPTER 1

Laila Eyvindr stepped off her plane at the Los Angeles International Airport, surrounded by dozens of humans. She readjusted her duffel bag and wheeled a small suitcase behind her. She shambled with the crowd away from the terminal and began the slow, frustrating task of trying to make it past the baggage claim and to the exit.

While humans had become so advanced over the millennia, she couldn't believe they had not found a better way to travel through the air. The aircraft stank of old sweat, and the seats had been stained, but as relieved as she was to get off the plane, the Los Angeles International Airport wasn't in much better shape. The tiles of the walkway were cracked, and the walls caked in grime. Parts of the building were under construction, but looked as though the work stopped decades before.

An unused terminal branched off to the right. A gate had been erected, blocking it off, and beyond were rows of makeshift tents whose inhabitants appeared to have taken up permanent residence. As she passed a gap in the makeshift gate, she couldn't help but notice a man within the shantytown wearing a stained airport staff uniform.

An airport worker living in the airport itself? That had to be against regulation. She shook her head and tore her eyes away from the tents.

The crowd stopped for some reason that Laila couldn't see. She noticed a little girl staring at her, or more specifically at her slightly pointed ears. They were the only distinct feature that revealed she wasn't just another human. She smiled at the little girl for a moment before she disappeared in the crowd.

Laila was tall and lithe with dark auburn hair. Her warm green eyes were set in an angular but delicate face with high cheekbones. As an Elf, she at least looked more like humans than most other Supernaturals. Aside from the ears, that is. It was for that reason she was hired by the National Security Agency or NSA. It made it easier to interact with humans if you looked like them.

Over the last year Laila had taken several American culture classes in Washington, D.C. that were designed to help Supernaturals fit in. Humans used the word Supernatural to define any creature that came from another world or had some sort of special powers. The label was too general in her opinion, but since she was to live among humans, she should at least be comfortable with their terminology.

As she stepped through the doors to the baggage claim, people shoved their way past her, rushing to the carousels. The luggage had yet to arrive, but still the humans hurried to find a place along the conveyor belt. Under different circumstances Laila might have laughed, but her cramped muscles and growing headache dampened her mood.

She couldn't wait to be out of there. She hadn't slept in nearly two days thanks to a series of layovers, delayed flights, and missed connections. Oh yes, the government had at least provided her with first class seats, but there was no way she could have let herself sleep knowing that the plane might crash for any number of reasons. All she wanted was a nice long shower and to sleep. Preferably for several days.

As she passed a man waiting for his luggage on the carousel, she saw another man in a threadbare coat slip his hand into the pocket of the first and remove a wallet. The thief took off at a brisk walk back towards the tents, while the victim continued to watch obliviously for his luggage. She couldn't just stand there while the pickpocket got away.

"Hey!" she shouted, taking off after the thief.

He looked over his shoulder but didn't stop. Laila shouldered her way through the crowd. She caught up to the man and grabbed him roughly by the collar of his coat.

"Where's the wallet?" she demanded, her grip like iron as she glared at the man.

"I don't know what you're talking about," said the man innocently.

"What's going on here?" demanded a security guard, stomping up to her.

She turned to the guard but didn't release her grip on the thief. "I caught this man stealing a wallet."

The guard looked over the thief with disinterest. "Was the wallet yours, Elf?"

"What?" she asked. "No, it belonged to a man over there." She indicated the luggage pick-up.

"Then I don't see what the problem is," said the guard disinterestedly.

Laila grit her teeth. His reaction was so much like the Elves of her homeland. If it wasn't their problem, then it wasn't their business. But she wasn't willing to turn a blind eye and walk away. That was not how she operated.

The thief pulled out the stolen wallet and passed the guard a fifty-dollar bill. The guard pocketed the bill with an appreciative nod. Laila's mouth nearly dropped open in shock.

"Now mind your own business, Elf. I'd hate to see you reported to the government for disturbing the peace. I've got friends in high places, and I'd hate to see you deported." The guard sneered at her.

She took a step closer and lowered her voice. "I'll let you in on a little secret. I work for the government."

With a dark smile she flashed him her badge from the Inter-Realm Security Agency, and any shred of bravado vanished from the man's expression. His reaction was priceless.

"Now I suggest you give me back the wallet and the money before I involve the local authorities." She held out her hand expectantly, and the thief and his security guard buddy handed over the stolen items, scowling.

"Thanks," she said cheerily as she turned on her heel and walked away.

She returned to the luggage carousel and found the wallet's owner. He frantically patted his pockets before snatching the wallet from Laila.

"Supernatural freak," he muttered under his breath as he hurried away.

"A thank-you would have been polite!" she called after him, not bothering to keep the annoyance from her voice. She shook her head.

Walking straight past the rest of the crowd at the baggage claim, she headed toward the exit.

"Miss Eyvindr?" a musical voice called from her left. A man approached her. He was an Elf too, though quite a bit older than she, and dressed in a well-tailored black suit. Laila's own suit was wrinkled from siting in the cramped airplane cabin, making her feel slightly self-conscious. She nodded, and without another word followed him out of the building to the black SUV waiting for them.

She slid into the back seat and welcomed the silence as they pulled away from the curb and into the night.

Despite the late hour, the streets were crowded with impatient humans trying to get to their destinations as quickly as possible. Shops and restaurants were open, and the parking lots were relatively full. She was amazed at how the city was thriving, considering that the people living here had nearly been annihilated five years ago.

Without turning around, the Elven escort spoke to her. "My name is Einar. I have orders to take you back to the Alfheim Consulate where you have been invited to stay until you can make suitable living arrangements."

Alfheim, the world Laila came from, was one world among seven that existed in parallel dimensions to the human world. While Earth was dominated by the human race, Alfheim was home to many different sentient races and kingdoms. Two of the largest city-states in Alfheim were Ingegard (the city of the Light Elves), and Tír na nÓg (the city of the Fae). Humans who accidentally stumbled through the natural inter-realm gateways had referred to it as "fairyland." But Alfheim was not as tame as children's stories would claim. There were deep woods and forgotten bogs where the more reclusive beings resided, all too ready to prey upon the unwary traveler. In the cities, cutthroat politics and intrigue reigned supreme, with plots to build and destroy reputations. Laila preferred to stay out of the politics.

Einar cleared his throat, bringing Laila back to the present.

"Sorry." She shook her head. "What were you saying?"

"I said," he began with annoyance, "that I have taken care of your paperwork to register you in the area. One of my colleagues has also arranged temporary housing in one of our guest suites at the consulate."

She just nodded and yawned.

The Alfheim Consulate was a large building. Unlike Earth and its human consulates and embassies, Alfheim and the other worlds preferred to house the ambassadors from several city-states in one building. The building and grounds were beautiful and reminded her of home. Before the SUV pulled underground into a parking lot, Laila could have sworn she recognized a few plants in the garden that were native to

Alfheim. Her throat felt tight at the memory of the people she had left behind, but now was not the time to get emotional.

Einar didn't bother to help her with her bags. Instead he waited in impatient and haughty silence until she had gathered her belongings and then led her to an elevator.

Laila hadn't even stepped into the hallway of the building when a human woman hurried over to Einar looking frazzled. She whispered something to her escort that Laila couldn't make out.

"If he was going to insist on picking her up, he should have just arranged to meet her at the airport himself," the Elf grumbled.

The woman hurried them down a hallway. Laila was so exhausted that she almost ran into the Elf when he stopped abruptly.

They were in a lobby with a human who had a slightly rugged look to him. His scruffy beard and unruly hair were a stark contrast to the prim hairstyles of the consulate staff. He was dressed in business casual with the sleeves of his dress shirt rolled up. His clothes were slightly wrinkled from sitting at a desk all day, and there were circles under his eyes from too many nights of missed sleep. Yet beneath the weariness, Laila could see strength and determination. He nodded curtly to her escort and the woman before turning to Laila.

"You must be Laila Eyvindr. My name is Colin Grayson, and I am the head of our team at the Inter-Realm Security Agency. I figured you could use a lift to the office this evening." He held out his hand, and she shook it firmly. The thought of working while so sleep-deprived was off-putting to say the least. But at least he was more pleasant than the other two.

"Fine, just allow me to take my luggage to my room, then—"

"That won't be necessary," he cut her off. "I have already made arrangements for you, just bring it along."

The Elf in the black suit opened his mouth to protest, but before he could get a word out, Colin bid him goodnight as he took Laila's duffel bag and led her to the door.

Laila almost laughed in response to the look of shock on the Elf's face as she followed Colin out the door.

Once they were on the road, Colin relaxed.

Laila raised an eyebrow. "Please excuse me if I sound rude, but it's been a long day. Would you mind telling me where I'll be staying?"

"Actually, I haven't figured that out yet. My tech who was tracking the flights expected you to arrive in the morning."

She nodded. "I was able to catch an earlier flight at the last minute." There was no way that she had wanted to sit around in an airport for another eight hours.

"I figured we would have time to find something for you at that point. But since you made it here early, I didn't have much choice other than to pick you up."

"I could have slept at the consulate."

He shook his head. "It's better if you stay away from those politicians at the consulate. They often have to be reminded that our purpose is to protect the humans from Supernatural threats, not to get caught up in a power struggle."

She tried to stifle a yawn, but he spotted it. After a moment's consideration, he pulled into a nearby shopping center with a drive-through, 24-hour coffee shop. Colin ignored the men loitering around the corner in the process of what appeared to be a drug deal.

Lovely, thought Laila.

"Drink's on me, what would you like?" he said, pulling out his wallet and scanning the menu. She was still not used to coffee, and it usually made her jittery, but she settled for mocha.

He ordered their drinks, and then added a fancy beverage that he explained was for one of their other team members. As they waited in silence for their drinks, Laila drifted off to sleep.

CHAPTER 2

Laila woke when the car came to a stop at the gates of an underground parking lot.

"Here we are," Colin said. He scanned his ID badge with its IRSA insignia and was granted access.

The Inter-Realm Security Agency, or IRSA, was a branch of the National Security Agency concerned with protecting the government and American citizens from threats by Supernaturals, particularly Demons.

Contrary to popular human belief, Demons are not evil spirits, or even a single species. Any creature, no matter if they are Elf, Troll, or even human, can be considered a Demon if they are a member of, or associate with members of the Demon political organization from Muspelheim, the most desolate of the realms where the worst otherworldly criminals and monsters are sent. This inter-realm prison is casually known as Hell. Through generations of religion and myth, humans had come to confuse Hell—whose inhabitants are very much alive—with the Realm of the Dead, where the souls of the dead traveled to whatever fate awaited them in the afterlife.

Demons are divided into two categories: Greater and Lessor Demons. The Greater Demons are members of the Demon political organization, who have been damned or sentenced to life in Hell. Those who have never been damned, but have been persuaded to work in the support of the Demon organization are known as Lessor Demons.

Damning is a sentence for life, and while it is supposedly impossible to escape from Hell, there were many that speculated that Greater Demons had escaped and initiated The Event. This had yet to be proven though, and so far there was no documentation of Greater Demons in other worlds. Laila wasn't even sure what the punishment would be for an escaped Greater Demon. A meeting between the governments of the various worlds would probably be called to determine the criminal's fate. The Gods could potentially become involved as well. A Death sentence would be far too merciful, and while she had a difficult time imagining a worse fate than damning, she was sure one of the Gods could devise a more severe punishment.

Laila took a sip of the mocha and followed Colin up to their office suites.

He informed her that the building was home to more than just the IRSA offices. It was also equipped with state-of-the-art prison cells to temporarily house Supernatural criminals until they could be moved to a more secure location. There was also a morgue, but it was not currently in use since a qualified Supernatural medical examiner had yet to be appointed. Next door was the Asclepius Hospital of Supernatural Medicine that specialized in treating otherworld visitors and Supernatural-related injuries.

The building was new and a sharp contrast to the filthy, chaotic airport. They reached their offices on the third floor and stepped out of the elevator. The other team members were sitting in a conference room whose walls were plastered with maps of the city. A large monitor for video conference calls rested at the end of a long table.

"Don't you have cases to be working on?" Colin said glaring at the two.

A gorgeous Fae woman rose from her chair and faced them.

"We've been a little distracted," the Fae said. She had long honey-blond hair in loose curls down her back and large purple eyes that were characteristic of the Fae. She also had curves that Marilyn Monroe would be jealous of. Definitely different from the long, lean figure that the Elves were known for, but Laila had long ago accepted that there was no changing her thin, willowy body that was deceptively strong and resilient.

"Laila, meet the team," Colin said, passing the sugary coffee drink to the Fae. "This is Alastrina Fiachra."

"You can call me Ali," she said, reaching for Laila's hand. "You have no idea how excited I was to hear that another otherworldly woman was going to be on the team! It's great to work with the guys, but you know..." She rolled her eyes and took a sip of her drink.

There was also a male in the room who was obviously a Vampire, as indicated by his red eyes and pale skin. He had short, spiky black hair and looked at her with mild curiosity. Laila masked her disapproval as she took in his appearance. He was dressed in distressed jeans, biker boots, and a black leather jacket. He looked as if he belonged on stage at a rock concert or in a biker bar. He didn't bother to shake her hand.

"I'm Darien," he grunted.

"Right," she said, trying to keep the distain out of her voice.

"You look a little tired to be working tonight," he pointed out.

"She's not here to work. I just need to find her a hotel for the night and she'll be on her way," Colin said, fishing around a cabinet for napkins.

"Oh, don't be ridiculous," Ali told him. "She can stay with me. I've got more than enough room. Besides, I doubt she has a car yet, so how else could she get around this city?"

Colin considered the offer for a moment, then nodded.

"Thank you," said Laila, a little surprised that Ali would open her home to a stranger. "That's very kind."

"Great!" Ali grinned. "Then we better head out now. Laila's had a long enough day as it is."

Ali's house turned out to be a converted building that had once been home to a business. The exterior still had the old sign for Fredrico's Automotive Repair painted on the brick wall.

The interior was cavernous and renovated with warm colors, soft fabrics and a collection of items that one would expect to see in Alfheim, such as glowing crystal sculptures and vibrant paintings that were so lifelike that they seemed to move. The kitchen was large and fully equipped with hardwood floors, stainless steel appliances and a granite bar that could seat six. The kitchen opened to a living area with leather sofas covered in colorful pillows and blankets and arranged around a coffee table. Paintings of otherworldly scenes decorated the walls and brightly colored baubles filled the shelves It was the perfect combination of Alfheim and Earth, and Laila instantly fell in love with it.

"Obviously," Ali began, "this part of the building was used by an auto mechanic. The upper two levels were used by a couple of lawyers. They all abandoned the place after The Event though, and I bought it in an auction. I thought it would be fun to really make this place my own." She stashed her purse on the counter and hung her coat on a hook in the hall between the garage and the kitchen.

"It must have cost you a fortune!"

Ali shrugged. "Not really. At that time all labor and materials were cheap. I was in the first group of Fae that were sent here, when humans were still trying to make sense of everything that had happened. They were desperate for work to support what remained of their lives and families."

She straightened up some dishes in the kitchen.

"You hungry? Can I make you something?"

"Oh no, thank you, I—"

The sound of footsteps down the hall caught Laila's attention. A girl of about twelve rounded the corner into the living room, but something was odd about her. Not physically, but she exuded an aura of power.

The girl was a Dragon.

Ali waved the Dragon over. "Erin, this is Laila, the new coworker I was telling you about. Laila, this is my sister, Erin."

Clearly they weren't biological sisters.

Dragons have two forms: their human form and their true Dragon form with wings, scales, and claws. In Dragon form, an adult could easily grow to be the size of a house. Even though Erin was in her human form, there were slight indications of her heritage. She had a defined jawline and slightly broader facial features. Her slightly disheveled black hair was shoulder length, and she wore a set of fluffy blue pajamas.

"Laila just arrived," Ali continued, "so she will be staying with us for a while."

Laila nodded. "If you will excuse me, I think I need some rest now." She figured she had better just shut up and get some sleep before she said something stupid. Dragons liked their respect, and according to their reputation they generally had nothing against eating anyone who annoyed them. Laila was running on far too little sleep to be tactful, and even a young Dragon in fluffy blue pajamas was someone to be cautious with.

She was shown to a suite on the second floor complete with a king-sized bed, walk-in closet, and the most glorious bathroom she had seen so far on Earth. It had double vanities with a large glass shower and a huge tub. The bathroom had an aquatic theme in shades of blue and green that once again mixed Earth life with Alfheim creatures. Her favorite part was the floor with its stone mosaic of a blue sea serpent.

Laila was hit with another wave of homesickness. When would she see the familiar streets of Ingegard? She missed the intricate craftsmanship of the buildings, where every detail was a work of art, and the way the distant music of magic echoed through the air.

It had been nearly a year since she had moved to Earth. She had received messages from her family a couple of times, but every message was the same: stop fooling around and come home. She knew it was rude to leave their messages unanswered, but she had explained her reasoning to them before she left. It seemed unnecessary to have to explain it to them again, and knowing that her family felt ashamed of her decision to leave cut her like a knife.

She definitely missed home and occasionally was tempted to listen to her family. But she knew that there was no point in returning. After all, the best way to work her way up to a position in the Royal Guard was to prove herself here in Midgard.

It didn't matter that she had spent over two decades training, or that she was at the top of her graduating class. She had even applied for the Royal Guard with the full support of the training academy staff. But Elves like tradition and rules. She would have to wait until she was 100 years old, and at the moment she was only 83.

So she would wait, and work. And maybe in a few years she would gain the experience to reapply.

Most of the others who trained with her had enlisted in the army. They had been taking as many applicants as they could after The Event. It was work, but not as appealing as working for the Royal Guard among the finest Elven warriors.

Many of her relatives, including her father, worked in the Royal Guard. Others held respected positions in the court. Her father was proud of her determination to join the Guard, but her mother still wished she would show more interest in politics and court life. Neither her mother nor her father was pleased with their only child's decision to come to Earth, but in her heart Laila knew that she was needed here more than at home.

Sighing, she traced the outline of a mosaic wave curling along the wall of the shower.

As tempted as she was to take a long, hot shower, Laila was a blink away from falling asleep right where she stood. So she quickly changed out of her wrinkled suit and crawled into bed.

CHAPTER 3

By the time Laila awoke it was almost noon. While she was slightly ashamed of the late hour, she knew that Ali would have said something if she was expected at work. So, rather than rushing to get ready, she enjoyed a leisurely bath.

The warm water was blissful and helped to sooth her body. She wished she could lie there all day. After dragging herself away from the luxurious bath, she opened her duffel bag and removed one of her many neatly folded black suits before heading down to the kitchen for breakfast.

Ali was already there in a pair of pink sweatpants and a matching T-shirt, making some scrambled eggs.

"Good morning! I hope you like eggs. I'm not much of a cook, but that is one thing I can actually make." She motioned to the refrigerator. "Help yourself—there's milk and juice, or I can make some more coffee."

"Thank you." Laila rummaged through the refrigerator for the juice and then settled into one of the bar stools.

"You're wearing *that* to the office?" asked Ali, eyeing the suit.

"Of course," said Laila, a little confused. "In D.C. everyone wears them. Don't you?"

"Nope!" laughed Ali. "I'm sorry, but you'll stick out like a sore thumb in that. You should probably change into something, well, a little more ordinary."

Laila ignored the suggestion. She preferred to look professional for the job.

"So, how many agents are there?" asked Laila.

"Just the four of us in L.A. Hopefully we'll expand, but there are so few Supernaturals applying for the position that we are spread pretty thin and way overworked. At least we have human technicians and support staff, and a small investigative team to help gather evidence and deal with crime scenes. They have enough training in otherworldly creatures to help us, but they don't have the strength to subdue the Supernaturals we normally deal with. So, we usually head up the investigations and deal with the Supernaturals, and then we call in the investigative team to collect evidence."

It made sense, but the lack of Supernatural backup wasn't particularly reassuring, considering that the only ones standing between the people of Los Angeles and any Supernatural threat were a Vampire, an Elf, one of the Fae, and Colin.

"Is Colin human?"

"He's a Werewolf. There are a number of families like his that have hidden their ability for generations." She spooned the eggs onto plates with buttered toast and slid Laila's across the bar.

Werewolves and other Weres fell under the category of Supernatural creatures known as Shifters, creatures that have the ability to morph into more than one form. In order for a Shifter to be considered a Were, one of their forms must be human, and the other was typically animal. Dragons were also considered to be Shifters and had a human looking form, however since they had elemental magic and resided in Alfheim, Dragons were not considered Weres. There were a

variety of other Supernatural creatures classified as Shifters because they could change their physical shape and appearance in
some way such as Dryads, who could take the shape of plants.
Fae did not fall under the category of Shifters though, because
the changes in appearance the Fae were able to create came
from magic that manipulated the viewer's perspective, rather
than a true physical change.

"So, if he's our supervisor he must have been working
with IRSA for quite a while," said Laila.

"Yeah," Ali said with a mouthful of eggs. "He's been
with IRSA since it started up. He was into some sort of law
enforcement before The Event, so when he announced his
abilities to the government, they picked him up and took him
to IRSA. I arrived shortly after he was transferred here to set
up an office. That was about four years ago."

Laila savored her eggs while Ali told her a little about
her transition. Eventually Erin made her way downstairs and
helped herself to a bowl of cereal.

"So," Laila asked her, "did you move to Los Angeles
to go to a human school?"

Dragons, like Elves, age much more slowly than humans.
While many of them chose to continue their education, it
would not be unheard of in Supernatural circles for young
Dragons to find work.

"Nope." She chewed on a spoonful of cereal. "Our
parents died, so I came to stay with Ali."

"Oh, I'm sorry." Laila didn't know what to say.

"Thanks, it happened a couple years ago," Ali explained. "My dad worked for the city guard in Tír na nÓg. He
was just arriving home from work when a criminal he'd been
searching for attacked. Both he and our mother were killed."

She exchanged a glance with her sister before continuing.

"But it was thanks to his job that he rescued Erin's egg. He
was traveling with a messenger through the Dragon Kingdom
and there had been some sort of attack. There were many dead

and wounded, and her egg was among the carnage. He sent the messenger on to the Dragons alone while he tried to find her birth parents, but they had been killed. No one stepped forward to claim her, so my parents decided that they would adopt her." She reached over the counter and messed up Erin's hair. Erin gave her an irritated look and tried to straighten it back out.

Laila imagined that Ali's parents must have been very kind to take in the orphaned Dragon. Her own mother would never consider such a thing, especially given her position with the Elven court. In fact, most Elves would have turned the Dragon away or sent her to an orphanage, claiming her own people should take care of her. But the Fae were much more open and caring. It was one of the things Laila admired about them. Their reputations were less important than following their hearts. Laila was about to mention this when she noticed the clock over Ali's shoulder.

"Gods! Shouldn't we be at the office by now?" It was almost one o'clock, and Laila didn't like the idea of being late the first day on the job.

"Don't worry, we generally work afternoons and most of the night. The Supernaturals are more active then, plus Darien can't join us until sundown." She gathered the dishes and arranged them in the dishwasher. "I'll just get dressed, and then we can head over."

The city baked in the midday sun. In daylight Laila observed that many of the buildings were in various stages of neglect or repair. There were many plain-looking apartment buildings and storefronts with power lines strung between them. Most buildings were painted in bland colors like tan or light grey, and everything was coated in a fine layer of dust.

"Everything's so… worn out," said Laila with distaste.

"If you think this is worn out, you should see other parts of the city." Ali glanced over at Laila. "This is actually one of the nicer areas. It's not as posh as Santa Monica, but at least the buildings are still standing and under repair."

It took them over a half hour to get to the office with the daytime traffic. Laila was fairly convinced that she could have walked there in less time than it took to fight the traffic, but Ali insisted it was better to drive in the city. They stopped at another drive-through coffee shop where Ali purchased another large sugary coffee drink like she'd had the night before. She offered Laila a sip, but she politely declined.

Laila followed Ali up to their floor but stopped at Colin's office. The door was open and he was on the phone, so she paused in the doorway.

"You've got to be kidding me! Get whatever information you can on the guy. There has to be a connection to the others somewhere." He noticed Laila and motioned for her to come in.

"Just see what you can find and send it to me. I'll take a look at it later. Thanks."

He hung up and massaged his neck.

"Nice suit," he said. "How are you feeling today?"

"Much better, thank you."

"Good to hear. I had a computer tech bring down a computer and phone to your office. I've got these for you as well," he said as he brought out a case from behind the desk. Inside was a government-issued handgun with a holster. There was also a stun gun and handcuffs. Although Laila preferred to use her magic, carrying the weapons was part of the protocol. She filled out the necessary forms as Colin continued.

"For your first case, you will be working with Darien. He's been on Earth the longest, but sometimes gets a bit distracted…. He normally works alone, but I think it will be good for you two to handle this case together."

He swiveled the computer screen so that Laila could look through the electronic file.

Apparently, there was a Supernatural harassing patrons in one of the local bars. There was no name, but there were descriptions that people had given of him. He looked like a human but was just a little too tall, angular, and muscular. He had reportedly visited the same bar a number of times in the last week. Each time he had been thrown out after either harassing women in the club or getting into fights with the men. Laila suspected he was from Svartalfheim, a world similar to Alfheim but with a harsher climate, so most of its cities existed underground.

"You haven't identified what he is, have you?" she asked Colin. "That would help us prepare to face him if he starts another fight."

He shook his head. "That's all the information we've got on him. I'm not sure if he's even documented."

All Supernaturals were required to get a visa and submit documentation on their race and their abilities. They would then receive an I.D. card, since an inter-dimensional passport had yet to be established. Laila had been given hers while she was in D.C., along with an IRSA I.D. card and badge.

"I want you and Darien to go to the bar tonight and see if the SNP shows up." He settled back into his chair.

"SNP?" asked Laila.

"Supernatural Person."

"Right," said Laila. She hadn't heard that one in D.C. "You'll find all the information in our database. Just call the support staff if you have any issues."

Darien arrived shortly after dusk. One of the myths that humans told about killing Vampires is true: the sun does turn them into a pile of ashes. That and anything sharp through the heart, though that would be a good bet to kill most beings anyway. Vampires usually find some way or another to amuse themselves during the day. Laila had met a Vampire back in Washington, D.C. who had accumulated a fortune by trading stocks during the day while she was stuck indoors. That said, many Vampires simply choose to sleep through the daylight hours, which conserves their strength so they are required to feed less often.

Colin had already briefed Darien the night before, so he only stopped long enough to pick Laila up before heading to the bar, which was on the eastern end of Santa Monica. The traffic was bad, but they hoped to get there before the night's rush began.

"You look official," snorted Darien as he drove.

"And you don't," said Laila, eyeing his ripped-up jeans and leather jacket. "Doesn't anyone dress for the job around here?"

Darien laughed. "Oh boy, you've got a lot to learn."

She ignored the comment.

"I assume you have some sort of magic, right?" The way Darien said it made the question somewhat insulting.

"Of course. Most Elves are gifted with magic, and healing in particular."

"Well, that's definitely helpful. At least for you mortals that don't heal very fast."

He was right about that. While Elves could live for thousands of years, they certainly weren't immortal. Elves also healed slowly like humans, so healing by magic was incredibly valuable. Laila, however, wasn't particularly skilled as a healer. Her strengths were in offensive and defensive magic adapted for combat.

"So, when were you turned?" she asked flippantly. It was normally seen as rude to ask a Vampire about his death, but she figured that if he was asking impolite questions, she didn't need to worry too much about etiquette.

"In 1724. I challenged this guy to a duel because I caught him talking to my fiancée. I didn't realize that he was a Vampire at the time, and naturally I didn't stand a chance. We met at dusk, and after he toyed with me for a while I realized that something about him wasn't right. He pierced my lung, and as I lay dying I asked him what he was. He told me. But being the good-natured man he is, he offered to change me, and I accepted." He shrugged.

She found it absurd that anyone would fight over such a petty affront.

"Had you fought other men before that?" she asked him, glancing sideways to see his reaction.

"Of course. A good thirty or so. I only killed a handful of men though. Dueling was very common among humans then. I guess you can say it was required by society when one gentleman offended the honor of another. Occasionally I would offend a man just so he would have to fight me." He laughed.

She wasn't sure how much of the story was true, but it made sense to her in a twisted sort of way. From what she'd seen so far, Darien constantly challenged the people around him, just as he had before he died. Apparently old habits die hard, particularly with the undead.

"What about your fiancée?" she asked, noticing there wasn't a wedding band on his finger.

"I broke off the engagement."

Before she had time to pry further, he pulled into the parking lot of the bar.

Darien flashed his badge at the bouncer standing by the door and asked him if the owner was there. The bouncer was a large, burly man, especially for a human. Laila was surprised that he hadn't been able to keep their Supernatural out of the establishment. He pointed to the woman who was restocking the bar.

The woman was a middle-aged human with dark brown hair pulled back into a ponytail. She easily hefted a crate of beer off a stack waiting by the bar. Her expression was grim and haunted, as with most of the survivors from The Event. She set the crate down as they approached.

"Can I help you?"

Darien casually took a seat at the bar. "I'm Special Agent Pavoni, and this is Special Agent Eyvindr. We are from IRSA. We heard you have a Supernatural patron who has been harassing your customers lately."

The woman breathed a sigh of relief.

"Right. My name is Angelique. That guy has been coming in here for the past two weeks. But every time we throw him out, he finds some way back in. He seems like he is particularly interested in one of the women who comes in here often. I'm just sick of dealing with the guy, and he's costing me business."

"Is there any information you can give us about him? Maybe if you noticed anything particularly unusual, like magic?" Laila asked her from across the bar.

She shrugged.

"Not really. The light isn't the best, and I don't see many Supernaturals around here. If you're willing to stay for a while, though, I can point him out to you if he shows up."

They had nothing else to do, so they decided to wait around and see if he would show. They took a booth opposite the bar where they could easily see Angelique. The seat was covered in greasy handprints, and the table was sticky. Laila wrinkled her nose and resisted the urge to wipe down the seat before sliding into the booth that was held together with more duct tape than vinyl.

The walls were decorated with peeling posters of pop singers and old, yellowed photographs of celebrities who had visited the bar over the years. Most of the photos were probably from before The Event, and they had the same man posing in most of them. She suspected that he was the previous owner. The humans in the photographs were happy and relaxed, so different from the grim survivors. Yet another reminder of how the humans' lives had drastically changed. With a sick feeling in her stomach Laila realized that most of the people in the photos had probably died during The Event.

The bar wasn't especially large but had lots of tables and chairs. There were stains from water damage on the ceiling, and the wooden floor was warped and coming loose in places. Laila wondered how they had managed to pass a health and safety inspection.

"Is something wrong?" asked Darien, watching her with a sneer.

"No." She kept her expression neutral.

"You're not used to places like this, are you?"

Laila ignored the bait.

"This bar's pretty decent. I've been here before. Wait until we get called out to Culver or the Old City."

When she didn't say anything, he continued.

"Yeah, there's a bit of a poverty gap here that you won't see in D.C." he lounged in the booth. "You've got the people with more money than they know what to do with. They're the ones who have the nice, new buildings. Then there are the people who struggle to make it by and squat wherever they find shelter."

"Like in the airport?" she asked.

He nodded. "They technically have to pay to live there in the airport. It's deducted from their pay, which is too low to begin with. No one's been enforcing a minimum wage since The Event."

"But there are plenty of abandoned buildings. Surely it would be better to live in one of those?"

"Some do," he said. "But it is hard to live without running water and electricity, and the utility companies have jacked the prices sky high. At least the airport workers have access to those amenities on site."

Laila shook her head in disbelief. "How can the government allow people to live like that?"

Darien shrugged. "The humans are still searching for structure and balance. Out here, people do what they have to in order to survive. The city's reverted to a wild western version of itself, and we're just trying to do what we can to keep the peace."

A silence settled around them as Laila processed this new information. This was not at all what she had expected. No one in her training courses had prepared her for what Los Angeles would actually be like. D.C. was so manicured with well-maintained buildings and homes, and few people lived on the streets. She had assumed Los Angeles would be the same. It was truly a disappointment, but Laila also realized that places such as this were in greater need of help.

The bartender brought Laila a glass of soda on the house, but they didn't carry bottled blood for Darien. Bottled blood had started to become more popular among places frequented by Vampires. It helped to keep them from feeling left out, and from feeding on the living customers.

They settled in to wait for their man.

CHAPTER 4

Gradually humans began to show up, and by ten the bar was relatively full. But the man they were waiting for had yet to show.

Darien apparently got bored with Laila's company and left to "question" some of the ladies at the bar. From what she could see, he seemed less interested in questioning the women about the SNP, and more interested in flirting. Laila shook her head.

Laila sat at the booth watching the humans with little interest. Angelique brought her another glass of soda and a basket of fries. She hesitated for a moment as if she were going to ask Laila a question, but then thought better of it and returned to the bar.

By now the bar was quite full. Most of the booths and tables were occupied, and music blasted over the dull roar of conversation. It was hard for Laila to make out what the people around her were saying, except for the person sitting in the booth behind her.

"No, we will wait a while longer," said a male voice directly behind her. "He was here almost every day last week, and with that temper I expect he puts on quite a show."

That was odd. Could he be looking for the same guy as she was?

Another male spoke from the opposite side of the table, but she couldn't make out what he said.

"True, it usually is shorter, but if he is as big as I've been told, it should take a lot to knock him out, and *that* is what the crowd likes. It builds suspense."

Laila couldn't hear anything more, but it didn't matter because Angelique hurried over to her and pointed out a man who had just walked through the door.

"That's him!"

He was definitely Supernatural. She could feel the energy that was seeping out of him; it was filled with the heat of lust and anger.

There are plenty of creatures that have that kind of energy, but this man's facial features and tattoos defined him as a Daeva. Supernatural creatures from the parallel realm of Jotunheim, Daevas aren't magically gifted but are extremely strong and surprisingly stealthy. They had made appearances in the ancient Middle East through a broken portal that accidentally connected to Earth and had caused quite a ruckus. Laila had met a few Daevas before, and they generally weren't an issue unless they were pissed off. And this one was.

The Daeva searched the crowd until he spotted the person he was looking for and took off across the bar. Laila slid out of the booth and tried to follow him as inconspicuously as possible to avoid drawing his attention. After all, the people of her realm and his had been at war for centuries, so treading lightly wouldn't hurt.

Keeping an eye on the Daeva, she found Darien who had been hitting on some poor human girl in a slinky dress with way too little material for Laila's taste.

"Our friend's here," she mouthed, grabbing him by the collar of his jacket.

With some hastily made promises of coming back, he left the girl sitting at her table.

"We are here to arrest a guy, not for you to pick up a date!" she hissed at him in exasperation as they edged their way around the crowd.

"Relax. I was just asking her a few questions about this guy."

Laila kept her mouth shut but decided she would definitely be having a word with Colin about Darien's "methods."

She had lost sight of the Daeva, but as they pushed through the crowd she could hear him yelling.

"You think you can tell me what to do, little man!?!" he roared above the music.

Laila knew she didn't have much time to get to him before he started a fight with the person he'd been looking for. Assuming that person was a human, he or she probably wouldn't last long. She reached for her stun gun, wondering if it would work on a creature like a Daeva. Finally, she shoved her way through the crowd in time to see the Daeva punch a human man in the face.

Laila was tall, but the Daeva was at least a foot taller than her and built like a mountain of muscle.

"Freeze!" She pointed the stun gun at him. "You're under arrest—"

Before she could finish, he lunged at her with a right hook aimed at her jaw. Ducking, she narrowly avoided the punch and pulled the trigger on the stun gun. The probes discharged, but the shock had little effect other than aggravating him further. *Shit,* thought Laila.

Darien slammed into the Daeva, knocking him off balance and giving her time to recover. Laila holstered the useless stun gun and prepared to cast a spell. The Daeva kicked Darien in the chest, hard enough to break several ribs, and sent him crashing into the bar patrons who were standing nearby.

Laila reached out and felt the magic that saturated

everything around her. She sent a blast of air from her fingertips that knocked the Daeva off his feet like an invisible punch.
While he was down, she gathered the magic once again to
freeze the air around him, binding him in place.

He roared in fury but couldn't do more than turn his
head to look at her. Calmly she walked over to him, manipulated the magic until he was kneeling with his hands behind his
back, and cuffed him.

She glanced around to look for the human. She didn't
worry about Darien—he would heal in a matter of minutes—
but the human could be badly injured after a punch like that.

The man seemed okay, but she had Darien take his
statement while paramedics who arrived on the scene checked
his injuries. Laila then borrowed Darien's phone to call for an
SUV to transport the Daeva back to headquarters.

As she turned back, she caught a glimpse of someone
walking away from the Daeva, but before she could question
him, the man had slipped out the door.

"Now do you get why we don't wear suits?" asked
Darien, shaking debris from his jeans.

Laila glared at the Vampire.

Back in her office at headquarters, Laila typed up her
report. The office was fairly small but had a window, a desk,
and a shiny new laptop computer that was fast as lightning.
She had to admit, she did love the technology that humans had
created. It rivaled magic in its uses and wasn't anywhere near as
exhausting to use.

There was also a fancy new cell phone in its box that
someone had left for her. She grabbed it on her way out of the
office, planning to look at it when she got home.

She uploaded the report and sent it to Colin before heading down the hall to his office to make sure he had
received the file. He was on the phone, and she didn't want to
disturb him so she turned to walk away, but he motioned for

her to wait.

She took a seat in a chair and waited until he ended his conversation and turned to her.

"I just wanted to let you know that I sent you my report," she said.

"You seemed to have had an eventful first night, from what Darien told me."

She shrugged. Laila had dealt with far worse than a pissed-off Daeva. "Nothing we couldn't handle. I just hope that human's all right." A thought popped into her head. "You do know that those stun guns are useless against the larger Supernaturals, right?"

He nodded. "Yes, that's a bit of an issue. I would stick to using magic on SNP's if I were you."

There was a chime from his computer. Colin immediately opened the message and scanned through it.

Laila glanced at his desk and noticed a single picture in a frame of a young woman. Not wanting to intrude, she returned her attention to their conversation.

"I thought I should also mention that Agent Pavoni seemed to have difficulty focusing on the task at hand. I caught him flirting with women in the bar."

"Yeah, he does that sometimes."

Laila frowned. That wasn't quite the response she'd been expecting, but she dropped the subject, for now.

There was a cardboard box sitting next to his desk crammed full of folders, and more piled on his desk.

Colin followed her gaze. "The Los Angeles Police Department sent those over."

"That's a lot of cases to be working on all at once," she observed. She also noticed that the file in front of him read "Missing Persons."

"Technically it's one case, or at least I suspect it is. Every one of these men was last seen brawling in a local bar before going missing. I'm beginning to think someone is purposely targeting SNP's."

"Laila, are you coming?" Ali called from the doorway, her car keys dangling from a finger.

Laila rose from her chair and wished Colin a good night, but he had already turned his attention to the box of missing persons files.

CHAPTER 5

When Laila woke, she heard voices coming from downstairs. There was an unfamiliar presence in the house, and whoever that person was, they were very powerful. Part of her gift with magic was that she could sense the energy of a person. It often came in handy in a fight, but also in determining someone's status in the otherworld societies, and from the power she was sensing, this person was off the charts.

Her curiosity got the better of her. Laila took a quick shower and pulled on another suit. After double-checking to ensure she was presentable, she followed the voices downstairs.

As she stepped into the living room, she had to stop herself from gasping. Lounging on a sofa was a Goddess.

The Goddess sat with her back to Laila. She was facing Ali who, much to Laila's astonishment, was wearing a purple satin bathrobe! She was starting to wonder at the Fae's sanity. No rational being greeted a Goddess wearing a bathrobe.

Ali noticed Laila watching.

"Oh! Laila! I hope we didn't wake you. This is Arduinna, Goddess of the Black Forest. Arduinna, this is my new roommate and coworker, Laila Eyvindr."

The Goddess stood and turned. She had long, curly black hair and eyes that were such a bright shade of green that they put Laila's to shame. Her posture was strong and confident, yet grounded and comfortable. She wore a short chiffon tunic dress in pale blue and a pair of leather sandals. She was beyond beautiful, practically glowing with an inner divine light.

Laila bowed deeply. She didn't even know what to say. She never expected to meet a God, particularly not in Ali's living room!

"I won't have any of that. Come on, and stand up. It's nice to meet you, Laila."

Arduinna held out her hand. Laila took it in a nice, firm handshake.

"It's nice to meet you too," she replied, feeling a little star-struck.

They took their seats again, and Laila followed suit. She helped herself to a cup of coffee from the pot that was sitting on the side table.

Ali acted as if having coffee with a Goddess in Los Angeles was a completely normal occurrence.

Arduinna turned to Laila.

"So, why did you decide to come to Earth? And why L.A.? It seems to me that Elves prefer to live in places that are less… polluted, or at least more connected to nature."

"Los Angeles wasn't exactly my choice. I decided to come and join IRSA to gain experience, and this is where I was needed."

"That's definitely true," Ali said, shifting in her seat. "This city is way too big not to have anyone with a real talent in magic. You never know when a Demon Sorcerer or, worse, a Necromancer might show up."

"Well, hopefully that is something you will not have to deal with," Arduinna replied somberly.

"How about you?" Laila asked the Goddess. "I didn't think the Gods left their realm often."

"Oh," she laughed. "Well, I don't care for the constant bickering of the other Gods. They are usually fighting for power and offending each other, so I prefer to stay on Earth back in my forest. I came to L.A. out of curiosity and met Ali when she was relatively new here."

The Goddess gave Ali a warm smile, as she sipped her tea.

"Do you live here now?" asked Laila.

"Oh, no! There is no way I could survive in a place with so little nature. I live in my forest, in Germany."

Laila nodded. She could understand that. It was much more difficult for her to cast spells here, since her magic was linked to nature. "It's true. I can practically feel the city draining my energy. But how did you get here?"

"Oh, I teleported. It's much more convenient for a chat than the human methods of transportation."

The idea of teleporting just to talk was insane. It took so much energy to teleport that most Sorcerers, including herself, were unable to accomplish it. Then again, Arduinna was a Goddess.

"Here," said Arduinna as she handed her a crystal from her pocket. "I embedded it with a transportation spell. It lasts for years and takes much less energy than casting the spell yourself. They only work two ways, though—to my forest and here. You can have it. Ali already has one, but this way you can come visit me if you ever need a break from the city."

"Thank you!" Laila exclaimed. This was truly an honor.

She carefully examined the crystal while Ali changed the subject. It looked like an ordinary quartz crystal, but if she concentrated, she could feel the energy pulsing in it. Crystals are great for focusing energy and hold spells better than most other objects.

Laila excused herself to find a safe place for the crystal in her room. This was certainly an unusual start to her morning. It was the first time Laila had ever met a Goddess. From the time she was a child, she'd been warned that that it was all too easy for Gods to take advantage of mortals and use them as disposable assets in their power games. But Arduinna seemed different. Laila felt like she was genuinely interested in the mortals.

Work that evening was pretty dull. She had a stack of paperwork to sort through and a couple of new case files to look into. At the bottom of the stack she found an envelope from LAPD with a note addressed to Colin. It was another missing person file. The office assistant who delivered the mail that morning had probably missed it.

Ready for any excuse to get out from behind her desk, Laila scooped it up and took it down the hall. She paused in the doorway for a moment, watching Colin pace back and forth.

"I think I have one of your files. It's another missing person case."

Colin took the folder. Laila watched as he dropped it on the stack with a sigh.

Laila hesitated and noticed that the wall behind his door was now covered in files and images. There was red string connecting them to various locations on a map. That was new. She hadn't noticed it yesterday.

"If you don't mind my asking, why do you think these cases are connected?" she asked as Colin hastily opened the envelope.

"There are rumors of illegal, Demon-run cage fights, but the only evidence I have are these missing person reports. And even those could be completely unrelated."

In Laila's opinion he was grasping at straws. The office was swamped with work. How could Colin justify wasting so much time on a hunch? But he was her supervisor, and questioning his judgment her first week on the job was not going to win her any favors.

"Is there anything I can do to help?" she asked, trying to be helpful.

"Not until I can come up with a lead. But if you hear

anything that could possibly be related, let me know."

Laila filed the information in the back of her mind as she returned to her office.

The hours passed, and Laila was beginning to develop a headache from staring at her computer screen by the time Ali sauntered into her office with a half-drunk blended iced coffee drink in her hand.

"T.G.I.F.!"

"What?" Laila said, glancing up from her computer.

"Oh, come on! Don't tell me they didn't teach you that in D.C.?"

Laila racked her brain but couldn't recall any code called T.G.I.F. What was with these people and acronyms?

"It's a human phrase. It means 'Thank God It's Friday!'"

"Really?" Laila mumbled absently as she saved the documents on her computer. Ali reached over and playfully snapped the screen of the laptop shut with a click.

"Don't even think of working through the weekend! You haven't even seen the city yet, and I saw your wardrobe. We are definitely going shopping. I can't take you clubbing in that." Ali made a face at her slacks and plain blouse.

"Wait, clubbing?" said Laila shocked, "Oh no, I—"

"You can't say no until you've tried it. If you absolutely hate it, I promise I won't make you go again."

Partying was not something Laila usually involved herself in. A crowd of people drinking in a room with loud music had never appealed to Laila. There were far too many ways for that to go wrong. But it was also pretty clear that there was no use in arguing with the Fae. Besides, a few more outfits would be nice. All the clothes she owned fit into the small carry-on bag she had brought, aside from the gear that IRSA had provided her. She really did need to expand her wardrobe.

CHAPTER 6

Laila tried to hold still, all too aware of the burning hot metal Ali held only millimeters from her scalp.

"This is completely unnecessary," grumbled Laila as she glared at the metal contraption. "I don't understand the appeal of singeing my hair to make it curl, and I'm sure a spell would be more efficient anyway."

"I'm almost done, just hold still." Ali released the lock of hair and pinned it up to let it set.

Ali had set up a station in Laila's bathroom, turning it into a makeshift salon. Erin was in the bedroom rummaging through a mountain of shopping bags. Not only had Laila purchased a couple of dresses, she'd also purchased regular street clothes that she could wear to work. She was starting to realize that suits were probably not the best option for the kind of work she would encounter here. Most of the cases she'd worked in D.C. involved routine arrests of SNPs for infractions or nonviolent misdemeanors, and they usually didn't run or fight. Many of those SNPs also had good lawyers who knew how to get the charges dismissed. When dealing with those cases suits were appropriate, but there were few of those cases here in Los Angeles.

Laila had to admit she had been impressed by the large shopping mall. It was like the street markets back home, but three floors tall and blissfully air-conditioned. Both Los Angeles and D.C. were quite a bit warmer than she was used to, and she had quickly developed a love for air conditioning.

The original structure of the pre-Event mall had allowed for individual storefronts with large signs for each shop's name. However, in the time since The Event, the building's original order and organization had been abandoned. Shopkeepers set up booths and stalls wherever space allowed.

Much to Laila's horror, Ali had informed her that most of the clothing in the mall had been salvaged from other shops across the state that had been abandoned during The Event. Ali insisted it was a legitimate business practice and prevented the clothing from going to waste, and that it was far cheaper than shopping the new brands that could be found in the shops in Santa Monica. But Laila couldn't help but think they were purchasing stolen goods.

In addition to clothing, Ali and Erin had also convinced her to buy new shoes and makeup. Laila rarely used makeup, but Ali insisted she buy the expensive, name-brand cosmetics.

The government had provided her with a large relocation bonus when she signed up to work on Earth. It was intended to help her settle into life in a new world. Laila was sure she had made a sizable dent in her bank account by the time they had finished.

"How about this one?" Erin called from the other room. Laila couldn't see which dress Erin referred to, but Ali shook her head.

"Not for tonight. Keep looking. There should be a black lace one in there somewhere," Ali replied. She pinned the last curl into place and spritzed it with hairspray.

Both Ali and Erin seemed to particularly enjoy the whole

process of getting dressed up and going out. They were listening to music and took turns telling Laila about the crazy experiences they'd had in the city. Even though this wasn't what Laila typically did for fun, she found herself smiling and laughing. It wasn't so bad, she supposed.

Her friends back home were quite different. Many of her Elven friends who were involved in the court or and politics, were more formal in their relationships. Social interaction typically meant formally arranged dinner parties and it would be considered highly unusual for them to help each other dress and prepare for the evening. Her friends from her training courses were more laid back, but usually their time spent together either involved training or a casual meal out. This experience was certainly different, but not in an unpleasant way.

Ali faced the mirror to finish her makeup, and Laila followed suit with her new cosmetics.

"Isn't Erin coming with us tonight?"

"No, not tonight." Ali touched up her eyeliner. "Technically she's old enough to get in, but the other people find it strange to have a 'kid' wandering around the club. Sometimes I use a glamour to make her look older, but it's a lot of work and energy."

"This?" Erin brought in a beautiful dress—a black lace sheath with an open back, short but not so short as to make Laila feel uncomfortable.

"Yes! Here." Ali passed it to Laila.

After the dress was on, Erin added a pair of strappy black stilettos. Laila couldn't help but smile. Thanks to Ali's guidance and help, she looked as glamourous as any celebrity.

"Normally," Ali explained, "I wouldn't have you wear this dress to a club here. It's too elegant. But tonight we're going to a Supernatural club owned by one of the local Fae. It's kind of upscale and has the charm of home mixed into the décor. There are plenty of Supernaturals, so it's easier to fit in with the crowd. Who knows? Maybe you'll even find someone to have a little fun with tonight."

"Um." Laila blushed.

"Oh no!" said Ali, embarrassed. "Are you engaged to someone back home?"

"No! Definitely not. I just think relationships are a distraction from work."

Laila had never had time for that when she was training. She had been too focused on her goal. Now she had her job to focus on. Romantic relationships were low on her list of priorities.

"But you've been in a relationship before, right?"

"I have." She had experimented with a few lovers before she started training at the academy. "I think I'm just not really the kind of person who is good with that sort of thing."

Ali raised an eyebrow. "Or maybe you avoid relationships because you don't like feeling vulnerable."

"What?"

Ali motioned for her to sit down so she could remove the pins in her hair.

"Love is a risk, and you tend to carefully assess risks. It's totally natural that you wouldn't want to let someone in who might hurt you."

Laila shifted uncomfortably. It wasn't as if she couldn't handle heartbreak. But there were other risks associated with relationships. They created weaknesses that could be exploited.

"Well, in any case, I have enough to adjust to as it is. I don't need a relationship complicating things."

"We'll see about that," Ali said with a mischievous grin. She finished arranging the curls and adding one last layer of hairspray. "Besides, there's nothing wrong with a casual fling," she winked.

Laila supposed Ali had a point. One of the nice things about living here in Midgard was that she wouldn't have to worry about people gossiping and spreading rumors like they did in her home city. In Ingegard, Elves who pushed the boundaries of the strict social norms or took new lovers would quickly find themselves the latest scandal of their social circle. Reputations were of greater significance there than here on Earth because a scandal, real or even just perceived, could quickly cost the individual not only their social standing, but also their career.

Here though, the stakes weren't quite as high and people seemed less concerned about their social standing. They were more like the Fae. It was refreshing, and it made Laila wonder how it would feel to be as free as Ali was with her actions. As tempting as it was to just be herself, there was still a part of her that felt reserved, but maybe tonight would be a good opportunity to try letting go of some of her inhibitions and relax.

To say that Laila had never been to a club at all would be a lie. She had visited a few since she arrived on Earth, but every time had been for an assignment. Club La Fae was very different from any of those.

It had marble floors and pillars with stone carvings of various creatures from Alfheim. There were booths draped with silk curtains, imported furniture from other worlds, and even glowing fairy lights floating around the ceiling.

There was a mix of different races lounging on chairs and dancing to the throbbing music. Most patrons were Supernaturals, but there were also many humans. Many were wearing designer brands, and the bottles of liquor behind the bar were each worth more than her paycheck.

"Wow," Laila breathed, staring in awe. It wasn't really a true representation of Alfheim—more like a twisted fairytale version—but it was fascinating nonetheless.

"I thought you might like it," said Ali winking as she led Laila deeper into the club.

The club was amazing, and so different from what she had imagined. She traced her finger along the vines expertly carved into the stone of a pillar. Even the music was different, sort of a blend of popular Alfheim and Earthly music. It made Laila think that clubbing with Ali might be more enjoyable that she'd initially thought. Ali seemed extremely satisfied with Laila's reaction.

"Ali! I haven't seen you in weeks!" A tall, graceful Fae man appeared behind them. He spoke in the common tongue of Alfheim.

He was very attractive and had the same purple eyes as Ali. He looked Laila up and down playfully. The Fae in general were playful and sexy people. They were very comfortable with flirting and flattery. This man was no exception.

"I don't think we've met. My name is Orin. I'm the owner of Club La Fae."

"Laila. I recently moved to the city." Laila shook his hand.

Whatever he was about to say next was cut off as the bouncer waved him over.

"If you will excuse me, I have something to take care of. Enjoy yourselves, ladies." He winked and left them, winding his way through the crowded club.

"A friend?" Laila asked as they walked to the dance floor.

"And sometimes an informant. He knows a lot about the local Supernatural community. He gives me information, and I get him help when he needs it."

The crowd writhed and swayed with the beat of the music, and Laila joined them. The beat was intoxicating, and it was nice to just enjoy the music and let the worries of the last couple of days sink to the back of her mind.

A good-looking human soon caught Ali's eye. She headed over to strike up a conversation.

Laila wondered if maybe she should take a leaf from Ali's book, but she wasn't into casual dating. After a while she found herself standing on the edge of the crowd, watching. Her feet were beginning to ache, as she really wasn't used to wearing heels.

"Care to join me for a drink?"

Laila jumped and realized that Orin was standing next to her, and was rather amused by her startled reaction.

"Sure, let me just…" Laila glanced behind her to find Ali dancing deep in the crowd, the human like putty in her hands.

"It seems Ali is a little preoccupied." He guided Laila out of the crowd.

He showed her into another room away from the dance floor. It was relatively quiet, and there were actual trees growing up from the floor, giving the appearance of a forest.

He sent a waiter off with their drink orders and took a seat in one of the booths.

"I hope you're enjoying yourself," he said with a smile.

"Yes, it's very… interesting here."

He raised his eyebrows.

"In a pleasant way," she added hastily. "The Supernaturals seem more comfortable here than other places I've been."

He nodded and smiled triumphantly. "That was my goal, to create a place where our world and Earth meet. Where people of different races can openly intermingle. I maintain a close eye on the place to keep out anyone looking for trouble. So far I've been pretty successful."

Laila nodded, and let down her guard a little. "It's hard to constantly be the outsider. And I don't think the humans know what to think of all the creatures suddenly appearing in their world. It's good to see that places like this exist."

The waiter came back with their drinks, and Orin raised his glass.

"To balance. May we all find the right balance in this world."

Laila followed suit and took a sip of the cocktail. It was delicious and fruity, and there was something familiar about it.

"What's in this?" she asked suspiciously.

"Just a taste of Fae liquor." He winked as he reassured her, "Don't worry, it's from my own private cabinet in my office. I don't let the humans anywhere near the stuff."

Fae liquor was much more potent, so it took a whole lot less for a human to get drunk off it. It wasn't illegal, but ridiculously expensive, so most bars didn't carry it.

"Did you take care of that issue earlier?" she asked as she took another sip of the drink.

"Oh, just the usual crowd upset they didn't get in." He tried to play it off nonchalantly, but his shifting eyes betrayed his discomfort.

"Does that happen often here?" she pried.

"Every once in a while, I suppose. This is a pretty popular place."

"And you see many Supernaturals in here."

"What are you getting at?" he asked suspiciously as he shifted in his seat.

"You wouldn't happen to know anything about disappearing Supernaturals, would you?"

"What?" he said sharply, suddenly serious. "You're one of Ali's colleagues, aren't you?"

"I'm just trying to ensure the safety of your patrons."

He sat there staring at his drink for a moment before answering quietly.

"I've heard rumors, but nothing more. This place is a little too refined for their taste. I didn't even think much of it. I thought it was just paranoid gossip."

He glanced around to make sure no one was listening. Laila nodded for him to continue.

"From what I've heard, Supernatural men show up at the bars in pretty low spirits, some of them too broke to pay their tabs. Then they get into a fight with someone, are kicked out of the facility, and are never heard from again. It seemed a little too dramatic to be true."

"Do you believe there's a group behind these disappearances?" she asked. This was already more information than Colin had given her. She wondered if Colin was aware.

He shrugged and finished his drink. "*If* that is happening, I don't think it's likely that there is only one person behind this. It would take at least two or three humans to capture a Supernatural male."

"So, they are looking for desperate men. Probably men who are in some bad situation to begin with."

"Don't forget aggressive. They were all in fights, from what I've heard."

Then it clicked.

The bar, the Daeva, the two men she overheard. They had been waiting for the same man because they thought they could abduct him. Or recruit him. However they operated.

"Damn." She pulled out her phone with excitement. "I think I've got something. Is there somewhere quiet where I can make a phone call?"

"My office." He stood and took her through a door behind the bar.

The office was chic and open. It had a well-equipped mini bar and lounge area. But what caught Laila's attention was the large section of the wall occupied by digital monitors. There were multiple cameras monitoring every angle of the club, and digital video recorders saving the video footage. There was also a one-way window overlooking the dance floor.

"A little paranoid?" She grinned at him.

"Like I said, I take the security of my customers very seriously."

"Is there anything else you may have heard or seen that might help?" she said while starting the call.

"Sorry, that's all I know. I can ask around to see what others have been hearing."

"That would be great."

At that moment Colin answered his phone.

"Colin, I may have some more information on that case. I think I even saw two of the men involved."

Orin stepped out of the room while she filled Colin in.

"It isn't much." She looked out a one-way window onto the dance floor. She didn't see Ali, so she was probably looking for her. Or she was off playing with her new boy toy.

"It's something, though," Colin said thoughtfully. "I'll see if I can find the security footage from the bar you were at so we can get a photo of these guys."

"Should I come with you?"

"No, I've got this. Enjoy your night. I'll see you on Monday."

Laila ended the call and sat down on the sofa. How was she supposed to go back to relaxing after that?

There was a knock on the door, and Orin entered.

"I put out a few calls, but nothing yet."

"Thank you so much." She grabbed a note pad from his desk. "Here's my number. Please call if anything else comes up."

"Oh, I will." He gave her a sly grin, and she suddenly wasn't so sure about giving him her phone number.

"Right. Well, I think I should be going," she said, moving towards the door.

"Oh, come now, don't let this spoil your evening," he said, taking a step closer. "How about another drink?"

Laila could feel an unseen force drawing her to him. He was very attractive, after all. What would be wrong if she just—

"Nice trick," she said, winking at him. "Don't think you're the first one to try their glamour on me."

He sighed and made a mock show of offense. "I would never!"

"Uh huh," she said with a smirk.

"Well, go if you must, but seriously, if you need *any-thing*…" He gave her a concerned look. Laila simply nodded and showed herself out.

"It was a pleasure to meet you!" he called from the doorway. "Please don't be a stranger."

"There you are!" Ali said from over the bar. She looked at Laila, then at the door to Orin's office. "I see you two have been getting better acquainted."

"It's not like that." Laila tried to ignore the blush that was creeping up her cheeks.

"Mmhmm."

"No, really—"

"There's no need to feel embarrassed."

Laila stalked off towards the door. Ali, who was still grinning like a cat that caught a mouse, followed close behind.

CHAPTER 7

Laila watched the passing streetlights as Ali drove them home. After the chaos in the club, she welcomed the calm of the warm summer night. It was 3 o'clock in the morning, and the ordinarily crowded streets of Santa Monica were now empty. The buildings in this area were new or recently renovated. Santa Monica had reemerged from The Event as the wealthiest city within the Los Angeles area. It was home to the wealthy entrepreneurs who had helped to rebuild society and raise the city from the post-apocalyptic ashes. It had become a playground for the wealthy with designer stores, restaurants, and a raging nightlife.

Venice Beach, where Ali and Laila lived, was still a popular place to live, but the buildings were mostly pre-apocalyptic and run-down by comparison. The residents had done a good job of maintaining the buildings and fixing places up. Its proximity to the ocean made it more desirable than other areas of Los Angeles, but property came with a lower price tag than in Santa Monica.

By contrast, the outlying areas south of the airport and

inland towards Hollywood were mostly abandoned. After her conversation with Darien, Laila had done some research into poorer outlying areas. The buildings there had been determined unfit for habitation by the city. Even so, she heard there were people who took their chances. She had yet to see these areas in person, though, and dreaded the thought of being called out there. Driving through deserted streets, searching through the gradually rotting structures people once called home, was an idea she found unsettling.

"How was it when you first arrived?" Laila asked Ali. "What was the city like?"

"Well," said Ali, pausing to think for a moment. "The people here were totally in shock. Most of them were completely alone, separated from loved ones, and many of them had no idea if any of their friends or family were still alive."

Ali paused to change lanes.

"Basically, they started to clean up the city because that was the first step in rebuilding society. It really helped to create jobs and give the people some sense of purpose. Once there was relatively safe housing and reliable food deliveries, things started to improve. Then they could have a home, a job, and their lives would be back to some degree of normalcy. But there is still a lot of room for improvement."

There was so much Laila felt she needed to know about the city, but the heavy topic was beginning to weigh on her. She decided to change the subject.

"Erin seems a lot older than she looks," Laila said with a yawn, as she glanced curiously at Ali.

"Yeah," Ali rolled her eyes, "that's a bit of an issue."

"What do you mean?"

"She isn't as young as she looks. She just stopped aging about ten years ago."

"What?" Her first thought was that many people would love to stop aging, but when you were stuck in the body of a kid? "How is that possible?"

"I think it has something to do with her Dragon heritage. I've tried reaching out to find a Dragon who might know, but they are very funny about revealing their culture and customs to strangers."

"Isn't it Erin's right to know what is going on with her body?" asked Laila shaking her head incredulously.

"You would think so." Ali turned down a side street. "But no one is talking. It's as if she doesn't exist to them."

Laila could hear the frustration in Ali's voice.

"Perhaps Erin's birth parents had something to do with this," Laila wondered.

"All I know," Ali said, pulling into their garage, "is that I have an adolescent Dragon who can't age, use magic, or even shift into her Dragon form. A perpetual pre-teen sister."

Ali cut the engine but didn't move to get out. Instead she rested her head on the steering wheel.

"I feel like I'm not doing enough, but there's no handbook on how to raise a Dragon." She sighed and glanced at Laila with a look of distress.

Laila wanted to help Ali, especially since the Fae had been so kind and welcoming. Among the Elves though, it was considered inappropriate and offensive to become involved in the family matters of another Elf. She remined herself that she wasn't among her own kind anymore though, and perhaps Ali would be more accepting of her desire to help.

"Don't worry," Laila reassured her, "I'm sure there is a way to contact the Dragons. If you would like, I'll help you figure this out. I can talk to some people back home in Alfheim. Maybe one of them will be able to contact a Dragon who is willing to help."

"Could you?" said Ali hopefully, glancing up from the steering wheel.

Laila nodded enthusiastically. "Of course. It's the least I can do. After all, you opened your home to me. If I wasn't staying here, I'd probably be working myself to death out of sheer boredom."

Ali snorted. "Sounds like Colin."

"How?"

"Because the only thing he ever has an interest in is work. I mean, I've even stopped by the office on weekends when I've forgotten something, only to find him pacing in his office."

"Surely he has something to take his mind off work. Hobbies? Or a girlfriend?"

Ali shrugged. "I don't know about hobbies, but he definitely doesn't have a girlfriend."

From the way Ali spoke, Laila could tell the Fae found Colin's work ethic concerning. Laila wanted to agree with Ali, but she also knew that she had a similar tendency to become absorbed in her work. Then again, Colin was human, and he required more time to rest and recover than she did. How long would Colin last if he just worked incessantly? Perhaps she should talk to him just to see if he was all right.

"Anyway," Ali yawned, opening her door, "I'm beat. I'm going to bed."

"This was really nice," said Laila as she slid out of the passenger seat, "I probably didn't seem too enthusiastic earlier, but I really did enjoy it."

"I'm glad," said Ali grinning as she led their way into the house.

"I've never really had many female friends that invite me out to places like that, and I never thought it would feel so good to do things together like this," explained Laila.

"Hey," said Ali laughing, "anytime you want to go out or do something girly, just say it. Erin is so sick of me dragging her to clubs and salons."

"I might take you up on that," said Laila with a smile.

The next morning Laila wandered down to breakfast. Erin was awake and performing a series of poses along with a woman on the television.

"It's called yoga," Erin explained as Laila ate her toast. "It's a kind of human exercise. Holding each pose helps your strength, balance, and flexibility."

Erin switched to a different position, lying down on her mat and stretching her back.

"Yoga's also good to relieve stress," Erin continued.

"Can I try?" Laila asked, finishing her breakfast.

"Sure," Erin shrugged.

Laila didn't see another of the fancy mats like Erin was using. She just took a spot on the carpet next to her and tried mimicking Erin.

"Good," the Dragon encouraged. "Now don't forget to breathe. Listen to the instructor on the TV—she'll help guide you."

It was actually more difficult than Laila expected. But she thoroughly enjoyed it.

"Morning," Ali muttered groggily from the stairs.

"We're doing yoga. Care to join?" Laila said enthusiastically.

"Ugh, no, thank you." She searched for some cereal in a cupboard.

Erin laughed. "Ali hates yoga."

"I don't hate yoga," Ali replied, pouring cereal into a bowl. "I just hate yoga in the mornings. And after work."

"The only way Ali will do yoga is if she is in a class full of hot guys," Erin whispered to Laila.

"I heard that!" Ali shot Erin a look. "Anyway, it's not like I don't exercise. I just like doing something a little more exciting. Like kickboxing."

The lesson on the television came to an end, and Erin switched it off.

"It's funny," Laila mused, "this yoga is a lot like the exercises I used to do when I first started using magic."

"How?" Erin rolled up her mat and put it in a cupboard.

"There are similar movements, but the intention is to use them to discipline your control over the magic. The breath helps in particular. Watch this…"

Sitting with her legs crossed, Laila rested her hands on her knees with her palms facing up. She closed her eyes, and reached for the strands of magic around her. With a deep breath and an upward intention, she cast a spell of light and when she opened her eyes, tiny glittering lights floated around the ceiling like a hundred fireflies.

"Woah!" said Erin admiring the lights, "that's amazing!"

Laila walked back to the kitchen to join Ali, who passed her a glass of water. The Fae watched the lights as well, but her look was more pensive and had a sense of longing.

"Well," said Erin, sliding into a seat at the bar. "I don't know about magic, but I always feel better when I do yoga in the mornings."

Erin took an apple from a bowl on the counter and added, "You can join me anytime you want. I try to do it every day."

Laila decided she would take Erin up on her offer.

"How long does that last?" asked Ali, as she waved at the lights above them. They were now wandering through the entire room almost as if they were exploring the space.

"Just ten minutes or so, why?"

"Oh," said Ali with a hint of sadness, "I thought they might last longer. They remind me of the fairy lights back home. It's nice."

"They kind of do, don't they?" asked Laila as one passed by her head.

"I miss the magic," said Ali with a sigh.

Laila nodded in agreement. Ali had done a great job of incorporating little touches of Alfheim into the decoration, but it still lacked the magic of their home world.

Ali shook herself out of her reverie and glanced at her phone.

"I got a text this morning," said Ali, leaning against the

sink. "A human guy I know wants to meet at a bar in the Old City. He sometimes has information on illegal activities. Do you want to come along?" she asked Laila.

As much as Laila dreaded going into the Old City, she knew that she needed to learn about the city. It would be better to take that first step now than to wait.

"Colin asked me to be on call tonight with Darien, but it's probably okay to join you, right?"

"Sure," Ali shrugged and laughed, "but just because you need to stay sober, doesn't mean I have to. I'm not on duty."

CHAPTER 8

The Old City, as Laila discovered, was actually what remained of Beverly Hills, Hollywood, and a few other historic cities. One of the current restoration projects involved preserving what remained of the film and celebrity history for which the city was once well known. Old streets, famous buildings, film studios, even private houses of late actors and actresses were slated to be transformed into museums honoring the entertainment days before The Event. Unfortunately, this project was only in its early stages.

For the time being, the Old City was home to a slew of unsavory types and ruled mostly by gangs. The police and other law enforcement officers tended to steer clear of the area unless absolutely necessary. They didn't have the resources required to deal with the sheer amount of illegal activity.

"Some of the old film studios have started opening up in the last few years," Ali explained as she pulled off the 405 freeway onto Wilshire Boulevard. "They're making new movies and television shows, but they aren't as good the ones made pre-Event. It will probably take a couple more years for the technology to catch back up."

Beverly Hills was deserted. It was 8 o'clock on a Sunday night, but they saw only the occasional driver. Most of the buildings looked abandoned as well. Large shops and hotels that were once glamorous were now standing dark and empty. Some were even collapsing.

"Where are we meeting this friend of yours?" Unless they were meeting in one of these deserted buildings, Laila didn't see where Ali's friend would possibly want to meet.

"There's a more populous sector up ahead. We'll meet him at a bar there."

Ali parked in an old underground parking structure.

"We'll have to walk from here," she mentioned as she got out.

Laila followed suit, pulling on a brown leather jacket that helped to cover the gun, badge, and other equipment on her belt.

They walked a couple of blocks before they came to a street that looked out of place. The curving road was paved with grey bricks rather than asphalt. The buildings were more stylized and elegant, and there were ornate lanterns lining the streets. The peeling black street sign was printed in gold lettering reading: RODEO.

"Rodeo Drive," Ali said with a dejected sigh. "It was once the center of shopping for top designer brands. I would like to have seen it before The Event."

Ali stared wistfully at the sign before continuing. "Now it's been taken over by low-end bars and shops for those who avoid the west side."

The "west side" meant the area surrounding and west of the 405—a massive highway that ran parallel to the coast about four miles inland—and included everything from Santa Monica south to the airport and west to Culver City.

This section of the city felt desolate and eerie leaving Laila wary and on edge. She felt as though they were being watched, but when Laila glanced around at the dark windows of the floors above them, she couldn't detect any sign of life, save for the noise floating out of the street-level businesses. Whereas the west side felt lively and chaotic, the Old City truly felt post-apocalyptic. Laila remained alert, keeping watch for anything suspicious.

Laila followed Ali up the walkway until they reached a non-descript pub that had taken up residence in an old restaurant. The restaurant had once been sophisticated and stylish. Some of its charm could still be seen beneath the layers of dirt, grime, and smoke stains.

A man waved at them from a table in one of the corners, and Ali walked toward him.

He was tall and muscular with short black hair, tan skin, and green eyes. He looked hot enough to be a model, and by the hungry way he was looking at Ali, it seemed their relationship might be more than strictly professional.

"Laila, this is Carlos." Ali took a seat. "Carlos, Laila."

He nodded to Laila and gave her a charming smile. "Damn, are all the ladies in your world as beautiful as you two?"

Laila raised an eyebrow at Ali, as they took their seats.

"Just an informant?" Laila asked smugly, her voice was low enough that Carlos wouldn't be able to hear over the dull roar of the crowded pub, but she spoke in the common tongue of Alfheim just to be sure.

"He particularly enjoys threesomes," whispered Ali with a wink.

Laila ignored the blush creeping up on her cheeks and quickly searched for a reply.

"I don't like to share," said Laila causing Ali to snort.

Carlos was certainly attractive, but he was an informant. That was a line Laila had no interest in crossing. Not to mention the fact that threesomes were definitely not Laila's thing.

"Your text sounded urgent this morning," Ali said, switching to English and changing the subject. The man sobered.

"Yeah, well, strange things have been happening. At least stranger than usual."

"Go on," Ali encouraged him.

"People have been disappearing. Without a word, they just vanish."

"People go missing every day. Not all of them are related to crimes," Laila pointed out casually as she took in the others sitting in the bar.

"But these people are the kind of folks who wouldn't just leave. Not without telling anyone. And if it were just one or two, I wouldn't think too much about it, but now there are several men I know who are missing."

"When did they go missing?" Ali asked.

"After work sometime. I stopped by their homes, but there was no sign they had packed anything. It was as if they had never gone home."

His story was beginning to sound familiar. Laila exchanged knowing glances with Ali.

"Is that all?" Ali shifted in her seat.

He shook his head.

"No. Other things have happened. People out here have been attacked by unusual creatures. The survivors told me that whatever attacked them didn't look like any animal. At least not anything from here on Earth."

"That's the first I've heard of this." Ali frowned.

"Why hasn't this been reported?" Laila asked.

"That's not the way things work out here," Carlos said as he turned his attention to Laila. "People out here are more private, and hesitant to get the cops involved."

Laila thought for a moment.

"Do you have any descriptions of these creatures?" she asked.

He shook his head.

The cell phone in Laila's pocket started ringing, and she excused herself to take the call outside.

"Hello?" she answered.

"It's Darien. Colin said you are on call too. There is some sort of spell or something that has been cast near the fence on the west side of LAX. They've got glowing runes by the airport's fence, and the security guards are worried that an SNP may be trying to break in. Do you think you can meet me there?"

"Sure, but I'm in the Old City at Rodeo Drive with Ali, meeting a contact of hers."

Laila glanced through the filthy window. She could see Ali and Carlos deep in flirtatious conversation.

"It looks like Ali may be a while," she added.

"No worries. I'm near the area, so I can pick you up in ten minutes."

"Thanks," she said, and ended the call.

After a quick explanation to Ali, Laila headed back down the street toward the main road.

The streetlamps were dim, and the last remaining light of day glowed faintly on the horizon. Laila's eyes slowly adjusted to the gloom.

When she reached the main road, she leaned against the wall, watching for any sign of movement in the night. The minutes ticked by in silence.

From the darkness, barely audible, came a cry.

Darien would be there any second, but if someone needed help…

She made up her mind and wandered down the sidewalk, searching for the source of the sound. The closer she drew, the more clearly she could hear the sobbing of a woman.

"Hello?" Laila called into the night.

There was no response, but the sobbing continued. Laila reached a covered entrance to one of the buildings. The pathway to the door faded to black, obscuring her view. From the shadows echoed the weeping.

"Hello? Ma'am, are you okay?" Laila's voice drifted into

the blackness. "Do you need help?"

Something felt very wrong. Waves of dread pulsed out of the darkness. Laila's stomach was in knots, and her instincts screamed to run, but she was frozen where she stood. In the gloom, she could barely make out a figure crouching against the wall.

"Ma'am," Laila repeated, her voice quavering, "Do you—"

The woman looked up at her. Her deathly white face was covered in claw marks, and her eyes were nothing but white glowing orbs. She looked human, but each disjointed moment revealed that this creature was anything but.

She looked at Laila and unleashed a bloodcurdling scream.

Laila stood there, unable to move, as the ghostly entity crawled slowly closer, stalking her prey. Ghosts existed in all realms and took various forms. Some were harmless whispers of a forgotten soul, while others were strong, undead beings that could inflict pain, maim, or even kill the living. There was no doubt in Laila's mind that this was the latter of the two.

She tried to scream, but no sound escaped her lips. In horror, Laila watched like a fly caught in a web as the Ghost reached out with a withered, claw-like hand to caress her cheek.

CHAPTER 9

Bright headlights appeared behind her, and the Ghost hissed and retreated to its dark hole. The spell on Laila broke, and she hastily backed away.

There was Darien behind her, pulling up along the curb. She looked back, but the creature was gone. Shaking, she climbed hastily into the sleek, black Mercedes. It wasn't his usual work-issued SUV, so it must have been his personal vehicle.

"You look like you've seen a Ghost." He chuckled.

"I'm pretty sure I just did." She stared into the darkened doorway. "Let's go."

She described the encounter while Darien drove. Darien, she discovered, was not fond of Ghosts. He explained that they were an occasional nuisance, and something IRSA was called on to deal with. By the time they reached the 405, Laila had mostly recovered from the experience.

"So, tell me about this incident at the airport." Laila glanced at the Vampire in the driver's seat.

"A security guard from the airport was doing a check

around the perimeter of the airport when he noticed some
strange markings by the fence. He described them as glowing
and orange."

"I don't suppose airport security has any idea of how they
got there?"

"Nope. That's your job." Darien grinned at her.

"Great."

Darien exited the highway and headed towards the sea. It
wasn't long before they saw the glowing lights of what seemed
to Laila, to be runes. They were burnt into the grass between
the road and the chain link fence of the Los Angeles International Airport's property. The other side of the road turned
into a beach that sloped down into the ocean. Gathered at the
location were a number of airport security vehicles.

They parked beside the vehicles and walked over to the
group of people assembled nearby. Laila recognized one of
them. It was the security guard she'd encountered the night she
arrived. He sank further back into the group of his colleagues
as Laila glared at him.

Darien spoke to the humans while Laila examined the
runes. She didn't recognize them at all. But she didn't have to
read them to break the spell that sustained them.

"Can you fix it?" one of the guards asked, shaken.

"I have to figure out what it does before I can find a way
to undo it." She pulled out her phone and snapped a picture.
She would have to find a way to decipher the text later.

Next, she walked over to the glowing symbols. Holding
her hands above the runes, she carefully felt for the energy that
would tell her their purpose.

"Huh," she said, stepping back.

"What is it?" Darien kept his voice low enough that the
others couldn't hear.

"It's a banishment spell."

"What for?"

She ran her fingers through her hair. "For a type of Spirit

or something. The spell has already ended. This is just the remains of it."

"Those guys over there are pretty freaked out by this. Is there anything you can do to stop the glowing?"

She waved her hand and the symbols faded into darkness.

"Should we tell them?" She gestured toward the others.

The Vampire shrugged.

Walking over to the group of them, Laila explained, "That was just the residual energy from a spell that was cast a couple of hours ago. Don't worry, it doesn't seem to be in any way related to the security of your airport. It was just a cleansing spell."

The security guards were confused and a little skeptical. It was only after she told them she would find whoever was responsible and make sure they kept away from airport property, that the guards eventually went back to the airport.

"Well," Darien stood next to her and watched the cars drive off, "that was a little anti-climactic."

"At least we know no one was trying to break into the airport," said Laila as she slid into the passenger's seat of the SUV, "but now we've got to track down this Witch and figure out why she's casting banishing spells near the airport."

Once they were on their way, Darien asked Laila if there was any news from Ali's contact, Carlos.

"I take it you've met the guy?" she asked.

"No, I just know of him. He's given us some useful tips though."

Laila stretched in her seat. "Basically, he confirmed that those disappearances that Colin's been investigating have also occurred in the Old City. He also mentioned there's been an increase in the number of unusual attacks. He thinks they are SNP-related."

"Do you think they're connected?" he asked as he turned down a street.

"It's hard to say," she sighed. "Would you mind dropping

me off at Ali's place?"

"Sure, but you really should get yourself a car," he said with a smirk.

Laila rolled her eyes. Then, all irritation vanished when a familiar feeling of dread returned.

"Do you hear that?" said Darien, slowing the car. "It sounds like someone's crying—"

Suddenly a woman appeared in the road before them with a scarred face and glowing white eyes.

"Shit!" Darien yelled, and swerved to miss the woman. Laila looked up in time to see the light pole, seconds before impact.

The car hit it with a sickening thud, throwing the two of them face first towards the dashboard. Luckily, Laila's airbag deployed.

"Darien!" Laila called, fighting to see around the airbag. There was no answer.

Looking over, she saw that his airbag hadn't worked. Instead, he had bashed his head against the steering wheel and was slumped in the seat, unconscious.

Laila untangled herself from her seatbelt and climbed out of the vehicle. From the hood of the car, she saw smoke starting to coil upward.

"Darien!" she screamed, and used her Elven strength to launch herself over the car. She landed nimbly on the other side and jerked the door open, just as flames began licking the hood.

The Vampire was still unconscious, but she was able to unbuckle and drag him out of reach of the flames.

"What—?" he groaned.

A sob jerked Laila's attention back to the scene. The Ghost was watching them from the shadows of a building.

"What the fuck is that?" Darien swore, scrambling to his feet.

"It's the Ghost I saw earlier in the Old City. It must have

followed us. We have to deal with it before it escapes and hurts someone else."

The specter shrieked, slowly inching towards them. An explosion from the Mercedes behind them lit up the street. Darien hissed and recoiled from the flames.

"Try fire," he said, as the creature slunk further back into the shadows. "Dead and undead don't like fire."

Quickly she cast a spell, encircling the creature in a cage of flames. It screamed and hissed at them.

"Now what!?!" she asked frantically. "You're undead, can't you tell it to go away?"

"It doesn't work like that!" he yelled over the creature's screams. "Can't you banish it or something?"

"I don't know how!"

"Well, we have to try something!"

Laila thought for a moment. She could still recall that energy signature from the runes by the airport. She might be able to cast a spell replicating it. But such an improvised spell could be dangerous. She had no way to tell if she was strong enough to complete it, and if she failed, they would be stuck with a very angry Ghost on their hands.

"Okay, here goes." She called up her magic and attempted the spell of banishment. There was an intense flash of orange light, and when her eyes adjusted, the creature had vanished. Thank the Gods!

"Is it gone?" asked the Vampire.

"I hope so."

They turned back towards the flaming wreckage of Darien's car.

"Well, shit," he said, as sirens screeched in the distance. At least someone in the area had thought to call the fire department.

Laila stumbled and grabbed hold of Darien's arm to steady herself as she was hit with a wave of dizziness.

"Are you okay?" Darien scooped her up and sat her gently

on the sidewalk.

"Yeah. It's just the backlash from the spell. I just need a moment." She rested her head on her knees and waited for the ringing in her ears to fade. Usually this didn't happen—Laila knew her limits for her magical stamina very well—but she had never cast a banishing spell before. Darien sat with her while they waited for the emergency response team.

A paramedic from the ambulance arrived and examined them both. Meanwhile, the firefighters worked on the car. Laila was a little weak from casting the spell, and she had a purple bruise beginning to form across her chest from the seatbelt, but she insisted that she was okay.

Another, rather pale, paramedic was nervously tending to Darien.

"Seriously?" The Vampire rolled his eyes. "I'm a freaking Vampire. That bandage won't do shit."

He ripped the bandage from his head and threw it on the ground as the paramedic backed away.

"What I really need is blood," he muttered. "Do you have anything on hand?"

The paramedic stared at him with wide, horrified eyes.

"Never mind," the Vampire muttered and hopped off the truck.

"Do you have everything under control here?" Laila followed as he stalked away.

"Yeah, my insurance will cover all this." He shrugged. "I was getting sick of the car anyway. Maybe I'll get a Ferrari."

Laila rolled her eyes and snorted. "That's what you get for taking a personal vehicle on a call."

"Yeah, looks like I'll be driving one of the office cars for the next few days."

"Well," she said, pulling out her phone, "in that case I will call a taxi. Do you need one?"

"No thanks, I'm fine. See you tomorrow."

CHAPTER 10

After a restless night of sleep with dreams haunted by angry Ghosts, Laila was not feeling ready for the day to begin. She changed into yoga pants and a t-shirt, then pulled her hair back into a ponytail before heading downstairs in search of coffee, and the will to go to work. No one else was up yet, so she started brewing the coffee while she made herself some toast. She was spreading a layer of peanut butter on the toast when a noise caught her attention.

Glancing up she saw someone else coming down the stairs, but it wasn't Ali or Erin.

"Um, Carlos, right?" she said as he reached the last step.

"Oh," he said, realizing she was there. "Yeah..."

His hair was wet, as if he'd tried to comb it back into place, and his t-shirt was wrinkled. She glanced from the human to the third floor where Ali's room was and back again. They must've brought their meeting back to the house last night.

"Coffee?" offered Laila, unsure of what else to say.

"No thanks," he said pulling on his jacket. "I should get

going."

"Nice to see you again," called Laila awkwardly as he stepped out the front door.

"What's going on?" mumbled Erin as she wandered down the hall and into the living room.

"Ugh, one of Ali's…um…" Laila searched for a polite way to put it.

"Oh, I get it," laughed Erin, "you caught one of Ali's guys doing the walk of shame."

The Dragon poured herself a glass of water.

"Which one was it this time?" asked Erin.

"Carlos."

Erin nodded, "Yeah, that's kind of a thing."

"Right," said Laila, searching for a way to change to the topic. "Should I set up the yoga mats?"

"Sure," Erin set her glass of water down, "I'm starving though, I need a snack then we can get started."

When the Dragon reached for an apple from a bowl on the counter, she accidentally knocked the glass over. It tipped over the edge of the counter, and Laila managed to catch it before the glass shattered on the floor. She used a spell that made the water float up from the floor and down the drain in the sink.

"Here you go," she said handing Erin the empty glass.

"Thanks," said Erin relived, "Ali would've been pissed. Do you think I'll be able to do stuff like that someday?"

"Sure," said Laila with a smile, "it just takes practice."

She did some yoga with Erin and drank another cup of coffee. Afterwards she felt more or less ready to handle the day.

Laila and Ali had just arrived at the office and were heading down the hall. They'd reached Colin's office when Ali stopped.

"Shoot, I left my coffee in the car," she said. "I'll be back."

Ali retuned to the elevator, leaving Laila in the hall.

"Hey, are you okay?" called Colin from his office. "I heard about the incident last night."

"Yeah, thanks for asking. I'm just a bit bruised up."

She continued down the hall, but paused as she remembered something.

"Did Ali inform you about the rumors from the Old City?"

"She mentioned it." He adjusted the cuff of his shirt. "She was going to speak to me about it today."

Laila nodded and stepped into her office.

After booting up her computer, she opened the web browser and started her research into the local Witches. She had a strong suspicion that it was a Witch who had left those runes out by the airport.

Unlike Elves, Dragons, Nymphs, and other elementals, Witches were born with a different form of magic. It couldn't be used without a conduit to magnify it, though, so they tended to use runes, incantations, and magical artifacts as aids.

Finding the Witches would be difficult if they were discreet about their abilities, as many habitually were. They had a rocky past with other humans, who had spent centuries persecuting and hunting them. Although they were now an accepted part of society, Laila could understand why Witches and Wizards remained wary.

On the positive side, her search did turn up a handful of magic shops, psychics, and herbalists who could potentially fit the profile.

After hours of staring at the computer, she was able to determine that a number of the prospects were actually fakes, since their web pages contained nothing like the remedies and cures she knew from her lessons on Witches back in Washington, D.C. Most of the others' pages suggested abilities that wouldn't match the power of the Witch she was seeking. Only one website appeared promising.

Lyn's Charms and Remedies was located in Venice Beach, right by the ocean. The home page showed carvings in a style that resembled the runes she and Darien had seen the night before. Laila found a number and called the shop, but the call went straight to voicemail.

"Hello, this is Lyn's Charms and Remedies. We are closed for the week, but will be open next week as usual. Our hours are 9 a.m. to 6 p.m. Mondays through Saturdays. If you have a specific inquiry, you can leave your name and number, and I'll get back to you as soon as possible."

Laila hung up and wrote down the information on a notepad. It seemed that she wouldn't be getting any answers for a few days.

Sighing, Laila opened her inbox and began sorting through her emails.

Later that day, she was still sitting in her office working on her computer. It had been another slow day for her, and she found it hard to focus with her lack of sleep. Ali and Darien had been called away to deal with separate issues. Down the hall, Laila could hear Colin talking on the phone.

She thought back to the conversation she had with Ali about Colin, and how he never seemed to stop working. Sure, there was plenty of work to be done, enough to keep the four of them working day and night. But that didn't mean they should sacrifice their physical and mental health for it.

Checking the clock, Laila saw it was nearly 9 o'clock. It was time for her dinner break. She hit the Save button on her file and logged out of her computer. Grabbing her jacket, she headed out the door.

Patiently, she waited for Colin to finish a phone call. She was determined to convince her Werewolf supervisor to join her for dinner. While she waited, Laila noticed that his diagram on the wall had spread so that it now covered the entire wall and was spreading to the other walls as well.

Colin hung up the phone, and she took her chance.

"Hey!" she said enthusiastically. "I'm on my way to dinner. You should come with me."

He frowned. "I should really finish this email."

"It's still going to be there when you come back. When was the last time you ate?"

"I'm not really hungry. You go ahead." He typed away on the computer as his stomach let out a growl so loud that his inner wolf would have been impressed.

"Come on," she nodded towards the door with a smirk. Reluctantly, Colin logged off his computer and followed her.

Laila was still trying to get a feel for the restaurants in the area, so she let Colin choose the place. They walked down the street in the warm Los Angeles night to a Japanese sushi restaurant. They took seats at a bar facing the chef. Laila had never eaten sushi before and was a little concerned about the idea of consuming raw flesh. Elves didn't really eat meat. They weren't strictly vegetarian, but they refused to raise animals for the purpose of slaughtering them. She decided to stay on the safe side and ordered some rolls that only contained vegetables.

"That's not really sushi," Colin laughed when she had completed her order. She just shrugged.

He seemed content to wait for their food in silence, so Laila took the initiative to start the conversation.

"How have you been lately?" she asked casually.

"Okay. Busy with work."

The waitress brought them their drinks. Laila opened the paper-wrapped straw and stuck it into her glass of water.

"So I've noticed." She took a sip. "Is it because of that missing persons case?"

"Yeah," he muttered, "it's just one of those cases."

"What does that mean?"

"It…" he began. "No matter how many SNP men vanish, there's just not enough evidence to show where they're going. Or who's involved, for that matter."

Laila nodded.

"I feel like there's something I'm not seeing. I keep going

over the files again and again, but I keep coming up blank."

"You could try taking a break from this case," she suggested.

"No!" he said incredulously. "There are too many potential victims."

He was too quick to defend himself. Laila sensed there was another reason.

The chef passed them the plates they had ordered. Laila's had fried vegetables wrapped in seaweed and rice. Colin had three plates with different combinations of raw fish, some perched on top of rice, some wrapped up in it. Laila watched as he used the chopsticks to pick the pieces up. She tried using them, but eventually gave up and picked one of her pieces up with her fingers.

"I know there are a lot of people involved in this," she said, "but it seems to me that you're taking this case personally."

Colin sat for a moment chewing his sushi. He took so long that Laila thought he wouldn't answer. Finally, he spoke.

"I was living up in Oregon when The Event started. I was a police officer in a small, quiet city. Not much ever happened there."

He popped another piece of sushi in his mouth before continuing.

"Anyway, I met the most amazing woman. Her name was Karina. We started dating, then one thing led to another and we got married."

The pain in his expression was heartbreaking.

"What happened?" Laila whispered.

"I came home from work and she was gone. She usually went jogging in the forest after work, but she should have been home by then. Her purse was still on the table, but her house key was gone. I knew something must have happened when she was out in the woods. I told my colleagues, but they were convinced that she had just decided she needed time for herself. The only one who believed me was my partner, James.

"James helped me call her friends and family to see if they had heard from her, but no one had. We followed the paths through the forest again and again, but there was no sign of her. Then things got worse and other people were reported missing.

"One day I got a call that there was a break-in, and I headed to the house in question with James. You can imagine my surprise when I found Karina wandering around the house. She was badly injured. I rushed to her, but…"

He took a deep, quivering breath.

"You don't have to continue," she told him gently.

"No," he sighed, shaking his head. "I-I need to say it."

She nodded, and he continued.

"When I went to hug her, she attacked me. James shot her in the leg, but she hardly seemed to notice. He tried to get her off me, but she wasn't herself. When he shot her in the head, she let go for a moment, and I scrambled out of the way. At this point we had heard stories from other countries about the living dead, and we knew that she was one of them. I couldn't think clearly. I had to find some way to bring her back. She would've killed me if James hadn't pushed me out the door. He told me to run, so I did. But he stayed behind to buy me more time. I watched as she ripped out his throat and killed my partner, my closest friend. I had to shift into my wolf shape in order to outrun her."

He swallowed hard.

"James rose as a Zombie as well, and for the rest of my time in Oregon I was pursued by their slowly decaying corpses. I was condemned to be followed for weeks by the monsters my wife and my best friend had become. It wasn't until I flew to D.C. and joined the hunt to stop the Necromancers that I was able to escape them."

They sat there in silence. Laila had no idea what to say. Colin had experienced things that no person should ever have to deal with. She could feel the anger boiling inside her. The Necromancers had caused such unspeakable pain and nearly destroyed life in this world. That was the real reason why she was there in Los Angeles, to prevent another worldwide disaster from occurring at the hands of the Demons.

She stared at the sushi lying forgotten on her plate. Laila understood why Colin would obsess over his current case. He knew better than anyone what it was like to have loved ones who vanished without a trace. Even so, Laila worried that this case was too personal for him to handle.

"What you suffered through," said Laila, shaking her head, "that was horrific. But you have to look at this situation logically. You can't help these people if you aren't functioning at your maximum. You need to give yourself time to rest, and to eat."

She waved her hand at the food in front of them. When he didn't respond, she continued.

"If you need help looking over the files or talking to witnesses, just ask, but please," she said as she held his gaze, "don't punish yourself for being a survivor."

He didn't reply, but just nodded. She could still see the torment in his eyes, and Laila wished there was something else she could do to ease his pain, but she didn't know what else to say. Most Elves would excuse themselves from the conversation in order to give Colin time to gather his composure, but Laila sensed that Colin needed support rather than isolation. So, she offered him companionable silence. It wasn't much, but it seemed to be all that Colin required.

They paid for their food and walked back to the office. Outside the IRSA building, Colin paused.

"Don't tell the others, please," he said in a low voice.

Laila gave him a small smile and nodded as she opened the door for him.

CHAPTER 11

Laila returned to her desk as she contemplated what Colin had told her about his past. She logged back onto her computer and opened her emails. There was one from a member of the support staff requesting she review a case. It occurred to her that she'd never seen the support staff in this office.

"That's odd," she muttered to herself.

Pushing herself away from the desk, she stood and thought to ask Colin about the mysterious lack of support staff. But when she approached his office, the door was shut.

On her way back to her office, she noticed that Darien was back from his call. He sat behind his desk working on a report. His short, black hair was disheveled and spiky, and he wore a skin-tight black T-shirt.

"Hey," she said from the doorway of his office, "we have support staff, right?"

"Yep," said the Vampire, not bothering to glance up from his monitor.

"Then why haven't I seen them?"

Darien chuckled. "They aren't much for conversation, at

least not with our kind. They're a little reclusive."

"What's that supposed to mean?" Laila frowned and leaned against the doorframe.

"I think it's easier if I just show you," he said with a wicked grin as he rose from his desk.

He had almost reached the doorway when a thought occurred to him.

"I almost forgot!" he said, returning to his desk. He fished around in one of the drawers and removed a box of Twinkies.

"What are those?" asked Laila raising an eyebrow.

"Bait."

She cast him a suspicious look as he led the way down the hall. They took the elevator up one more floor and then followed a short hallway that ended with a single door. Laila hadn't realized there were offices up on this level. Darien opened the door labeled "Storage" and stepped into the dimly lit room, motioning for Laila to follow him.

"Laila, meet the support staff." He switched on the light switch with a click.

There were about half a dozen humans sitting at workstations throughout the room that grumbled and glared at Darien. They were dressed casually and seemed quite at home at their workstations. Many of them had mini-fridges, and she recognized a variety of energy drinks. There were also many desk lamps in use. It seemed they avoided using the overhead fluorescent lights that were standard throughout the building. To Laila's annoyance, she noticed one of them was playing a game on his computer. So, this was the team that screened their cases?

"What are *you* doing here?" groaned the nearest man to them.

"Chill out," said Darien, slapping the box of Twinkies on the man's desk. "Look, I've brought you a snack!"

The man glowered at Darien. "You know I'm gluten intolerant."

"Yeah, me too," said the Vampire, slapping him on the back.

The humans eyed Laila suspiciously. She gave them an awkward smile, but they continued to stare at her blankly.

"Guys, this is Laila Eyvindr, the newest member of our team," said Darien. He smiled, showing his fangs as he walked through the room. A few of them murmured hellos, but the rest watched the Vampire warily and shifted in their seats.

"There's a reason we moved to the storage room," said a woman scowling as Darien stopped to examine a cat figurine sitting on her desk.

"Yeah," chimed in another. "Don't you have enough cases to work on?"

Laila didn't know what Darien had done to these poor humans, but it was clear they weren't welcome. She grabbed his arm and dragged him out of the room.

"So sorry for disturbing you, have nice day!" she said with a sweet smile as the humans glared at her.

When she'd shut the door behind them, she turned to the Vampire.

"What the hell is wrong with you?" she asked, exasperated as she hurried down the hall after the Vampire.

Darien laughed and punched the button for the elevator. "Relax, I'm just having a bit of fun."

"You were tormenting them!"

"It's not my fault they're jumpy, or that they are easy to mess with."

Laila shook her head and stepped into the elevator. The doors shut and reopened at their floor.

"There you are!" said Ali, approaching them. "Where were you?"

"I was introducing Laila to the support staff," said Darien innocently.

"Really?" she asked with annoyance.

"I was going to introduce her to the investigative team as

well. Want to join us?"

Ali shook her head. "If you're not careful, you'll be kicked out of this office, Darien."

"Nah, you guys need me too much," said Darien with an evil grin.

Laila and Ali rolled their eyes simultaneously.

"Hey, that was pretty good," Darien gestured at their eyes, "did you guys practice that?"

Laila ignored him and turned to Ali.

"What's going on? Why were you looking for us?" asked Laila.

"Right," said Ali, "there's been an incident near Santa Monica. Someone was trying to smuggle Fire Salamanders into the city. They've escaped, and the smugglers are trying to re-capture them. We need to find the Fire Salamanders and arrest the smugglers before they go back into hiding."

"What about Colin?" she asked.

Ali waved her hand dismissively. "He said he's in the mid-dle of something."

"Right," snorted Darien. "We'll grab what we need and meet you in the garage. We'll take an SUV."

They sprinted down the hall. Darien snatched his leather duster from his office, and Laila grabbed her brown blazer. She'd opted for a pair of jeans, a tan T-shirt, and a sturdy pair of black knee-high boots. She'd decided that suits were not the best idea after all, at least not in this city.

The three of them piled into the car. Darien switched on the siren and the lights that were hidden in the dash as they pulled onto the street.

"Fire Salamanders are aggressive, not to mention they can coat themselves in flammable slime. Who the hell would want to transport those?" asked Laila incredulously, swiveling around in her seat to look at Ali who flipped through a file on her phone.

"Rumor has it their slime has a compound in it that can be

used in explosives," Ali replied as she pulled up a message on her phone.

"Great," said Darien, "just what we need, more bombs and fire! Looks like I'll handle the smugglers. If I get near those Fire Salamanders, I'm a pile of ashes."

Up ahead they could already see the traffic piling up, so they wouldn't get much further by car. Darien pulled off Lincoln Boulevard and onto a side road, parking the SUV.

"Ugh!" exclaimed Ali as she examined the street before them. "I hate walking."

They hopped out of the car. The others started down the street, but Laila stopped them.

"Hold on, what about vests?" She opened the trunk and pulled her bulletproof vest on before grabbing two more.

"We've got to go!" said Ali shaking her head.

Laila shoved the other vests into their owners' hands. "Then put them on while we walk."

"I'm going on ahead," said Darien, strapping his vest on. "You two can catch up."

"Be careful!" called Ali as he sprinted down the street.

It was amazing how fast Vampires could move without the need for oxygen. Laila envied him as she and Ali sprinted down the street, weaving through the cars at a much slower rate. She noticed Ali struggling to keep up and slowed her pace slightly.

The orange glow of fire in the distance caught her attention, and she knew they were heading in the right direction. Terrified humans fled in the opposite direction as Laila sprinted past them and their abandoned cars, and into an intersection where chaos had erupted.

"Well, shit," panted Ali beside her as they stared at the automobile-sized Fire Salamander that blazed like a miniature inferno. "I hope we've got some burn cream at home."

CHAPTER 12

"How the hell did they even transport those things?" cried Ali.

"I have no idea, but I see two more." Laila pointed further up the street. "I can extinguish the fire, but we need some way to contain them."

"I'm on it. I'll see if I can find the vehicle they were transported in." She took off through the swarm of humans that were running for cover.

Fire Salamanders of Jotunheim are quite different from their earthly brethren. Often found in hot springs and crater lakes common to various mountainous regions of Jotunheim, Fire Salamanders are large, amphibious creatures that are capable of surviving in extreme temperatures. Their skin secretes a slime that the creature can ignite at will to scare off predators.

In this unfamiliar environment, these frightened salamanders were blazing like bonfires.

"Okay, buddy," said Laila, approaching the first Fire Salamander. "Easy now."

She reached out with her magic, feeling the fire. Gently,

she forced the flames to shrink and extinguish. Luckily, Fire Salamanders are relatively harmless once their flames are extinguished. That is, unless they attempt to sit on you.

"There we go," she said, rubbing the slimy skin of the salamander's nose. She coaxed it over to the others, where she repeated the process.

Someone suddenly rammed into Laila, knocking her off her feet. It spooked the Fire Salamander, which reignited its fire.

The man pinned Laila to the ground, strangling her. It was one of the smugglers. Clearly he wasn't letting his Fire Salamanders go without a fight. She reached for her stun gun and jammed it into the man's side. The shock caused him to release her. Laila threw the human off her and cuffed his hands behind his back.

At that moment a semi-truck pulled up, and Ali hopped out of the driver's seat.

"The smugglers were transporting them in here." Ali jerked her thumb at the truck behind her. "The it's charred on the inside."

"Great, let's see if we can get them back inside."

Laila once again extinguished the Fire Salamander's protective flames, while Ali used her charm magic to lure the creature into the back of the truck. It lumbered into the vehicle, and Laila shut the door behind it.

"Great," she said, "one down and two to go."

They spotted the other two up another block and managed to lure them back to the truck the same way. They had just secured the door when a shot rang out behind them.

"Shit!" swore Ali, ducking.

Laila immediately threw up a magical shield around them as a group of armed humans approached them.

"Drop your weapons and put your hands up!" shouted Laila. "You are under arrest for the illegal trafficking of—"

One of the humans fired again. The shield stopped the

bullet, but the smugglers showed no sign of backing down.

"They never listen," said Ali, rolling her eyes. "Looks like we'll be using force."

"But they're human!" protested Laila in shock.

"So what?" said Ali.

"According to code 126—"

"Screw the code! They're shooting at us!" Ali drew her gun. "Do what you have to, just try to avoid killing them."

"What!?!"

This was most definitely not how she'd been trained. Humans were not to be harmed unless absolutely necessary. Then again, Ali had a point. These humans were shooting to kill.

Ali stepped forward and fired at the first man's leg. "Last chance!"

He howled in pain and clutched his leg. The other humans glanced at each other before taking cover. Still, they continued to shoot. Ali ducked behind a car for cover, carefully timing her shots.

Laila approached the first man. She reached out to his gun with her magic and fused its insides together, rendering the gun useless. It took him a moment before he realized his gun was no longer operable. He stepped forward and swung the useless weapon at her. She ducked and jabbed him in the stomach. The man doubled over, coughing and trying to catch his breath.

She reached into the asphalt with her magic, calling to the earthy materials to wrap themselves around the smuggler's feet. He tried to move, but his feet were stuck fast in the asphalt. Laila restrained his hands with a pair of handcuffs as he shouted a string of profanity at her.

Turning, she saw that Ali had managed to wound two of her attackers, but two more were bearing down on her.

"Where the hell is Darien!?!" fumed Ali.

Laila charged the closest, tackling him to the ground. She wrenched the gun from his grip and tossed it aside, out of reach. He swung at her with a right hook, but she blocked and stuck him in the ribcage with her stun gun. While he was stunned, she cuffed him as well.

The final man turned to her and took aim. She lashed out at him with a small bolt of electricity, just strong enough to stun him. He dropped to his knees as Ali walked over to cuff him.

"I leave you two alone for five minutes, and you manage to tear up an entire intersection!" said Darien, approaching with two more smugglers. He eyed the cars littered with bullet holes.

"Hey, weren't *you* supposed to handle the smugglers?" Ali hoisted her captive to his feet. "What happened to that idea?"

Sirens sounded in the distance as police cars approached. Three squad cars pulled up, and they were joined by four police officers.

"Oh, good!" said Ali, passing off her prisoner to the nearest police officer. "You can take the smugglers from here. Those three will need an ambulance." She jerked her thumb over her shoulder at the three humans who'd been shot.

The officer frowned but led the smuggler to his car, reading the man his rights. Laila and Darien helped the officers load up the rest of the smugglers.

In the distance Laila spotted a news crew and cringed. The intersection was a mess, and there was no doubt this would be making the morning news.

"What the—" started one officer, staring at the man whose feet were trapped in asphalt.

"Oh, sorry," said Laila, releasing the man's feet. "There you go."

She returned the asphalt to its normal position before turning to the rest of her team. Ali was deep in conversation with one of the officers, who shook his head.

"Hey," said Ali innocently, "we've got a truckload of Fire Salamanders to deal with. It's the least you can do to help out."

"Whatever," said the officer. "But you're the ones filling out the reports."

"Of course," said Ali, with a dazzling smile. Laila could feel the magic rolling off the Fae. The officer looked confused for a moment before returning to his car.

"Let's get out of here," said Darien in a bored tone. "Which one of you is driving the truck? 'Cause there's no way I'm driving one of those things around."

"I've got it," said Ali, swinging up into the driver's seat. "I'll meet you two back at the office."

Laila and Darien walked back down the street as more police officers arrived to sort out the mess of traffic the incident had caused. Darien waved at them as they passed.

"I can't believe I just attacked humans." Laila shook her head. "We are supposed to be protecting them."

Darien rolled his eyes. "Get over it. If they pose a threat, then they need to be dealt with. Don't overthink it."

"But if word gets back to D.C.—"

"Ha!" blurted out Darien. "Like they give a damn about what happens out here. We do what we have to do to keep things calm around here, and if that means bending the rules, then so be it."

Laila wanted to respond, but a valid argument escaped her.

CHAPTER 13

"I think it might be done," said Erin, peering into the oven.

"The timer still says five minutes," responded Laila, scanning an email from Colin.

Erin shrugged and went to search for a drink in the fridge.

After the Fire Salamander incident the night before, Laila and Ali had been swamped with paperwork all day, and Laila had been itching to do something that didn't involve staring at a computer screen. So, she'd found a recipe that looked easy enough and decided to cook for the others.

The timer beeped, and Ali searched for a pair of oven mitts to remove the casserole dish from the oven.

"Erin, do you know where the oven mitts went?" asked Ali frowning as she searched through various drawers.

"Here," said Laila, opening the oven. She used a spell that created a glittering blue shield around her hands as she pulled the hot casserole dish out of the oven. To Laila's horror, the top was charred black.

Laila groaned.

"Don't worry," said Ali, as Laila set the casserole on the counter. "I'm sure it tastes fine." She scooped out generous portions onto three plates and slid them across the counter to the bar where Laila and Erin took their seats.

Erin was the first to take a bite. Her expression morphed from suspicious, to surprised, and finally disgusted as she struggled to swallow the food.

"Okay," said Erin, spitting out the mouthful of casserole. "I think it's clear to say that the kitchen is off limits for Laila."

"Erin!" Ali glared at her sister before taking a bite. She chewed for a moment. "Oh…"

"Yeah," said Erin.

"What?" asked Laila uncertainly as she took a bite. Immediately she regretted it.

Laila sprinted to the trashcan, where she spat out the horrible spicy casserole. It was soggy and burnt at the same time. How that was even possible, she didn't know.

"Gods!" she said, eyes watering. She reached for her glass of water, but it did nothing to calm the burning.

"You know," said Erin, "even after that, I still can't breathe fire, but it was a nice try anyway." She winked, a smile playing across her lips.

Laila didn't know whether she should laugh or cry.

"I'm sorry." She sighed and leaned back against the counter. "I thought it would be nice to have a home-cooked meal for once."

"It's the thought that counts." Ali nudged her with an elbow. "And now we know that you aren't perfect!"

Laila gave her a confused look.

"Well, the guys and I were talking about how you're basically good at everything, that you have no weakness," explained Ali with a grin as she poked her fork in Laila's direction.

"Oh, seriously?" Laila rolled her eyes and swatted at Ali playfully.

❖ 90 ❖

"Well, I'd definitely say that cooking isn't one of her strong suits," said Erin, scooping her plate of casserole into the trash. "I don't know about you guys, but I vote we go out for dinner."

"I'll get my purse," said Laila on her way to the stairs.

They piled into the car and Ali started the engine.

"Where to?" asked Ali.

"The pub," said Erin. "I could kill for a burger! But can you use your glamour this time? They always give me crap in there."

Laila gave Ali a quizzical glance.

"Erin doesn't like to be the only 'kid' in the pub," explained Ali. "Even though they'll still allow her in as long as they're serving food."

"I see," said Laila laughing.

"It's not my fault I won't age," muttered Erin in the back seat.

"How do you want to look tonight?" asked Ali.

Erin thought for a moment. "Long blue and black hair, with extra eyeliner."

Ali glanced over at Laila and gave her a wicked grin. Looking over her shoulder, Laila had to suppress a snicker. Erin now appeared to be wrinkled old hag with gray hair and beady black eyes. Ali put a finger to her lips.

"How do I look?" asked Erin.

"You definitely look old enough to go to a bar," said Laila with a straight face.

"Awesome!"

Laila leaned back in her seat and exchanged another glace with Ali as they pulled into the parking lot of the pub.

There was a small crowd gathered before a television screen watching some kind of sporting event. Laila had no idea what the sport was called, she'd never bothered to take the time to learn about the games that humans played. Loud music came from speakers throughout the place drowning out the noise from the sport spectators gathered at the bar. The pub was dimly lit from old lamps that hung from the ceiling, and the tables and chairs were old, but sturdy. They found an empty table in the back and waited for the waiter.

"I'll be right back," said Erin. "I want to see this in a mirror."

"Okay," said Ali casually as her sister—in little old lady form—weaved her way through the tables to the back of the pub.

"Wait for it," said Ali motioning for Laila to listen.

Five seconds later they heard a screech in the bathroom. A door banged open somewhere down the hall, and Erin came stomping back to the table. She planted her hands on her hips and glared at Ali and Laila who laughed hysterically.

"You lied to me," she said to Laila, who was wiping the tears from her eyes.

"No, I didn't. I told you that you look old enough to go to the pub," Laila pointed out with a grin.

"And that you certainly do!" howled Ali.

"I look like I live in a gingerbread house and eat children!" Laila snorted, and tried to cover her smile.

"Okay," said Ali, "here you go."

There was a shimmer of magic around Erin as her appearance shifted again. This time Erin looked like a young woman, in her early twenties, with raven hair and dark eye makeup.

"Did I get it?" her sister asked.

"Nice!" said Erin, examining her reflection in the glass of the window.

Erin retreated to the bathroom once more. After she had gone, Laila turned to Ali.

"So, I talked to Colin yesterday."

"Oh?" asked the Fae. "And how did that go?"

"Good, actually. I think I understand where he's coming from."

"What do you mean?"

Laila hesitated. "I understand why these missing persons cases mean so much to him. Why he's working so hard to solve it."

"I'd be careful if I were you. Colin's a good guy, but don't let him pull you into his bad habits. Just because he's working himself to death chasing nonexistent leads doesn't mean you should too."

"Of course," said Laila. "But this case is sort of personal for him."

"Stop right there," said Ali. "There's a reason we are not supposed to take on cases we are personally connected to. Colin's judgement is clouded, and if something actually does goes wrong, he'll drag you down with him. The last thing any of us need is to get pulled into some bad situation because Colin's not thinking straight."

"I know," said Laila with a frown, "But that's why he needs someone watching his back. To make sure he doesn't do something irrational."

"I'm telling you, it's not worth it." Ali shook her head and gave Laila a pointed look.

"There are people out there that are missing. Shouldn't I do whatever I can to find them?" Laila eyes begged Ali to see the situation from her perspective.

Ali placed her hand on Laila's arm. "I get it, I really do. I admire your drive, but please be careful."

Laila looked out the window at the dark street beyond.

"I want to make a difference," said Laila after a moment, "that's why I came to Midgard. After I was rejected as a guards woman, I was told to try the army. But, I didn't want to sit around in an army barrack back in Alfheim waiting for the day I might be needed. I signed on for this job because I can do something that actually helps people."

Laila turned to her head to find Ali watching her with curiosity. She had to resist the urge to shift under the intense gaze of the Fae.

"I think you're finally starting to open up," said the Fae as a smile spread across her face.

"What do you mean?" asked Laila self-consciously.

Ali laughed. "It's not a bad thing. I swear, you Elves are so ridiculous sometimes. Just be yourself. If you want to help people, do it. It you want to laugh, then laugh. Life's too short to care about what people think."

Laila smiled and glanced down at the sticky table they were seated at.

"That's so Fae," said Laila shaking her head.

"What is?" asked Erin as she returned from the bathroom.

"Allowing yourself to be open to your emotions and desires," said Ali dramatically with a flourish.

"Yeah, that's way too philosophical for me," said Erin rolling her eyes as she pulled a menu closer. "I'm hungry, did you guys order yet?"

CHAPTER 14

The rest of the week passed without incident, and it was Saturday when Laila found herself sorting through a stack of take-out brochures with Ali.

"I still don't understand why we don't have this in Alf-heim." Laila glanced at a menu for a Thai restaurant. "The idea that you can just have someone bring your meal to your house is such a wonderful idea, and very practical."

"Why don't we just get pizza?" Erin called from the sofa.

"You always want pizza," Ali teased.

"I don't mind," Laila chimed in.

"Fine, but no pineapple." Ali picked up the phone and dialed the number.

Laila decided she would not be experimenting in the kitchen again any time soon. It didn't help that many ingredients she was used to using didn't exist in this realm. It was also clear that the sisters weren't particularly good at cooking either, although they could work their way through pasta, scrambled eggs, and a few other simple, Earthly dishes.

Laila took a seat on one of the leather sofas and watched

Erin flip through the movies in their database. Ali insisted that the old fantasy films would help Laila understand the impression humans had of Supernaturals. The creatures in the films were horribly cheesy, but she admitted that the humans were incredibly creative in finding ways to create special effects magic and violence.

"Ugh!" Erin groaned. "I've seen every one of these at least twice!"

"Didn't you download a new Ghost movie or something?" Ali frowned.

"I think I've had enough Ghosts for one week…" Laila shuddered at the memory of her ghostly attacker from the previous weekend.

"Are you sure that thing didn't follow you back here?" Erin glanced suspiciously at Laila. "I really don't want to find a Ghost standing at the end of the hall."

"Don't worry, I got rid of it." At least she hoped she had. But she hadn't seen the Ghost since she banished it, so she was fairly certain it wasn't following her anymore.

"Erin," Ali said, changing the subject, "you've got to find something to do all day other than watching movies. What about those online classes I keep paying for?"

"Yeah, but they're getting boring now. I can only handle so many history and language courses online." The Dragon flopped on the couch in exasperation.

"Well, you should be taking something more practical anyways," said Ali. "You can't even talk to other people in those languages."

"Why not?" Laila asked looking from one sister to the other.

"They're 'dead' languages. They're preserved in writing, but no one has a clue how to speak them," explained Ali.

"Yeah, that's why they're cool," said Erin, "it's like deciphering a secret code!"

"You're kind of strange, you know that Erin?" Ali joined

Erin on a sofa.

"If I wasn't perpetually stuck as a kid, I could sign up for a university program without everybody acting all weird. Then at least I could meet new people and actually attend classes," Erin pouted.

"Well next semester you should take something different. Maybe Spanish, or Dwarfish?"

"What's that language that Trolls speak?" asked Erin perking up.

Ali rolled her eyes.

As the sisters continued their conversation, Laila realized she still hadn't contacted anyone from back home. She knew she should call and try asking her mother if she knew anyone who could help Erin. But that would involve talking to her mother, who was probably still annoyed about Laila's abrupt departure. She sighed as she made up her mind.

"Ali, do you have a scrying bowl?" Laila asked, rising from her seat on the sofa.

"Yeah. It's not in very good shape, but it works." Ali retrieved the bowl from a cabinet and handed it to her. Laila set it on the kitchen counter.

The old, worn bowl was made of solid silver. It was slightly tarnished and dented in a few places but looked operational. Laila poured water into the shallow bowl, filling it to the rim.

"I know someone who might be able to help connect you with the Dragons," explained Laila, "but this call might get a little awkward."

Using her magic, Laila reached out toward the water. She pictured her mother's face.

"Ragna Eyvindr," she whispered. She knew her mother kept a scrying glass with her at all times, just as humans do with their cell phones.

The water turned a shimmery grey color, swirling like mist. Then the water stilled, revealing her mother's face.

"Hi, Mother!" Laila said cheerfully.

As she recognized who her caller was, Lady Ragna Eyvindr's expression shifted from surprise to ire. Laila immediately regretted making the call.

"One year," Ragna said with cool indignation. In typical Elven fashion, her mother's anger was controlled and as cold as her stony expression. "It has been nearly one year since you left and not a word, not a call, nothing!"

Laila grimaced. She was definitely not looking forward to this conversation, but she'd promised Ali she would try to find a way to help connect Erin with other Dragons who could help her with her stunted growth.

Ali and Erin stared silently from their seats on the sofa. Laila shrugged at them with a half-smile and returned her attention to her mother, who was still lecturing her.

"Yes mother, I agree, it was rude of me to wait so long before calling. But life has been very busy here in Midgard. The humans are still recovering from The Event and there is a lot of work to be done."

"There is plenty of work for you back in Alfheim! I demand you give up this nonsense and return at once!"

"Look, I know you don't understand my decision, but you need to respect that it was my decision to make. Not yours, not father's, mine."

Her mother opened her mouth to speak, but Laila continued.

"I'm calling because I need your advice."

"Why would you possibly need my advice?" her mother snapped.

"Because this is a matter concerning Dragons."

Laila could tell she had caught her mother's attention. It wasn't often that she went to her mother for help. Ragna watched her pensively for a moment before nodding for Laila to continue.

"A friend of mine is a Dragon foundling taken in by a Fae family. Her Fae parents were not able to locate her birth parents or any other relatives, so they raised her. However, her magic and ability to shift have not developed. She is not able to physically mature either, so she is trapped in the body of a child."

"I've heard of this once before," Ragna said thoughtfully. "Dragons require a special form of training that, supposedly, only another mature Dragon can give."

"The family has been unable to contact the Dragons, though."

The slightest hint of a frown creased her mother's brow. "This is a delicate matter for Dragons, but perhaps if you provide me with a description of this Dragonling and any other details regarding where she was found, I may be able to ask after her family. I often travel to their kingdom, and one of my contacts there may be able to assist."

Laila waved Ali over to the bowl on the counter.

"Mother, this is my friend, Ali. She is the older sister of the Dragon."

Ragna inclined her head in a bow. "It's a pleasure to meet you."

"Likewise," Ali said, returning the bow.

Ali told Ragna as many details as she could, while Laila's mother took notes. When they were finished, Ragna returned her attention to Laila.

"I will do what is in my power to help your friend, but on the condition that you call at least once a month."

Laila nodded hesitantly. She loved her mother, she truly did, but her mother was very opinionated on every aspect of Laila's life. It made their relationship difficult at times. It was a big part of the reason Laila had avoided calling her mother in the last year.

"How's father?" Laila asked after a lengthy pause.

"He'd be better if you'd ever have the decency to speak to him." her mother chide.

Her mother's words cut like a knife. She did feel bad that

it had been so long since she'd spoken to her father. They were much closer than she and her mother were, but Laila worried that the homesickness would be overwhelming if she spoke with him. Elves were expected to always be in control of their emotion, and she worried what her parents would think if she were to become emotional. She was waiting for the right moment to speak to her father, but deep down she knew it would be difficult no matter what.

Ragna's stony expression softened ever so slightly, as if she knew what Laila was thinking.

"He misses you a lot," her mother said, "it was difficult for him when you left.

"I know," said Laila quietly, "I'll call soon. I promise."

Laila released the spell, and her mother's image faded. Laila sighed and massaged her temples as she tried to suppress the feeling of guilt that left her feeling wrung out.

"Well," said Ali, "I can definitely see the resemblance."

"Is she always like that?" Erin asked. "She sounds so formal, and stuck up."

"Erin!" Ali glared at her.

"What?"

Laila laughed. "Usually, but it could have been worse. Much worse."

The doorbell rang.

"I'll get it!" Erin jumped off the sofa and hurried to the door.

"Thank you," Ali said, putting the scrying bowl back in its cupboard. "I don't think Erin understands how important this is, but if your mother is able to put her in contact with her Dragon relatives, it could open so many doors for her."

Laila took a stack of plates from a cabinet and carried them to the table. "My mother seemed pretty confident. I don't think she would have agreed to help if she wasn't."

Knowing her mother, Laila suspected she was probably also eager to help because it would give her an opportunity to find new contacts and potential political allies in the Dragon Kingdom. It was a game of politics to her mother. But Laila didn't tell Ali that. It was just one of the things Laila found distasteful and why she avoided the political intrigue in her home city of Ingegard.

"Seriously, though." Ali passed her the napkins. "No one here has done anything like this to help me."

Laila met her gaze with a knowing look.

"Of course I'm going to help," said Laila as she smiled warmly, "You two are the only friends I have here. You took me in when I needed a place to stay and continue to show me the positive side to living in L.A. I want to help you in any way I can."

To Laila's surprise, Ali responded with a hug. Physical contact like hugging was less common among Elves, but Laila relaxed, wrapping her arms around the Fae.

It suddenly occurred to Laila that soon she would have to move out and find her own accommodations. She was surprised by how much the thought saddened her. After all, she would see Ali at work. But going home to an empty and silent apartment would take some getting used to.

"I'm also going to start searching for an apartment," said Laila, stepping out of the hug and looking away, "I didn't mean to impose on you this long."

"Oh," said Ali, her expression changing suddenly, "um, of course."

"Is everything okay?" asked Laila, felling a little confused by Ali's reaction.

"Yeah, no, everything's fine. There's no rush, take your time." Ali smiled, but this time it didn't reach her eyes, and Laila detected a hint of sadness in her voice. "There's no rush, seriously, take all the time you need."

Laila heard the door shut, and Erin returned with a large pizza box.

"Nice and hot!" said Erin with a big grin as she set the

pizza on the counter.

Ali opened a cabinet and pulled out paper plates and napkins. "Alright Erin, I'll get drinks and you pick a movie so we can get this movie night started."

As Laila helped herself to a couple slices of pizza and took a seat on the sofa, she wondered if Ali enjoyed her company as much as she liked spending time with Ali.

CHAPTER 15

It was only 10 a.m., and Laila and Ali were already at the office. When they stopped for coffee Ali added an extra two shots of espresso to her usual iced coffee drink, but then again, this was an early morning call by their standards. Even Laila ordered a standard cup of coffee, hoping the caffeine would kick in before their interview.

They were called in early to speak with an SNP male who had been attacked the night before. As they walked down the hall, Colin stuck his head out of his office doorway.

"Laila! I finally received the surveillance footage from that bar you and Darien visited the other week. You mentioned that the two men sitting behind you seemed suspicious. Are these the men?"

He passed some papers to her. Among them were photographs from the night she was at the bar with Darien.

"That's them. These are the men I overheard." There was no mistaking it. There was even a photo of them sitting in the booth behind her where she had overheard their conversation.

"I made a few phone calls and managed to track down

some even shadier bars to check out later this week. You should come with me, since you know what we are looking for."

"Sure." Laila didn't want him out there investigating on his own.

"Okay, we'll plan to start searching on Thursday. We may have to try a few places before we can find anything."

He was clearly excited to get another lead. He headed back into his office, leaving Laila and Ali standing in the hallway.

They grabbed what they needed from their offices and walked to the hospital next door.

"Seriously!" Ali said, exasperated. "It's like he never sleeps. He was still there working when we left last night. I mean it's not unheard of for him to do this kind of thing, but this has been going on too long this time."

She finished her coffee and tossed the cup in a recycle bin. Laila threw away her empty cup as well.

"Well, at least he has a lead," said Laila.

Ali shook her head, but before she could respond, they reached the sliding glass doors of the Asclepius Hospital of Supernatural Medicine. There was a peppy young receptionist behind the front desk.

"Good morning! How can I help you?"

"We're looking for a patient by the name of Enrique Gonzales." Laila showed the young woman her badge.

The receptionist's manicured fingernails clacked on the keyboard as she searched the computer.

"He's on floor three, in room 3201."

They thanked her and headed to the elevators.

"So, it appears that Enrique Gonzales was attacked last night on his way home from work," Ali said as she scrolled through a file on her cell phone. "Gonzales is a Werecat, specifically a bobcat. He claims the men who attacked him were some kind of SNPs."

They asked a nurse for directions to the room, and she

pointed down a hall.

"Please be careful," the nurse warned them. "The patient and his family are quite upset. Security has been keeping a close eye on them."

"Thank you, but I think we can handle them," said Laila as she gave the nurse a smile.

"What do you think that's about?" Ali muttered softly.

"Probably the attack."

They found the door, and Ali knocked.

"Come in," a male voice called gruffly.

She opened the door and they stepped into the room.

It was small and plain, in faded shades of green and white. A man in his mid-thirties was lying in bed. He had a cast on his arm and a large bandage on his forehead. Dark purple bruises spread across his swollen face and down his arms. He was conscious and speaking to another man in the room. Both men stopped talking and scowled as they took in Laila's pointed ears, and Ali's violet eyes.

"Hello, Mr. Gonzales. I'm Agent Fiachra, and this is my colleague, Agent Eyvindr. We'd like to ask you some questions about last night if you're feeling up to it."

There was another man occupying the chair in the corner, possibly a brother, who stood.

"I think my cousin's been through enough already. Why don't you let him rest?" He took a step forward.

"I already told the *human* police everything I know," Enrique Gonzales growled, "why don't you go talk to them?"

"Yes," said Ali, "but we specialize in dealing with Supernatural-related crimes. We would like to hear what happened directly from you to be sure we have as much information as possible."

"Fine," said Enrique, not bothering to hide the annoyance in his voice.

His cousin mumbled something under his breath and returned to his seat.

Laila watched them for a moment before speaking.

"Why don't you start at the beginning? What happened last night when you were leaving work?"

"I closed up Martin's Liquor and left around eight like I normally do, and started walking home. See, I live about two miles away and usually drive, but my car is in the shop, so I walked. It's not the best part of Culver City, but it always seemed safe enough to me."

He winced as he shifted in bed.

"Anyways, I was taking a shortcut down an alley behind one of those bars off of Jefferson when someone grabbed the back of my shirt. I mean, I didn't even hear the guy—just one second I was alone and the next he was there."

He shook his head, exchanging glances with his cousin.

"See, that just doesn't happen to us. We've got sharp eyes and good ears. So it's not easy to sneak up on us. You know?"

"What happened after you were grabbed?" Ali encouraged him.

"I punched the guy in the face. I think I broke his nose 'cuz he let me go. But another one of those freaks was blocking my way."

"Why did you call them that?" asked Laila.

"What?"

"Why did you call your attackers 'freaks?'"

"I don't know," he said looking away from the agents.

"Can you describe them?" Laila asked.

"No, it was too dark." He still refused to make eye-contact, which Laila found unusual.

"When you were on the phone with the operator, you told them the attackers were Supernaturals," Laila clarified.

"Yeah, they were."

"How do you know if you couldn't see them?" Laila looked up from her notes.

"I just knew."

"Was the attacker someone you know?" she asked suspiciously.

Enrique's cousin said something to him sharply in Spanish and Enrique replied, gesturing at the two agents.

Ali calmly added, "I know that it may seem obvious to you that the attackers are Supernaturals, but there are many different kinds of Supernaturals out there, and we need as much information as possible so that we can identify who did this. This is for your safety as well as ours Mr. Gonzalez."

"I just know," he spat.

"Maybe you heard them say something?" she suggested.

"Yeah. I tried to fight them off, but they kicked my ass. When I was lying on the ground, they said something about me being the wrong guy, that I was just human."

"So, you didn't reveal you are a Were when you were fighting?" Laila frowned. "You didn't shift?"

"No, old habits die hard." He picked bitterly at the cast on his arm.

It appeared that he was not going to give them anything more. It bothered Laila that he hadn't explained how he knew his attackers weren't human, and she felt like he was covering for someone. Perhaps he was covering for the attacker, but why? In any case, he seemed unwilling to reveal any more details about the event. Laila's gut told her there was more to that part of the story, maybe something that could help them identify his attacker.

"Back to my previous question, Mr. Gonzales," Laila continued tentatively. "How did you know they were Supernaturals? Was it the way they moved? Or how they fought—"

"I just know!" he snapped. "Who the hell else would jump a guy like that? We were doing just fine here until all of you started crawling out of the woodwork."

It was Laila and Ali's turn to exchange glances.

"I'm sorry you feel that way," Ali proceeded cautiously. "But we are—"

"You're what? Here to help?" The other man jumped out

of his chair and stepped forward so he was nose-to-nose with Ali. "It's freaks like you that are to blame! Where the hell were you when they were beating the shit out of my cousin? If you would just crawl back into the hole you came from, we could have some peace of mind, instead of getting jumped in the streets by God knows what!"

"Sir, I'm going to have to ask you to please take your seat." Laila hoped he would see reason and calm down, but instead he spat in her face.

"Get the hell out of our city!" he screamed.

Laila wiped the saliva off her face as calmly as she could. She could have given him a lecture on respecting a federal officer, but instead she calmly stepped out of the room, with Ali following shortly behind.

"Well, that didn't go as planned," Laila said when they were out of earshot of the room. "Do you think he's hiding something about his attacker?"

"Maybe," said Ali, "perhaps the connection he had to the attacker might have to do with illegal activity, or maybe he thinks the person will retaliate. It's hard to say."

"Do you think that has any connection with the case Colin's working on?"

"Possibly, but it's hard to tell whether Supernaturals are responsible for this when these men think so poorly of them in general."

It was somewhat ironic, considering that the two men were technically Supernaturals themselves.

Ali stopped an older male nurse in the hallway.

"Please make sure that no otherworldly staff members enter room 3201, and if they do, please ensure they are accompanied by security."

He nodded and hurried on his way.

"Better safe than sorry," Ali explained as she shrugged.

"I'm going to call Colin and see if he can come over." Laila dialed his number. "Maybe they will be more open to speaking with someone from the same background."

After that encounter, Laila was not planning to return to room 3201 any time soon. She phoned Colin and gave him a quick rundown on the interview. He agreed with Laila and told her he would be over soon to try speaking with the victim.

"Here," Ali handed her an antibacterial wipe from a dispenser by the elevators.

"Thanks," Laila muttered, wiping the remaining spit from her face and hand. "Is that a common reception from people here in L.A.?"

"Sometimes," Ali sighed. "I don't know if it's gotten better or worse over the last few years."

Ali sat on a bench. Laila joined her. "I once saved a human woman in a car wreck," Ali said. "The car was burning, and I just happened to see it. When I got her safely out, she took one look at my Fae eyes and screamed something about being touched by a *'demon from hell'.*" She rolled her eyes.

"I even went to the hospital to check on her when the ambulance took her away. She told me to get out of her room or she would call security. But when I left, her daughter stopped me in the hall, hugged me and thanked me for saving her mother.

"Even though the person I saved wasn't grateful that I was there, it was good to know that there was someone who didn't care where I was born or what I looked like. They were just grateful that I was kind enough to risk my life for a stranger in need."

Laila leaned her head against the wall. She didn't know what to think. Of all the scenarios that had run through her head, she hadn't expected people to be so hostile. For the first time since she arrived, her determination started to waver.

"Did you get used to it?" Laila asked staring out the window.

Ali thought for a moment and chose her words carefully.

"Yes and no. I learned to be prepared for it so they

wouldn't catch me off guard, but I don't intend to get used to it. I prefer to have more faith in the humankind's ability to accept us, and hope one day they will see that for all our differences, we are actually pretty similar."

Ali rose and nodded towards the elevator.

"Come on," she said, "Let's get out of here. I can't stand the smell of hospitals."

Laila snorted, and followed Ali into the elevator.

CHAPTER 16

Since she had spent Monday dealing with the Were in the hospital, Laila decided to wait until Tuesday to visit the Witch at Lyn's Charms and Remedies. Hopefully she would finally get some answers about the runes left by the airport.

Laila asked Ali to drop her off at the waterfront in Venice Beach on their way to work. Ali had to meet with a witness and couldn't join her, so Laila would have to take a taxi back to work.

It was noon, and the day was hot. People lounged on the beach taking in the sun while the surf roared in the distance.

The ocean was beautiful. There were no oceans near the city where she had been raised, and Laila hadn't had much time to spend by the sea since her arrival. She had been close to the ocean the other night at the airport, but couldn't see much of it in the dark. Now that it was day, she marveled at the water stretching across the horizon.

Reluctantly she pulled her attention away from the ocean and back to the buildings along the beach.

The sign for Lyn's Charms and Remedies was hand-painted, with sea creatures curling around the letters. The front window displayed crystals, rocks, and shells adorned with intricate designs made up of runes.

A bell jingled when Laila entered. The tiny shop was less ocean-themed from the inside, but every bit of space was crammed with objects. There were shelves of bottles behind the counter. The glass display cases along the walls were filled with everything from scrying bowls and enchanted necklaces to other artifacts whose purpose Laila could only guess. No shelf space was left unused. Even the counter overflowed with odds and ends.

"I'll be there in just a minute!" a woman's voice called from a back room hidden by a beaded curtain. Laila looked over the objects on display as she waited.

The beads parted, and out stepped a woman in jeans and a woven halter-top. She was most likely in her late twenties and had bleached blonde, curly hair. She wore no makeup but had a nose piercing and several ear piercings. She also had multiple tattoos.

"Sorry about that. How can I…" She stopped mid-sentence and gave Laila a once-over.

"Well," said the Witch. She grinned and put her hands on her hips. "I'll admit, you are the first Elf I've seen in here."

Laila laughed as the human woman stuck out her hand.

"My name's Lyn. Looking for anything in particular?"

Laila shook her hand. "Special Agent Laila Eyvindr, I work for IRSA. I'm looking for some information. I was hoping you could tell me about the origin of these. They were found about a week ago close to the airport."

As she showed the Witch the picture she had taken near the airport, Lyn grimaced.

"Yeah, I cast the spell myself. I had a series of rather distressed clients who had encountered a Ghost out on that road. Normally I wouldn't go out to the site, but it had caused more than one person to drive off the road."

Lyn slipped onto a stool behind the register and pulled some pictures out of a drawer.

"These," she continued, "are photos from one of the accidents. No one was hurt, but the car was pretty damaged, and the driver was very shaken up. Since multiple customers had come to me about it, I decided to head out there and help the Spirit on its journey forward. I didn't think anyone would mind." She frowned, looking nervous as she watched Laila.

"Well," Laila said as she flipped through the photos, "airport security found those runes and thought someone was trying to break into the airport."

"Great," the Witch groaned and rested her head in her hands. "Are you going to arrest me or something?"

"No. But next time, I want you to contact me first."

Laila handed her a business card with her contact information. The Witch looked at her a bit suspiciously, so Laila clarified.

"There is a lot of work to be done in order to keep this city safe, and I'm the only one with a talent for magic on the local team. So, perhaps we can make a deal. You inform me about unusual Supernatural activity that you may need to deal with, and when I need someone with your skills, I'll give you a call, and make sure to compensate you for your time."

Lyn watched her for a moment, studying the Elf.

"I like the way you think," she said thoughtfully. "It's a deal. Anything else I can help you with?"

"Perhaps," Laila hesitated. "I had an encounter of my own. That night, before I went to this location by the airport, I was in the Old City. I saw something. I'm pretty sure it was a Ghost."

She flashed back to the hideous woman who had crawled towards her in the night and shivered.

"Go on." Lyn sorted through the contents of the counter as Laila continued.

"It had glowing white eyes. Its face was scarred, like it had been trying to claw its eyes out, and it was crying. It followed me, and when my colleague and I left the airport, it reappeared, causing my colleague to crash his car."

"Shit. That's a nasty one. Is it still out there?" the Witch asked.

"I don't think so. I trapped it with fire and tried to create a spell that would mimic the magical composition of yours. It vanished, so…" Laila shrugged.

Lyn tapped her fingers on the counter, thinking. She then got up, unlocked a cabinet, and started rummaging through it.

"I can check and see if there is anything following you… aha! Here we go!"

She held up a shard of glass surrounded with gold.

"This lens will show me whatever is tracking you," she said, holding it up to her eye. "If it isn't following you any-more, I think it is safe to assume it's gone."

"Anything?" Laila said anxiously as Lyn examined her through the glass.

"Nope," she shook her head. "Either the Ghost is gone, or it's stopped haunting you."

That was a relief. The last thing Laila needed was that Ghost following her.

Lyn returned to her desk and scribbled a note on a note-card.

"Here's my cell number." She passed Laila the paper.

"Thank you," she said, typing the number into her contacts list. "What do I owe you for the Ghost screening?"

"Ah, that was nothing," Lyn waved her off with a smile. "See you around."

CHAPTER 17

"As you know, there have been a series of disappearances involving SNP males within the city," Colin began. He had assembled the rest of the IRSA team for a meeting in the conference room.

Darien lounged with his motorcycle boots resting on the table, while Ali sipped her usual oversized blended iced coffee. Laila sat with the others and patiently waited for Colin to continue.

Colin indicated the map behind him. "The red pins mark the locations where the missing men were last seen. Most of these are concentrated in specific areas of Los Angeles. All of these men were involved in physical altercations in or outside of bars on the nights they disappeared.

"Additionally, Laila overheard a conversation between two men at the bar where she and Darien arrested the Daeva. It appears these men were there at the bar scouting for the Daeva as well."

"That could support the rumor we've heard of Demons gathering men for some sort of fighting force," Darien mused.

"That is all the more reason to get to the bottom of this." Colin exchanged a grim look with the Vampire. "That's why I propose we start out searching these areas tomorrow night."

This was the first Laila had heard of recent Demon activity. But if the disappearances were Demon-related... Laila suppressed a shudder.

"What does the blue pin represent?" Darien asked indicating the pin on the map before them.

"The location where Enrique Gonzales was found." Colin took a sip from his coffee mug sitting in front of him.

"The Were from the hospital?" asked Ali.

"Yes," Colin frowned. "He wasn't exactly forthcoming with information when I spoke with him either. I don't think it's likely that it is related to the other disappearances, but I've included it just in case."

"It's a shame he couldn't give a better description of his attackers," Darien muttered.

"If these are Demon-related," Laila began, "then I should be able to identify anyone involved."

"What do you mean?" Colin asked with interest.

"Hell has a very distinct energy signature that attaches itself to those who dwell there. It's strong enough that traces of that energy attach to any individual who has spent a significant period of time near a Demon who has escaped from Muspelheim."

"Why didn't you recognize it on those two scouts you overheard?" Darien asked her.

"I wasn't looking for it," she explained. "It's not like a smell that you recognize without searching for it. I have to reach out with my magic and actively feel for it."

Laila was not crazy about the idea of actively seeking out Demons. The Demons were cautious, and the only reason they would risk drawing the attention of the authorities would be if they were convinced they could deal with whoever came looking for them. And while the IRSA team here in Los Angeles was committed to their duty to protect the city, there were only four of them up against escaped Supernatural criminals of the worst nature. Whatever step the team took next would have to be extremely cautious.

Ali spoke up. "It seems clear to me that the safest option is for Laila and me to check out the bars. The scouts don't seem interested in women, so we should be less of a target."

Colin shook his head. "No, I'm definitely going in there. I might be able to get one of them to talk."

Laila saw a flash of annoyance cross Ali's face before she reined in her emotions. Darien looked none too pleased either.

"Colin," said Darien, "don't you think you're rushing into this? If there really are Demons involved, then why don't we take it slow? We could speak to the bartenders and ask them to report any suspicious customers."

"How?" Colin asked. "We only have photographs of two men involved, and there is no way the bartenders will be able to tell if their customers have lingering Demonic energy hanging around them."

"This is ridiculous!" shouted Ali. "These are fucking Demons we're talking about. They are not your ordinary criminals, Colin. If they think you're onto them, they'll kill you before you have a chance to put up a fight."

"Ali's right," said Darien. "You are not going to drag us into a suicide mission."

"This is our job!" roared Colin. "Grow a fucking spine!"

Laila sat in silence as the others argued back and forth. She had to agree that Colin wasn't thinking the situation through. But she also knew how personal this was to him. Her thoughts turned to his late wife.

However, his emotional involvement could compromise the entire investigation. That was exactly why Elves were raised to keep their emotions to themselves. But if Laila convinced him to let her work with him, perhaps she could stop him from doing anything reckless.

"I've got an idea," she said, interrupting the others. "We will take it slow. Colin and I will start visiting the bars on the map tomorrow night. We will not engage the Demons or those working with them. We'll just observe," she emphasized while looking pointedly at Colin. "Once we have enough information and evidence, the four of us will set a trap to arrest one or two of them. We can even contact other IRSA teams for backup. Then we can bargain with them for more information."

The others considered her plan for a moment before nodding in agreement.

It took a while before they agreed on a course of action for the next few weeks. By the time they had finished the meeting, it was one o'clock in the morning, and Laila and Ali were more than ready to head home early.

They drove in silence, the two of them lost in their own thoughts, and were surprised to find a visitor waiting for them when they arrived at the house.

Arduinna and Erin sat in the great room sipping tea from large coffee mugs. The Goddess rose to greet them.

"Hey! What brings you here so late in the day?" Ali asked, hugging the Goddess.

"I awoke with a premonition and wanted to check and see if everything is okay." Arduinna was normally a proud, strong, and sure presence (as one would expect of a huntress Goddess). So, Laila found the concern written on Arduinna's face disconcerting.

Laila frowned. "What do you mean, a premonition?" She and Ali joined the other two in the living room.

"Often, I have dreams of the past, present, and future. It is common among the Gods to have these dreams, and they often show us when to intervene in mortal life. Sometimes they are clear, but most often not...

"In any case, I awoke from a premonition dream that was very unclear. All I know was that something was stalking the streets of Los Angeles." She shuddered.

"Can you tell when this took place?" Ali asked.

"No." The Goddess shook her head. "It could have been any time. I couldn't even tell what manner of creature was out there, or if it was a physical threat at all. Sometimes these dreams are metaphorical in nature."

Arduinna sighed and took a sip of her tea before continuing.

"I know there is a lot of information that I don't have, but please be careful. I fear this is a horror yet to come, and with your jobs at IRSA, I fear you would be the ones to face it."

Laila shivered. All this talk of Demons and premonitions was beginning to get to her. The others seemed to feel the same.

"Laila met a human Witch yesterday," Ali said, changing the subject.

"Really?" Arduinna asked. "There are not as many as there once were. They were once hunted here, but they've resurfaced in recent years thanks to the changing opinions on magic."

"She was interesting." Laila shifted to a more comfortable position on the sofa. "She sounds like someone we could call if we need any magic-related help. Particularly with Ghosts. There was a nasty one following me last week, but the Witch had some sort of magical device that could show if the Ghost was gone."

"That's a relief," Erin muttered sleepily.

"Erin," Ali said, "why don't you go to sleep?"

Erin opened her mouth to protest but yawned instead. Arduinna chuckled.

"I should be going anyway." The Goddess stood. "You two seem to have had a long day. I just wanted to make sure that you were OK."

After Arduinna teleported out and Erin retreated to her room, Ali and Laila were left to clear up the coffee mugs.

"Do you think Arduinna's premonition has anything to do with Colin's missing persons case?" Ali asked. "I mean, that's some pretty close timing."

"That occurred to me as well. But I fear it could be something even worse." Laila loaded mugs into the dishwasher. Ali slid onto one of the bar stools with a tub of chocolate ice cream.

"I know you want to help him, but I'm worried he can't think clearly. I'm seriously considering going over his head on this matter and getting D.C. involved. I won't let him endanger the entire team so he can find out who has been taking the men. *Especially* if Demons are involved. There's just not enough of us for that."

"That's why I'm not letting him go out there on his own," Laila reminded her. "I've got this under control."

"But what if he drags you down with him?" Frustrated, the Fae ran her fingers through her hair. "Just because you're new doesn't mean you have to prove yourself to Colin."

"What?" Laila asked in surprise. "I'm not helping him to prove my loyalty. I'm trying to help him move on. I just know if he gets to the bottom of this, it'll help him deal with his past and he'll start focusing on other cases. It won't mend the wounds he's sustained, but it will help him to feel like he is making a difference for others."

Laila took a seat next to Ali, who watched her with exasperation.

"Look," Ali pleaded. "I'm not your sister, but I am your friend. I don't want you to get hurt for Colin's sake. Please be careful, okay?"

Laila smiled at her. "It means a lot to me that you're so worried, but I'm not looking to take any unnecessary risks. If things get out of hand, I'll get Colin out of there before he can do anything reckless. Even if I have to throw him over my shoulder and carry him out."

"I would pay to see that." Ali chuckled. She took a deep breath and sighed. "But seriously, if he does something stupid, leave him and get the hell out of there. It's his own damn fault if he gets himself killed."

Laila nodded. Ali passed her a spoon and pointed to the tub of ice cream. Laila scooped out a spoonful of ice cream.

"You know," said Laila, "sometimes I wonder what it would've been like to have a sister, or even a brother."

Ali chuckled, and glanced down the hall in the direction of her sister's room. "Yeah, well, it's a lot of work, but Erin's worth it. I don't know what I'd do without her."

Laila received an alert on her phone. It was from an apartment complex. Ali watched Laila as she unlocked her phone and opened the link. After skimming through the listing, Laila passed the phone to Ali.

"What do you think?"

"It's sort of basic," said Ali, wrinkling her nose in distaste, "and it's tiny."

"But it's affordable, and close to work," said Laila brightly.

It was nowhere near as welcoming and homey as Ali's house, but maybe she could add some color or something to make the apartment seem more lively. There wasn't much space to have guests over, and the apartment complex didn't accept pets, but maybe she could get away with a fish or two. She would miss the company though.

Ali continued to look at the listing with distain.

"You know," Ali said after a moment, "Why don't you just stay with us? We've got plenty of room here. We could figure out rent, and utilities, and it would be better than throwing your money away for that dumpy apartment."

"I couldn't do that," said Laila with a half-hearted smile, "as nice as your offer is, I've imposed long enough."

"You're not imposing," said Ali nudging Laila with her elbow, "it's been nice having someone else around. Things have been hard since my parents died. I built this place thinking they would come and visit, but now it just seems so big and empty. Having you in the house makes it seem less lonely."

Laila didn't know what to say. It hadn't occurred to her

that Ali liked having someone else around. She liked living with Ali, in this big colorful house. It really was starting to feel like home, and she didn't want to give that up.

"But what about Erin?" asked Laila, trying not to feel too hopeful.

"I already talked to her about it. She thinks it's fine, especially since any rent money you pay would go towards all her online classes."

It felt too good to be true.

"You know you want to," said Ali, poking her in the ribs with a grin.

"Okay!" said Laila laughing, "I'll stay."

Ali smiled triumphantly as she returned the remaining ice cream to the freezer.

CHAPTER 18

The next night Laila and Colin took their seats at a small table in the first bar on Colin's list. It was a country-western bar, with a group of people dancing on a large dance floor surrounded by tables for easy viewing. The bar was run-down and shabby, but the patrons seemed to be enjoying themselves. Cowboy wannabes with hats and boots tried to pick up the girls with flannel shirts and tiny denim shorts, but nothing out of the ordinary seemed to be going on.

It was Wednesday, so it wasn't unusual for business to be slow. They decided to try their luck and wait around, so Colin ordered them a couple of drinks. The alcohol consumed by humans had less effect on Laila, but she ordered a soda because she and Colin were working.

Both of them were dressed casually. Laila wore a white shirt and dark-wash skinny jeans with black combat boots. A brown leather jacket helped to conceal her firearm and badge on her belt. Colin had on a plain grey t-shirt, jeans, and a jacket.

"Do you recognize anyone?" Colin asked her.

"No, but they could have sent someone else." She absently traced the pattern of initials that had been branded into the wood of the table with her slender Elven finger. She was quickly growing tired of the loud music. Maybe she should just scan the room and get it over with so they could move on.

She waited until after the waiter had returned with their drinks before magically feeling out the room.

"OK, here it goes, Colin," she whispered. "If someone feels what I'm doing, they may run, or come after us. So be prepared."

He nodded and let his eyes casually wander around the room. Laila took a deep breath and exhaled, allowing her magic to reach out into the room, like tendrils of a vine. She searched, but there was no lingering Demonic energy.

"I've got nothing." Laila leaned back, blinking away the drowsiness that always came with such trances.

"We should wait, though," Colin said warily. "It's still early."

They sat in silence watching the bar and sipping their drinks. Laila could feel the tension creeping into Colin's body. She thought back to the warnings Ali had given her. The signs of his obsession were growing. His hair was disheveled, there were circles under his eyes, and he had forgotten to shave.

She was fairly confident that she could keep the Werewolf from doing anything rash. But once again she worried Colin was rushing into this investigation.

After an hour his patience had reached its breaking point.

"Can you check again?" he asked.

Laila was quite sure that no one, let alone an SNP, had entered the bar, but she kept her opinion to herself.

Once again she closed her eyes and reached out, feeling the energy of the people in the room. But still she felt nothing but the thrum of ordinary human life force.

She shook her head, and Colin stood impatiently.

"Let's go. The guys we're looking for aren't here."

Laila stopped at the cash register on their way out to pay

CAUGHT BY DEMONS

for their drinks. By the time she had finished, Colin was waiting in the car with the engine running.

The next five bars were busts as well. They didn't bother to stay at the first four after Laila scanned the energy in the room. At the fifth she picked up on some Supernatural energy, but it was just a Vampire looking for a good time, and a potential snack. It wasn't illegal for Vampires to drink from humans, so long as the human consented. They let him be, since he didn't seem to be bothering anyone.

Colin was becoming more anxious with every bar they left. Elves were patient by nature, and Laila questioned her supervisor's excitability. Surely, he knew that searching like this was a shot in the dark?

But then, finally, Laila sensed something.

They had pulled up to a tiny hole-in-the-wall bar. Laila could tell by the energy there, that someone had been in recent contact with a Demon. The residual energy was faintly attached to the two SNP's in question, but it was still there nonetheless.

"This is it. I can sense there's someone in there." Laila pulled out her phone. "We should call the others."

Colin shook his head. "It's going to take too long for them to get here. We should go in and I.D. these guys while we can."

"The second they notice our guns and badges, they'll take off."

"Not if we leave them behind."

"*What?*" Laila stared at him in shock. "Colin, I realize that you are pretty lax when it comes to decorum. But that is throwing all protocol out the window!"

"Look, I get it. You are fresh out of training, but out here we can't afford to follow protocol in every situation. We have to take risks and bend the rules out here. There are four of us in the entire city against God knows how many of them."

"This is insane!" she hissed. He was going to get them both killed. "The rest of the team will be here in fifteen minutes. Maybe less. We can wait."

"We are so close, and we can't lose this opportunity."

They sat there glaring at each other in the dim orange light from a distant street lamp. Laila once again recalled the conversation they had had about Colin's wife. Her instincts told her to wait for backup, but Colin was desperate. Laila had a feeling he was going in there with or without her.

"Fine," Laila sighed. "But I'm calling for backup, and we won't make any move to engage them before the others arrive."

"Deal." He began removing his badge and other items from his belt, and then stored them in a safe built into the center divider of the car.

"I won't know who we are looking for until we are inside." She passed him her gun and other articles.

"Okay, let me know when you see them."

The bar was a mess. The tables were grimy, the floor covered in a thick layer of dirt. The place stank of booze, vomit, and sweat.

There were a number of SNPs there. They seemed to be Shapeshifters mostly, but a few were from other realms.

Then there were the two men she was after. The energy that clung to them wasn't particularly strong. They were probably the grunts stuck at the bottom of the food chain trying to work their way up to more power. They looked human, but looks could be deceiving, and Laila had a feeling they were using some kind of glamour to disguise themselves.

Colin jerked his thumb at a couple of open seats at the bar and ordered them drinks. They sat there for a moment.

"Do you see the two men sitting at the table behind us?" she asked.

He nodded.

"They're the ones."

The seconds ticked by, and she could feel Colin tense beside her. Laila checked her phone. Darien and Ali still hadn't arrived, and Laila was worried that Colin might try to engage the men.

Suddenly he got up and muttered something about the bathroom. Laila caught his gaze, scowling, and gave a small shake of her head. He ignored her but left in the opposite direction of their marks.

Laila relaxed ever so slightly and glanced nonchalantly about the bar to get a glimpse of their targets, but a squeal distracted her and she jerked her head around to see Colin removing his hand from the squealing woman's ass.

Laila's jaw dropped. What the hell was that about?

The woman's date seemed none too amused. He grabbed Colin by the shirt.

"What the fuck 'you think you're doin'?"

"It's a compliment. A girl like that could do better than an ugly dick like you!" Colin gave him a drunken grin.

"YOU SON OF A BITCH!!!" the guy roared and shoved him into a table. Colin quickly recovered and punched him in the face. The man apparently had friends though—that or just a couple of guys looking for a fight—because three more men went after Colin.

"Shit!" Laila muttered. She rolled her eyes and joined in, ignoring the bartender's protests.

Doing her best not to injure anyone too badly, she grabbed the man closest to her around the neck with one arm and swept his feet out from under him, throwing him to the ground and knocking the breath out of him. She dodged a punch from another and kicked him in the groin, incapacitating him. He dropped to the floor as well.

"Break it up!" yelled the bartender. "I swear to God I'll call the cops on your sorry asses if you don't get the hell out of my bar!"

Laila shoved another man out of the way, grabbed Colin by the front of his shirt, and dragged him out of the mess and through the door.

They stood there in the cool night air, panting. Colin turned to her.

"What the hell was that!?!" She spun him around so he was facing her.

"I was trying to spark their interest." He shrugged.

"Without backup?"

"They're on their way," he reasoned.

Laila massaged her temples and took a deep breath to calm herself.

"Do you think it worked?" he asked.

"I guess we'll find out," she muttered and shrank back into the shadow of the building.

"Well, I'm definitely glad to have you in a bar fight."

"You should have at least started a fight with me and kept the humans out of it." She frowned at him.

He shrugged. "More convincing this way."

Laila was about to argue when the other men piled out of the bar. She and Colin inched further into an alley to stay out of sight. They didn't need to start another fight in the streets.

"Did you see them leave?" Laila searched the crowd, looking for the two men they were after.

"I'm pretty sure they're still in there."

A sound behind them made Laila turn in time to see a dark figure hook his arm around Colin's neck. It was one of the men they had been searching for.

She lunged, but the other man appeared, wrenching her arm behind her painfully.

"Let him go!" she snarled. They ignored her.

"Leave him. He's a Werewolf, I can smell it. We don't want another mangy mutt," her captor spat. "This one's the real prize. A better fighter too."

Colin was still struggling and starting to shift. Laila thrust her elbow into her captor's stomach and twisted out of his grasp. But she wasn't fast enough to stop Colin's attacker. He bashed the Werewolf's head against the cement wall, and Colin crumpled.

"Colin!" Laila screamed, but the two men grabbed her and

shoved a piece of material in her mouth to silence her. She gagged and struggled against them as they dragged her down the alley, but even with her Elf strength, their combined force was too much for her.

Laila's mind raced. Was Colin okay? Where was back up? They should've been here by now. Would they be able to find her? She gave one last glance to Colin's motionless body before she was taken around a corner.

CHAPTER 19

Laila was in trouble. She tried to make as much noise as possible, hoping that Ali and Darien would have arrived. But no one appeared to help her.

She was led down the street and through a long back alley before entering a shabby, two-story office building. There was a cracked and faded sign hanging above the doorway that Laila couldn't make out. She was fairly certain it didn't matter, as the Demons had probably broken in anyway.

One of the men knocked. Another goon answered the door and motioned for them to come in.

The room was dimly lit by a lamp sitting on a cardboard box. It revealed peeling wallpaper and stained carpeting that was covered in a thick layer of dust. A few men stood by in the shadows, but there was one man seated in a folding chair in the middle of the room.

He could have been a businessman. The SNP had slick, black hair and wore a clean and sharp-looking suit, a contrast to the dilapidated room. His eyes were as cold as steel, and he had the vibe of a Shapeshifter of some kind. The hellish energy surrounding him was much stronger than around the others, but still he was not a Greater Demon, one who had been imprisoned in Hell. Regardless, all of these men were involved with the Demon organization. They had fraternized with the damned and were considered to be Lesser Demons by association.

He stood.

"Welcome!" he said with a smile, which faded as he slowly looked her over.

He turned to the men who had brought them there. "What did I tell you?" he warned, his voice dangerously slow. "Do not attract attention. I could hear you from two blocks away!"

The two men exchanged glances, and the taller one said, "But boss, they—"

He didn't have time to finish his sentence because the boss's head shifted, his pupils became slanted, and scales covered him. Before anyone could move, he grabbed the henchman and tossed him through the wall into the next room. He nodded to the man who had let them in, who then went into the other room.

Thor's hammer, this guy's insane, thought Laila, spitting the gag out of her mouth.

The boss brought his attention back to her, his fangs now extended. It was entirely possible that he was venomous. He shook his head as it changed back to his human face.

"Please excuse my behavior." He mopped his forehead with a handkerchief that he pulled out of his pocket. "Sorry about that, miss. These boys here have such bad manners. Unfortunately, we are not looking for ladies. I don't think a woman, even an Elf, is strong enough to handle this job."

Laila's stomach dropped. She had seen too much. There was no way they were going to let her walk out of there alive. But if she switched tactics, perhaps she would convince them to take her instead of killing her. She had no idea where they would take her, but anywhere was better than a morgue.

Or perhaps there was still time to escape? If she caught them off guard, she might be able to slip out the door behind them. She was outnumbered, but there was still a chance.

"Oh, I see. You're one of those men," she said, giving the Shifter an appraising look. Brazenly she looked over the men in the room, silently challenging them.

"I'm sure," she said boldly, "anything these idiots could do, I could do twice as well."

Some of them grumbled and shifted. The Shapeshifter checked his watch. Laila knew he only had moments to decide what to do with her. She'd made enough noise back in the alley to draw attention. It wouldn't be long before her teammates, or the police, came to investigate. She needed more time, and a distraction.

One of the henchmen rested his hand on her shoulder. She grabbed his arm, flipping him over her shoulder. He landed on one of his buddies in a heap of tangled limbs. Laila lashed out, sending a blast of fire towards the Shifter, who ducked.

"Grab her!" he screamed.

Someone grabbed her from behind. She reached behind her, digging her nails into his face and raking them across flesh. The man screamed but didn't let go. Another approached her from the front. She kicked, smashing his nose with the heel of her boot. He howled and collapsed, grabbing his broken nose.

Laila returned her attention to the man holding her, but there was movement behind Laila, and she felt a needle stab into her neck. She clawed at the hands that were holding her captive, but whatever was in the syringe made her hands heavy and clumsy. Her vision went dark, and she fought until she was pulled down into unconsciousness.

Colin growled and shifted back into his human shape. His head ached fiercely. Gingerly he reached up to feel it, and his fingers came away wet with blood.

He was lying in the alley where he and Laila had been attacked, but there was no sign of the Elf.

Carefully he stood and made his way back to the street. An SUV pulled up, and Ali jumped out.

"Gods! What happened?" she said, examining his head.

"We were jumped by the Demons' henchmen."

"Where's Laila?" Darien suddenly appeared, with unnatural speed.

"Gone," he growled. "They took her. I didn't see where they went."

In an instant Darien was gone, tracking the Elf.

Colin sat on the curb. Clearly Laila was the better equipped of the two, as their attackers had said. They took the skilled Elf and left him lying by a dumpster. He hated these Demons with every fiber of his being.

He hated Laila as well for her strength and magic. But the second he thought it, he regretted it. He had been an idiot going in there, and she knew it. She had tried to stop him. But he wouldn't listen.

"Colin?" Ali sat next to him on the curb. "Are you okay?"

He snarled at her, and she backed up.

"Hey!" She glared at him.

"Sorry," he grumbled. He sat there in silence, even ignoring Darien's return.

Ali pulled the Vampire aside. "Did you find anything?"

"Not really." He shook his head. "I tracked them to an abandoned office building, but they left by car before I arrived, and the trail went cold."

"No! We have to…" She faltered.

Darien's hand on her shoulder stopped her.

"Ali, they're gone. There is no way we can track them. We don't even know what vehicle to look for."

Ali let out a long string of profanity so strong that Darien stared in shock. Ali knew it had been a bad idea for Laila to go with Colin.

She looked at Colin, who had been ignoring them. He wasn't even attempting to do anything. Laila had put her life on the line to help him. It was his fault she was abducted, and now all he could do was mope in the gutter.

CHAPTER 20

Laila fought to gain consciousness, but her head was in a fog. The feeling was as though she were floating underwater and struggling to find the surface. She could hear vague noises. There were people around her, but she couldn't tell where she was or why she was there.

She remembered she had been out drinking with Colin. No, not drinking—searching the bars. But for what? And why did she feel so strange?

She tried to move but could do little more than roll over on the hard stone where she lay.

There had been a room, an office with men in suits. And their leader had fangs. He was a Shifter.

The memories returned, plowing into her mind like a semi-truck. She bolted upright but immediately regretted it as a wave of dizziness hit her, and she collapsed with a groan.

Where was she? And more importantly, what had happened to Colin? She sent a quick prayer to any of the Gods that might be listening, hoping that he was alive.

As the drugs she had been given wore off, she observed

her surroundings. She was locked in a dingy cell, one of six that made up a cellblock in the concrete room. There were no windows, and the only light came from harsh exposed bulbs hanging in the corridor outside the cells. The walls were old, and small cracks reached like spider webs along them. The steel bars of the cell were new, so it seemed that the building had been repurposed. What the building could have once been, though, she had no idea.

There were others kept in various cells throughout the room, all of whom were SNP males. They looked worn and had minor injuries. They paid little attention to her.

She seemed to be uninjured but couldn't shake the feeling that something was off. She noticed a pair of metal bands around her wrists. Not handcuffs like she normally carried, but thick metal bracelets with glowing stones and inscriptions on them.

The language of the inscriptions was not familiar to her. It was probably some language used in Muspelheim. The cuffs were heavily enchanted, probably to keep her in the building or to bind her magic. In any case she knew how nasty those enchantments could be, so she decided not to chance a spell.

The door at the end of the room opened, and Demon henchmen dragged two other men back to their cells. The men were bloody and bruised, but worse than the physical injuries were the feral looks in their eyes. The only thing keeping them alive was the basic animalistic urge to survive, no matter the cost.

"Who's next?" one of the Demons said, checking a clipboard. "We need to stall a bit longer, and we've already gone through tonight's lineup."

The other noticed she was awake.

"How about this one?" He grinned darkly.

"What?" She stood as they unlocked the cell door. Her heart was beating so loudly she was sure they could hear it. She lunged and tried to slip past him, but the opening was too small.

He grabbed her arm and roughly yanked her out of her cell.

"Save your energy, you'll need it."

She could feel the adrenaline coursing through her veins. If she fought them off, could she run? She looked around, but they were in a labyrinth of hallways. It would be impossible for her to escape without knowing where she was running.

There were cheers from a crowd that echoed through the hall. They took her to a set of heavy steel doors. Through them was a massive arena. It must once have been a factory, but huge platforms with seats had been erected, reminiscent of the ancient Roman amphitheaters.

The arena had a stage where two men were currently fighting. She stood on the lowered outer circle of the fighting ring, which was separated from the inner circle by a metal rail.

Of the two men that were fighting, one was a Troll, and the other was a Svartálfr or Dark Elf.

She was not fond of Trolls. They had been at war with the people of Alfheim several times. They were really tough to deal with, stubborn and extremely strong. Most sensible people avoided a fight with them at all costs.

Svartalfar, on the other hand, were ancient relatives of Laila's people, the Light Elves. Legend had it that the two races were once one people. For political reasons, a group of the Elves had decided to leave Alfheim to start their own state in another realm, now known as Svartalfheim. The two races of Elves still had little to do with each other, even after many ages had passed. He could potentially be an ally, but that was assuming he was interested in helping her, and in Laila's experience, Dark Elves were usually only interested in helping themselves.

The Troll attacked the Dark Elf with a battered sledgehammer while the Elf nimbly dodged. When he saw an opening, the Dark Elf attacked with the broadsword he was holding but missed. The Troll swung again, and when the Elf ducked, he sliced the Troll's hamstrings. The Troll roared in pain and collapsed.

"A devastating blow for the Troll!" an announcer called over the loudspeaker.

The announcer was right. Despite the Troll's desperate attempts to keep the Elf at bay, he eventually disarmed the Troll and stood over him, pointing his sword at the Troll's throat. The crowd roared with enthusiasm.

It was the audience in particular that disturbed her. She had expected to see it full of Demons and their cronies, but as she scanned the arena she realized that, apart from the employees milling around, the audience was entirely filled with ordinary humans.

She was disgusted. The very people that she was here trying to protect stood cheering on this grisly sport.

"The Master of the Games has made his decision," the announcer called. "Finish him!"

The crowd cheered even louder as the Svartálfr plunged his sword into the Troll's neck. He had to repeatedly hack at the flesh because of the Troll's tough hide. It was a bloody and horrendous execution. Finally, the Troll shuddered one last time and was still. The crowd was silent as the Dark Elf cleaned his sword on the Troll's lifeless body. He then stood and thrust the sword into the air.

The crowd erupted into yet another rowdy cheer. The Dark Elf stood there savoring his victory as two Demons dragged away the heavy, mutilated corpse, trailing bits of gore behind them.

Laila seethed with anger. She had known that she would face something horrific, but this? She didn't have time to dwell on it, though, because her two Demons started pushing her up into the arena.

She stood there panicking for a moment. Did they expect her to fight this armed killer without a weapon? But instead of attacking her, the Dark Elf sauntered past, jumped down from the arena, and winked at her.

Movement on the other side of the arena caught her attention. A smallish figure—a Goblin—was crawling onto the platform. Goblins are similar to Trolls, but only about four feet tall. They do have sharp teeth, though, capable of taking a chunk out of someone's arm without a problem.

This one was taunting the audience and making rude gestures. The audience started shouting at him, and a couple of people even threw things.

"Ladies and gentlemen!" the announcer called over the speakers. "We have a special treat for you tonight! As you've noticed, the fool is back once again, but tonight we welcome a new warrior to the arena. For the first time, a woman graces our stage! A Light Elf too!"

The audience cheered, and one of the Demons shoved her forward.

"Hey!" she shouted to him, "What about my weapon?"

The Demon chuckled at her. "What about your weapon? Enjoy your fight."

She turned toward the Goblin who was thrusting his pelvis at her.

This was completely absurd, she thought. Maybe this was all just a very disturbing and messed-up nightmare.

A gong sounded from somewhere. Apparently it was the cue to start, because the Goblin ran at her with a demented grin.

Of course, she was much faster than him. She dodged out of the way, pivoted on one foot and kicked him in the side. He stumbled from the force of the kick and seemed surprised that she was fighting back.

He shouted something at her, but Laila didn't speak Goblin. She ignored him, stepped in and punched his nose. She found the resulting crunch satisfying.

The Goblin howled in pain as blood gushed down his nose. Whatever humor he possessed vanished. He bared his pointed teeth and slashed at her with his claws. Jumping back, she barely avoided the swipe. He rammed into her, knocking her to the ground and pinning her there. His clawed hands wrapped around her neck in a vise-like grip.

Her head spun from the impact with the floor, and she clawed at the goblin's hands, whose claws dug deeper into her flesh. She rammed her palm into his already broken nose.

His grip loosened in shock, and she used her legs to throw him off her.

She was on her feet instantly, and before he could plan his next move, she sent a roundhouse kick to his head. He crumpled to the ground, unconscious.

The crowd once again roared, and she heard the announcer over the speakers.

"Looks like the pussycat's got claws! But will she kill him?"

A jolt of panic struck Laila. She wasn't a killer.

She looked at the mess she had made of the Goblin's face. She was disgusted with herself for what she had done. The Goblin didn't deserve to die like this.

Luckily, she didn't have to kill. The man they called the Master of the Games shook his head.

"Sorry, folks, but the Goblin lives another night!" the announcer called.

Laila sighed with relief as the crowd protested. She turned to leave, wanting to get as far from that damned arena as she could.

"Where do you think you're going?" a rich, even, beautiful voice called over the rumble of the crowd.

CHAPTER 21

The Master of the Games leaned against the railing of his balcony, but she couldn't clearly see his face. Not with the bright arena lights shining in her eyes.

Two of the Demons approached her from the sides, blocking the exits. She turned and glared up at their leader.

"Come now, that's no way for a proper lady to act. Didn't they teach you manners in Alfheim, my little warrior princess? Bow to your master."

She fumed. She was not this man's servant to order around. She stood her ground and didn't move.

"He said, bow!" one of the Demons hissed in her ear.

"No."

The other Demon punched her in the stomach. She doubled over and dropped to her knees, gasping for air.

"Now was that so hard?" the Master of the Games purred.

She glanced back up at him but was helpless to do anything but struggle to breathe.

"Take her away." He turned and walked through a doorway and out of sight.

The same two guards grabbed her and dragged her back out of the ring. They led her down the labyrinth of halls back to her cell, where they unceremoniously thrust her into the cell and locked the door behind her.

She sat on her knees for a moment. Her head ached from hitting the floor, and her stomach did too. She was also exhausted. The drugs they had used on her must still be in her system. She placed her hands on the back of her head and started calling her magic to heal herself.

"I wouldn't do that, *princess*," a man to her left said.

She ignored him. She just wanted the spinning to stop. The magic came to her fingertips, and as it touched her, electricity jolted though her body from the cuffs on her wrists. She screamed in pain, and the magic slipped out of her grasp. The electricity stopped, leaving Laila to lie frozen on the floor of her cell.

"Don't say I didn't warn you," the man said smugly.

Laila noticed it was the Dark Elf from earlier. Apparently, he occupied the cell next to hers. Great.

"Light Elves never listen," he continued. "They always think they're right. So stubborn." He shook his head very patronizingly.

She gritted her teeth, forcing words out of her mouth. "At least I'm not a murderer."

"Survive here long enough and you will be, princess."

"Bastard!" she yelled at him.

"Hey!" a guard said, lumbering down the hallway. "Shut up down there!"

"What are you going to do about it?" She glared at the guard, challenging him to open the cell door. Instead he pulled out a remote, pointed it at her, and the cuffs sent another jolt of electricity through her body. She clenched her teeth, trying not to cry out, for what felt like an eternity. Finally, he stopped torturing her and wandered back down the hall.

She lay there in pain. Slowly the ability to move came back

to her weakened muscles. She crawled further from the door and curled up on the hard cement floor. She could tell the Dark Elf was watching her, so she turned her back to him and almost immediately drifted into an exhausted sleep.

She awoke to the clattering of plates being shoved into the cells, followed by cups of water. Stiff from the previous night's activity and from sleeping on bare cement, she got up to investigate the contents of the plate.

Breakfast appeared to be a couple of slices of bread and some sort of meat. She didn't bother to ask what, since there was no choice but to eat it or starve. Anyway, she was ravenous. She had no idea how long it had been since she last ate. The food and water seemed at least to help stop her growling stomach.

"Here!" a gentle voice called in English from the cage on her right, whose occupant she hadn't seen last night. He was a Dwarf, about three and a half feet tall. He had scraggly brown hair and a scruffy beard. His hands were tough and scarred, as if he was used to doing hard manual labor. His eyes were tired but kind. He was holding his cup of water out to her.

"Take it," he insisted, placing it in her hands through the bars of the cell. "You need it more than I do. You probably haven't had anything to drink since they captured you."

"Thank you," she said, taking the cup. "That's very kind."

That this stranger showed her such a kindness in this desolate hellhole was astonishing. Perhaps there was a catch. She watched him suspiciously for a moment but saw nothing but a deep sorrow in his eyes.

"I have four daughters, all strong, clever girls. As a father, it would kill me if I ever found out that one of them was trapped in a place like this. It's no place for a girl like you. My name's Torsten, by the way."

"Thanks, Torsten. This is no place for anyone. It's beyond cruel what they're doing here," she said, savoring the water.

"How long have you been here?"

"I'm not sure. Months, probably. At this point it's hard to believe that I'll ever get out of here, but the hope of getting out of this damned place is all that keeps me going." He sighed deeply and rested his head against the wall. "We're not killers—none of us here are—but in this place it's kill or be killed. If you refuse to fight, you earn the seat of honor at a public execution."

Laila suppressed a shiver at the thought.

"How is it that this place has been kept secret for so long? With the size of that crowd, you would think the government would have heard about it by now," she probed, trying to gather what information she could. Maybe she could at least figure out the location.

"I'm not entirely sure. Perhaps it's because the Demons that run this place have tight security, or because the people who come to watch the violence are addicted to it like a drug. The Event hit the humans pretty hard, and such a catastrophe does something to you. A lot of the survivors lasted as long as they could because they were cunning and lucky, or because they were ruthless and aggressive. Now the danger is over, but those humans who come here miss the violence. I think they value the thrill of the fights too much to let the cops catch wind of this."

"If they value their thrills so much, why aren't they the ones out there fighting?" she said bitterly and passed the cup back to the dwarf.

"Because, *princess*," the Dark Elf said in the other cell, "we're not from here. We're different, scary."

Despite the poor accommodations, the Dark Elf at least appeared well rested, or at least in better condition than she felt.

"Jerrik's right," Torsten said, nodding to the other man. "The humans aren't fond of newcomers, even of their own kind. Their history is full of examples of cruelty, not unlike the histories of our worlds."

The Dark Elf shifted in his cell.

"What the Dwarf is trying to say is that humans have been put on a pedestal by the other worlds as frail and innocent creatures, but they are just the same as any other race. There are the good and halfway decent ones, and then there are the others who would watch and laugh as innocent people were slaughtered in front of them."

Silence hung over them as the weight of Jerrik's words sank in. They watched as a guard passed and eyed them before moving on down the row of cells and out of the room.

Jerrik stared at her through the bars, his expression unreadable. Laila ignored him, hoping to discourage any further conversation on his part, but he was the first to break the silence.

"So, princess, why did you decide to come over to Earth?"

"Stop calling me that!" she snapped at him. "I'm no princess, and my name is Laila."

"What made you come to Midgard, *Laila?*" Midgard was the name their peoples shared for Earth.

Laila knew that revealing the truth that she was working for the government was obviously a bad idea. Anyone in this place would be only too eager to sell her out to the Demons. She chose her words carefully.

"My career wasn't going according to plan. I decided to come to Earth where I could make a fresh start."

"Oh? And what career was that?"

"That's none of your business."

"So dismissive and aloof in a friendly conversation," he chuckled, amused that he was getting under her skin. She tried to ignore him.

"You have more in common with me than you would ever care to admit." He crouched down next to her, leaning against the bars. "After all, you've ended up here like me."

"What's that supposed to mean?"

"Look around—this isn't exactly high society. We're the

greedy ones who were looking to make a quick buck, like some of the Demons promised us. The ones who couldn't make enough money to feed themselves or their families. Every single one of us ended up here because we were desperate and aggressive, and the Demons took advantage of that."

He leaned closer, and she resisted the urge to scoot away.

He continued, "I was tempted by the money, and the glory. They told me I could be some hotshot fighter and make as much money as I needed. I didn't realize that my only way out would be in a body bag." He stood there for a moment, and underneath his arrogance she could see pain and misery. She almost felt sorry for him, but then the smug arrogance returned.

"Better watch yourself, Elf." He winked at her and then moved to the back of the cell where he could lean against the wall.

She'd had enough of him anyway and decided to meditate. Perhaps it would help her to organize her thoughts and come up with a plan to get out of there.

CHAPTER 22

Ali ran her fingers through her hair, struggling to put her frustration into words. It had been two days since Laila was abducted by Demons, and so far, they had no leads.

After a long, frustrating day of work she had come home to find Arduinna sitting in the living room, with two mugs of tea waiting for them.

"I just feel so helpless," said Ali, staring into her mug. "We should be out there doing something. Instead, Colin is locked in his office sorting through files he's been through twenty times before."

"Perhaps he thinks there is a detail that could help?" offered the Goddess.

Ali sighed. "Maybe, but I feel like he's avoiding the rest of us."

She'd made several attempts throughout the day to get the team together so that they could plan their next step, but Colin kept making excuses about calls or emails that needed his immediate attention.

"Maybe he's ashamed of what happened that night," said

Arduinna, tucking her feet under her. "I mean, it sounds like he's at fault for bringing Laila into that situation."

"I tried to warn her." Ali shook her head. "Laila was so insistent though. She thought she could keep Colin out of trouble."

"Elves are interesting creatures," said Arduinna thoughtfully. "They place a lot of pride in duty and honor. I don't know Laila well, but if Colin had convinced her that it was her duty to see this investigation through, you couldn't stop her even if you tied her to a chair."

"Yep," sighed Ali. "That sounds like Laila, all right."

Laila's patience was astonishing to Ali. She was determined and dedicated, but also stubborn as hell. Sure, Laila was new to the team and probably felt as though she had to make a good impression.

"I have to do something." Ali set her mug down. "I should see if Darien's heard anything."

She stood and walked over to the counter where her phone sat, but there were no missed calls or new messages.

"You just got home," said Arduinna gently, "you need to rest."

"But she could be injured, or dead!" Ali started pacing. "She just joined the team. How could we let this happen?"

"Don't be ridiculous," said Arduinna sternly. "She may be new, but she's far from inexperienced. That training she received for the Royal Guard in Ingegard is nothing to overlook. It's one of the toughest training courses created by any of the mortals and takes nearly twenty years to complete. I'm sure she has everything under control."

Ali knew the Goddess was right, and honestly, Laila was better prepared to deal with this sort of situation than she was.

"Isn't there something we can do?" Ali returned to her seat on the sofa. "I mean, you're a Goddess. Can't you use your powers to locate her?"

Arduinna shook her head. "Only if she was lost in my

forest. I have no way to track her here."

"What about another God? Maybe a local one?"

"Oh no," she said grimly. "We are not going there. There is a reason I avoid other immortals. They are devious and cunning. If you went to them for help, you would end up in a worse situation that you started in. There is always a price, and it is generally very high."

Ali took a deep breath, trying to calm down. This was all too much.

"Ali," said Arduinna, scooting closer to Ali on the sofa. "We will find Laila."

She nodded.

Arduinna hesitated before asking, "Why are you so distraught? Laila seems like a nice person and all, but you've only known her a couple of weeks."

"I don't know," Ali shrugged. "It's been good to have Laila around. She's one of us. An SNP. It's nice to have someone from Alfheim who just understands what it's like to move here and feel alone and isolated. Since she moved in, this house has felt more like a sanctuary for us, more like our own little piece of Alfheim.

"Or," continued Ali, "maybe it's because this could've happened to any of us on the team. And if I was the one missing, and Erin was left here all alone, would anyone be trying to find me?"

That thought had been eating at her for a long time. What would Erin do if she were kidnapped or killed? They had no other relatives, at least none who had made their presence known. Would Erin be placed in a human foster home? Would she have to fend for herself trapped as a perpetual child?

Arduinna wrapped her arm around Ali's shoulder and squeezed. "We'll figure this out one way or another. I could try searching on other planes for clues. Maybe one of the beings that walks between the worlds can sense something that I can't."

"Thank you," said Ali, feeling weary to her core. Maybe Arduinna was right, and she needed rest. Maybe this would all make more sense in the morning.

Arduinna rose from the sofa. "If I find anything, I'll let you know."

Ali stood as well and gave Arduinna a hug. "Thank you."

When Arduinna took a step back, the air around her shimmered, and the Goddess was gone.

Ali sunk back onto the sofa and rested her head on the armrest. She needed sleep, but the guilt was still there.

"I can help too," said Erin walking into the living room in her fluffy purple sweatpants and an old band T-shirt. She sat on the sofa next to Ali and pulled her knees up to her chin.

"What are you talking about?" asked Ali.

"If there is someone out there kidnapping Supernaturals, I have a feeling someone will be talking about it on the Internet in some chat room or something. I know this guy. I met him through an online game. If anyone could find something like that on shady webpages and forums, I bet he can."

"That sounds sketchy," said Ali skeptically.

Erin shrugged. "Maybe, but what if he finds something?"

"Then there'll be a price."

"Look," said Erin, "just let me just talk to him and see. Trust me."

Ali frowned. "I am not going to drag you into this."

"I want to help," insisted Erin. "Please, just let me try."

"Fine," said Ali. "But asking that guy is as far as you go. I don't want you poking around and getting into trouble."

Erin rolled her eyes. "You're turning into mom, you know."

"Am not!" said Ali indignantly.

"You totally are." Erin stood up with a grin. "You better get some sleep, old lady."

"Oh, now you've gone too far!" Ali threw a decorative pillow at her sister. It missed, and Erin stuck her tongue out before disappearing down the hall, laughing as she went.

There were more fights that night. The guards escorted prisoners from their cells one at a time. Laila had assumed they were led straight to the arena, as she had been the previous night. When they came for her, though, they took her to a smaller cell closer to the arena. She guessed it helped to keep up the pace if the next fighters were closer at hand.

There were actually small windows in the tiny cells, and Laila's allowed her to see out to the arena. She observed the fights from there, taking mental notes on the fighters, guards, arena, and anything else that might be of importance to her. Lesser Demons patrolled the hallways during the day as well as when the games were in progress. The majority of them were actually human, but there were a few SNPs among their ranks as well either from Jotunheim or Midgard.

From what she could gather of the structure of the match-es, Jerrik seemed to be their top fighter, and the others worked their way up the ranks to try to beat him. The other fighters were an eclectic bunch of SNPs who were mostly foreign to Earth. She noted once again that she was the only female.

In the fights, the men were both armed and unarmed. She couldn't see a pattern other than whatever made their fighting abilities more amusing to the audience. And it seemed as if the fighters were killed only occasionally, since most of the fights ended with a knockout.

She didn't see Torsten fight, even though he was taken away periodically, but Jerrik was in the arena again tonight. He may be a pain in the ass, she thought, but he was an excellent fighter. Each action was swift and deadly, but so effortless. A master had probably trained him, and they generally demanded a high price. If he had trained under one, it was no wonder he had been looking to make an extra buck.

She was pulled away from his entrancing fight when some-one approached her cell. It was one of the Demons, but this one looked important. He was Fae.

The Demon looked her over with slow, calculating eyes

that made her extremely uncomfortable. Whoever he was, he made Jerrik look positively charming. He wore a long, fitted coat over an expensive-looking shirt and slacks, and his long, platinum blond hair was braided. He was wealthy, probably influential, and definitely dangerous.

"You are an interesting one, aren't you, dear girl?" He spoke slowly, and the words rolled off his tongue like silk. She knew that voice—he was the Master of the Games. She didn't respond, and he didn't appear to expect her to.

"I don't normally accept women here, but I think you will do just fine."

He motioned one of the guards to come forward and unlock her cell door.

"You're up next."

"Nice suit," Laila sneered, "won't it get dirty when I kick your ass in the ring?"

The Fae's arm lashed out, and he wrapped his hand around her throat in a vise-like grip. Before she could react, she was blasted with a wave of seething Demonic energy. There was no mistaking that he was a Greater Demon who had once been a prisoner in Hell. Since a sentence to Hell was a sentence for life, that meant he'd found a way to break out of his prison. Laila just hoped that she would be the one with the pleasure of sending him through the one-way portal back to Hell. But his very presence was alarming. If he had managed to escape, she was sure others had as well.

He leaned in so his nose was just brushing her ear.

"You've got a lot of nerve for a someone in your position. Your life belongs to me now, and I will do with it what I please." He released her, and Laila doubled over, coughing and gasping for breath.

He gestured to the guards. "You will bring her to the ring with whatever force necessary." He turned to Laila. She glared daggers at him, but he only chuckled before continuing.

"I picked out a spear for you to fight with. I hope you

know how to use one." He turned to leave, then paused. "Oh, one more thing—don't kill your opponent, please."

CHAPTER 23

Swiftly the guards led her down the hall and out into the arena. True to the Demon's word, she was supplied with a spear before being shoved into the ring once again. She made a mental note to ask the other prisoners about this Master of the Games later. Assuming she made it out of the fight alive.

"And here is our newest gladiator," called the announcer, "our very own Warrior Princess!!!"

Laila was already annoyed by his voice, not to mention his lack of creativity in choosing names. She ignored his string of objectifying comments and turned her attention to her opponent.

This time her opponent was a human, but a Shapeshifter. Like the victim from the hospital, this man was obviously a cat Shifter. Every movement he made was feline in quality. His many visible scars told her that he was one of the veteran warriors here, so she would have to be cautious. He too was armed, but with a stave instead of a spear, and although it lacked a blade she knew this weapon could be all too dangerous.

She heard the gong, and it was time to begin. She didn't hesitate but cut to the left with the blade of the spear, then feinted right and struck him left in the ribs with the opposite end. He hadn't expected it and roared with pain. She didn't hear anything break, but that didn't mean much.

He took revenge with a barrage of attacks. All she had time to do was parry. It was clear that he had training, probably in human martial arts of some sort. She was patient, though, and conserved her energy as best she could while she waited for an opening. He swung for her head, but rather than blocking, she ducked. But she was too slow on her recovery and didn't see him as he swept her feet out from under her.

The impact was jarring, but she recovered in time to roll out of the way of his next attack and stand. For a human, this guy was fast, but as an Elf, she was faster. On his next attack she bound his stave, trapping it between the floor and her spear. Laila kicked him hard in the stomach while wrenching the stave out of his grasp and throwing it aside. Quickly he grabbed her, catching her off guard, and threw her to the ground. She watched with a silent curse as her spear went skidding across the arena floor.

She was at a disadvantage and knew it. As a Werecat, he might still have the ability to shift, and once he turned into whatever monstrous cat he was, he would slice her to ribbons.

She pulled him close and used her legs to throw him off her.

She scrambled to her spear, but just as she grasped it, a searing pain sliced down her back. She screamed and turned, shoving the spear into whatever part of his body she could reach. Her opponent cried out and collapsed, the spear in his side. The fight was over.

The audience screamed and cheered.

Laila's back throbbed, but she could tell that the cuts were pretty shallow, and there would be no lasting damage except for some scars. She just hoped that there was a healer on hand.

It hurt to move, and an injury like this would slow her down considerably. To her annoyance, she also noticed that the back of her shirt was shredded.

Much to her relief, there was a medic of sorts, a grizzly looking Water Dragon in his human form. He oversaw a number of patients in the concrete room with a handful of cots where she and her competitor were led after the fight. The floors were caked in a layer of dried blood, and the Water Dragon's clothes were covered in blood as well. Laila noticed he didn't wear the same cuffs as the prisoners, and decided he was probably another Demon, rather than a prisoner.

He tended to the Werecat first, frowning as he examined the wound. Her opponent was injured pretty badly, but hopefully not beyond a healer's ability to mend. If he recovered without infection, he probably wouldn't be able to fight for a while though.

Water Dragons had some ability to heal the body, but not like Elves. Laila watched skeptically as he worked, gritting her teeth as her own wound bled wishing he would allow her to take the cuffs off to heal herself. But by the time he finished healing the Werecat and got to work on her, he barely healed her enough to stanch the flow of blood from her wounds with his magic before sending her away. It still hurt like hell, but at least the wounds were closed.

A small voice in the back of her head taunted her for how quickly she had nearly taken to killing. She shoved the thought away. They had both survived, and that was what mattered.

Back in her cell she was left with the problem of her tattered clothing. The Werecat had managed to not only cut through the shirt, but through the back of the bra as well. She sighed, it was a new one she had purchased just two weeks ago.

Was it really only two weeks ago? she thought. In the span of a few days her life had turned completely upside down. Now she was a prisoner, and her hopes of escape were diminishing. The hallways were crawling with Demons and their henchmen, not to mention that she had no idea how to get out of the building. Up to this point all she had seen was her cell, the hallway leading to the arena, and the arena itself.

She sighed again and got to work repairing her clothes. With a blush she realized that Jerrik was watching her with mild interest, as were a number of other men in the room. She ignored them and managed to tie the bra into place, wincing at how it rubbed against her wound.

The back of the shirt was in pieces, although the front was fine. She managed to tie that together as well. At least her jeans were still intact, although they were covered in bloodstains. Once her clothing was repaired as well as she could manage, Laila curled into a ball on the floor, taking care not to lay on her wounds, and fell asleep to the whispered conversations of the men in the surrounding cells, wishing she could be anywhere in all the worlds but there.

She was running as fast as she could down the hall with the guards close behind her, gaining on her with every step she took. Even through the exhaustion she pushed herself as hard as she could, using every ounce of energy she had left. The men in the cells tried to grab her through their bars as she passed. Suddenly she tripped and went sprawling on the ground.

The guards were upon her instantly, tearing at her clothing, grabbing for her and strangling her. She fought them, but there were too many. Her strength was failing, and there was nothing she could do about it. They were crushing her.

A dazzling bright light appeared before her, and the men were tossed aside like rag dolls. Laila squinted, trying to see through the brilliant, pale light. It dimmed, and Laila found herself in a white, foggy dreamscape. The men and the hallway had just been a dream.

The light was still there, radiating from a woman so incredibly beautiful that all Laila could do was stare up at her in awe.

The mist coiled around her flowing, white gown and hair. But the most dazzling feature was her eyes, which were an unearthly electric blue.

"Little Elf," she said with a warm but commanding voice, "do not allow yourself to fall into despair. Your spirit and will are strong, as is your mortal body."

"I don't know what to do! There are so many guards. I have no idea where I am, and I'm surrounded by men who would see me dead! Please help me! Save me from this place!"

She thought that the Goddess gave her a look of pity, but her divine features were hard to read.

"I cannot take you from that place. It is not the order of things. All I can offer is my advice. Stay strong, have faith in yourself, but also in those who are trapped with you. They need a savior, and you are the one chosen for the task. Never be ashamed of who and what you are, or of the path before you. You are a woman, a warrior, and an Elf. But you are also so much more. So, wear your identity proudly."

She hesitated a moment, then added, "You are on a long and dangerous path. Fate has much in store for you, and this is just the beginning."

Before Laila could speak, the Goddess vanished. Laila was left alone in the endless dreamscape.

Laila wondered at the meaning of the Goddess's words. What was this just the beginning of? The Gods rarely spoke to mortals, especially a Goddess as powerful as this one. She didn't even know which Goddess it was. She sent a prayer of thanks out into the universe in any case.

She looked around, but there was nothing in sight, not even a star or planet in the sky, just an endless expanse of mist. She wasn't sure how long she had been walking when she heard a familiar voice. It was the Goddess Arduinna of the Black Forest.

"Laila? Is that you?" called Arduinna as she emerged through the mist. She hurried over to Laila's side. She too was glowing with a white light, although nowhere near as brilliantly as the other Goddess.

"Arduinna! It's so good to see you! Where are we?" Laila said while scrambling to her feet.

"We are on the Astral Plane. I've been looking for someone who might be able to track you from here. I didn't realize you could actually project yourself here."

Laila shook her head. "No, I have no idea how to do that, but I think the other Goddess brought me here."

"Which one?" she said, looking around as if she might be able to spot her still.

"I'm not sure, she didn't identify herself, and the light surrounding her shone so brightly that I can't even remember what she looked like."

"That could have been any number of them, but she must have her reasons if she didn't reveal her identity." Arduinna gave her a concerned look, and she took in the Elf's condition.

"Can you take me back with you?" Perhaps this was Laila's chance to escape her prison.

"I'm sorry, I wish I could, but you are only here in spirit. The only way to return to the mortal worlds is to go back to where your body remains physically. Only a God has the strength to materialize, but it is impossible for us to take a mortal with us without killing them. If you tell me where you are, though, I can send Ali to find you."

"I have no idea where I am. They drugged me, and I awoke in a cell. We, the prisoners, are basically gladiators, and they have these cuffs that bind my magic. There is a Greater Demon running the operation and many Lesser Demons working with him. I have no idea how their boss escaped from Muspelheim, but we've got a big problem here."

The Goddess sat on a pile of mist and shook her head. "That's bad, really bad. We'll have to find out how they are escaping before we have another inter-world war on our hands."

"Wait!" A thought came to Laila. "How is Colin? Did the

others find him? Is he okay?"

"Yes, he's fine. A little foggy on the details of that night from what Ali said, but they found him stumbling out of an alley behind a bar."

At least he was okay. That was one worry off her mind.

"I can help send you back to your body. I sense you have been here too long already," Arduinna offered.

Laila hated the idea of retuning to that wretched place, but she knew there was no other choice.

"Please tell the others that I am alive, and that I will contact them at the IRSA office as soon as I escape." If she escaped.

"They will be waiting." She hugged Laila. "Take care, my dear girl, and when you are back, come to my forest. I want to help train your magic. You have a lot of potential that is being unused. I'm not sure how I missed it before."

And with that Laila's vision began to fade, and she awoke to the noise of men arguing around her.

CHAPTER 24

"How the hell did she do that!?! She can't use magic with the cuffs. We saw her try it before!" said someone in a frantic whisper.

"Shut up! Someone's coming!"

"Roll her over, quick!"

Hands hastily rolled her over so that she was facing the bars of the cell door. Laila had no idea what was going on. She opened her eyes as a guard came walking down the hall. He glared at the prisoners in the surrounding cells, but just kept walking and rounded a corner out of sight.

"What's going on?" she asked no one in particular as she sat upright.

"You tell us, princess!" Jerrik snorted. "You're the one who managed to heal yourself. How did you do it?"

"What are you talking about?" It was then she realized that the pain in her back was completely gone. Sure, the healer had used some magic on her after the fight, but it was not enough for a full recovery. Even if he had, there would still be the usual stiff and tender feeling that came with using magic to heal. It felt as if nothing had happened.

"So, you didn't do that?" he said, pointing to her lower back.

If she twisted, she could just barely make out the ends of the four long gashes from under her ruined shirt. At least they had been gashes. Now there were four silver lines that that glowed faintly as if there were a blue light within them. They were beautiful and fascinating.

"No," she replied in shock, "I didn't."

"How did those get there, then?" said one of the men on the other side of the walkway.

"I don't know," she said, although the truth was that one of the Goddesses must have healed her. She sent a silent prayer of thanks.

"You were glowing! I've never seen anything like it!" another said.

She just told them that she had no idea what had happened. The men didn't seem satisfied with her answer, but they would have to live with that. After all, she wasn't really sure what happened and was not ready to confide in them the experience she had had on the Astral Plane. Eventually they dropped the matter.

How strange, she thought, to have an encounter with two Goddesses in one night. She wasn't sure that it was a particularly good thing. History of the worlds was full of stories where Gods appeared and something disastrous happened. There were a lot of politics surrounding them as well, and it was best for mortals to stay out of it. For better or worse, though, she had gotten the attention of two of them. Arduinna was one thing. She was connected to a mortal world and liked to fit within it. The other Goddess was another matter. She was clearly very powerful, but Laila had no idea who she was or why she had come to her.

Arduinna had mentioned something too, she remembered. The Goddess spoke of her potential and hoped to help Laila develop and hone her magic. She wasn't sure what that entailed, but when a Goddess—even a minor one—was offering to train you, it was best not to pass up that opportunity.

With little else to do, Laila decided to carefully examine the cuffs. They were very familiar to her now, but she was no closer to deciphering the language of the inscriptions. They did contain a spell of binding though. It was also clear that there was no physical way for her to remove them. They might as well have been forged around her wrists.

She sighed. If only there was a way for her to break the spell...

A thought occurred to her, and her heart raced with excitement.

There were three ways to break a spell. First, the person who cast the spell could lift it. The second was that another spell could be used to counter it. The third way was the most difficult. It didn't involve casting a spell but altering the present one. It was like untangling a ball of silk threads. It was extremely difficult and time-consuming, but theoretically it could be done. Like picking a magical lock. She had never attempted to unravel a spell before, but in this case, it could be her ticket out of there. Just as long as the cuffs didn't detect that she was using magic.

Laila shifted against the concrete wall until she found a comfortable position and then began to meditate, slowly sinking into a trance. It wasn't necessary to be in a trance, but it allowed her to see the strands of magic with greater clarity.

Very carefully, she reached out and began to examine the spell, seeing how the strands of magic were intertwined. As slowly and gently as she could, she began to untangle them, fearing she would trigger the cuffs if she moved too fast.

It was grueling, but little by little she made progress. Down to the last two strands, Laila hardly dared to breathe. She was seconds away from breaking the spell, and that much closer to freedom!

She forced herself to remain calm and took a deep breath to steady herself. Slowly she unraveled the strands. There were just inches to go, centimeters, millimeters…

She gritted her teeth and barely held back her scream as pain coursed through her body. It jerked her out of her trance, and she felt the strands coil back together.

She opened her eyes, body still throbbing with pain, and noticed that she, once again, had everyone's attention. Great.

"There is a way of rearranging the spell on the cuffs without technically using magic, but apparently the cuffs can still detect it," she explained.

"There are charms to break the spells," Torsten said. "I've seen the guards use them before."

Some of the others nodded in agreement.

"But they don't let us anywhere close to them. Believe me, I tried," Jerrik grumbled.

"Okay, we just need to examine this situation with fresh eyes," she said.

Jerrik snorted. "What are you? A cop?"

"No. I just read a lot of detective novels." It was a pretty lame excuse, but at least it kept her identity safe. For now.

Jerrik Torhild didn't have anything against the Light Elves, but he knew this one was hiding something. He thought it was too much of a coincidence that she was the first woman here.

She was far too good a fighter to be an ordinary Elf. Sure, it was common for both of their peoples to learn how to fight, particularly with the wars over the years. He had the best training money could buy, and he knew a warrior when he saw one. She was graceful and deadly in the ring. What was she doing here in this realm? And how had she been captured by the Demons? Not to mention the glowing blue scars. They had now faded and had a similar color to moonstones.

Knowing how reserved she was, Jerrik refused to believe that she had been accidentally discovered like the rest of them.

He wouldn't expect to find her in a drunken brawl at a bar. There was definitely more to her story, and he was determined to uncover it.

CHAPTER 25

Darien and Colin sat quietly in the conference room as Ali finished informing them of Arduinna's encounter with Laila in the Astral Plane. It was a relief to know that she was still alive. But they were far from figuring out how to rescue her.

Since Laila had vanished, Ali and Darien had spent their time pacing in the office and scouring every lead they could. The walls of the conference room were covered in maps of the city that they used to track every location of anyone possibly connected with her disappearance. They had even taken to the streets looking for anyone with the smallest scrap of information. Each time they came up empty-handed.

Colin was still shutting himself up in the office, much to Ali's annoyance. He had contributed minimally to the actual investigation, and Ali suspected he was avoiding them. She'd been tempted to exclude him from the meeting, but Darien insisted that Colin should be present.

"So, now what?" Ali directed the question at Colin.

"We still have nothing." He didn't even bother to look at her.

"Then I'm going out there." She glared at her supervisor. "And I'll find her the same way she found those Demons."

"Absolutely not!" he growled at her. "If anyone goes, I will."

"Enough of that bullshit!" she screamed. "Don't you brush me aside. We are a freaking team here! You've been sitting on your ass in that office doing Gods know what, while Darien and I have been investigating."

Colin's face turned red, and he tried to interrupt her, but Ali wasn't finished.

"It's your damn fault we have an agent missing! If you had let me go with Laila instead of—"

"What?" he snarled, every bit the wolf he was. "What could you have possibly done that I—"

A loud bang startled them.

In the blink of an eye, Darien was standing between them. The table they had been sitting at, now had a large dent from where he had slammed his fist into it. His fangs were bared.

"Shut up, both of you!" the Vampire hissed. "Throwing yourselves at the Demons like a fat, juicy steak is not going to solve this."

Darien continued to stare both of them down until they backed off. Once the Vampire was sure they weren't going to rip each other's throats out, he continued.

"We need everybody on board with cool heads. No, we don't have any more information on where they are, but we know Laila is alive. We have to trust that she knows what she's doing and prepare for when we hear from her."

"He's right," Ali said coolly. "Laila can handle herself."

There was more malice in her voice than was necessary. Darien shot her a warning look.

Without another word, Ali stormed out of the conference room.

Darien sighed and glanced at his supervisor. Colin had become quite withdrawn since he and Laila were attacked. Darien knew that the Werewolf was fighting some internal battle, and that he didn't need Ali's constant criticism, but she had a point.

"You can't keep doing that," Darien told him motioning to the doorway Ali had just left through.

"Doing what?" Colin muttered.

"Brooding and moping around the office."

Colin stared blankly at the Vampire, so Darien continued.

"I don't know where this is coming from because I have never seen you act like this before, but you need to shape up."

Darien shut the conference room door and took a seat on the opposite side of his supervisor.

"Colin, do you realize that your job is on the line? Right now I'm the only thing stopping Ali from involving your superiors in D.C. You seem pretty indifferent at the moment, but I know it would kill you if you allow this team to fall apart."

"What more can I do? We can't act until we have more information." Colin glared at him.

"That didn't stop you before." Darien sat there challenging the Were, figuring the canine instinct would kick in and wake Colin up.

"You're the supervisor," Darien hissed, "start acting like it."

Ali slammed her car door shut and shoved the key into the ignition. She wasn't sure where she was going, but anywhere was better than headquarters, so she pulled out of the parking garage and took off into the night.

It made absolutely no sense to her. She had told Colin that Laila was alive. They even had some idea of what the Demons were doing. So why was he so indifferent? They were talking about Laila's life, not rush hour traffic.

Silently she fumed and turned onto Lincoln Boulevard. Her phone went off, and she glanced at the screen. It was Darien.

She rolled her eyes and ignored it. At the moment she was

not ready to talk to him.

Ali continued driving, just trying to put some distance between her and the office. It was not until she pulled into a parking lot that Ali realized where she was. She parked the car, got out, and looked up at the Club La Fae.

It was Saturday night, and the line wrapped around the block. Ordinarily she would be standing in line and enjoying a night out, but not tonight. Ali ignored the line and walked up to the bouncer.

"I need to speak with Orin, please."

She recognized the bouncer. He often worked the Saturday night shift. He took a look at Ali's grim expression and ushered her through the door.

"He should be in the office," said the bouncer before returning his attention to the line.

She walked up to the bar. The bartenders rushed back and forth, but she waved at one and indicated the hidden office door. The bartender nodded before returning his attention to the next order. Ali opened the door and climbed the stairs to Orin's office.

"Ali!" said the Fae man cheerfully as she stepped into the room. His face fell as he took a closer look at her. "Gods, is everything ok?"

Ali shook her head and stepped into his embrace. "No, it's really not."

He motioned for her to sit on a sofa. "Can I get you something to drink?"

She shook her head. "Maybe later. I think I just need a moment."

"Do you want to talk?" he asked, sitting next to her.

"It's a long story."

"I've got plenty of time." He grabbed her hand, and Ali felt a trickle of warm, calming energy seep into her body.

As always, Orin was dressed to impress. He wore a designer suit, and it looked amazing on him. Then again, he could make a cloth sack look sexy.

Ali knew it was his magic that was influencing her thoughts, but it also helped to relax her.

"Laila was abducted. She's alive for now, but there's no way to know where she is."

"What!?!" said Orin, jerking back. "Does this have to do with those men disappearing? She mentioned that to me when she was here."

Ali nodded. "My dick of a boss got her kidnapped, and now he's being an ass about it."

"The Werewolf?"

"Yep."

"What about the Vampire?" he asked.

"He's trying to keep the peace," she said bitterly.

"Isn't that a good thing?"

Ali paused for a second. She knew Orin was right, but she was done putting up with Colin's shit.

Her phone rang. It was Darien again.

"Are you going to answer that?" Orin pointed to the phone in her hand.

She glared at him, then hesitantly she answered the call. "Hello?"

"Finally, you pick up!" said Darien. "Where are you? I searched the entire building, then noticed your car was gone."

"I needed some space," she said shortly.

"Look," he said. "I know you're upset, and I am too, but arguing with Colin isn't going to help."

Ali did not respond.

"Where are you?" he asked finally. "We need to figure out how we're going to deal with this, and I'd prefer to talk in person."

"I'm at the Club La Fae with Orin."

"Okay, I'm on my way."

Ali ended the call and crammed the phone back into her pocket.

"So?" asked Orin.

"Darien's on his way," she said, feeling moody.

"Good," said the club owner cheerfully as he stood. "You need him in your corner."

"Why do you have to be so reasonable?" she grumbled.

He walked around to the backside of the sofa and massaged her shoulders, allowing traces of his magic to trickle in and soothe her. Ali wasn't sure why she had come to the club, but she was happy she had. Sometimes it just felt good to be around other Fae.

"You need to be careful," said Orin softly. "Our kind is very sensitive. Fae form bonds quickly, and we tend to get carried away by our emotions."

He leaned over the sofa and looked at Ali. "We might be used to this, but you are surrounded by others who are not. Don't be so hard on these Weres and Vampires. I don't think they understand the situation the way we do."

Slowly Ali nodded. Fae were ruled by their hearts. It was part of what attracted others to them, but it was also their weakness.

"I don't suppose you've heard anything about these disappearances?" she asked, changing the subject.

"Unfortunately, no," said Orin. "I'm sorry, Ali, I really am."

An intercom on his desk crackled to life.

"Hey, Orin," came the voice of the bouncer. "There's a Vampire with a badge looking for someone called Ali."

Orin hurried over to the desk. "Thank you. Send him in, please, and have someone show him to my office."

A minute later there was a knock on the door, and Darien entered the office. Orin raised an eyebrow at the Vampire's clothes. They were his usual grunge-meets-goth apparel. Ali ignored the other Fae. She crossed her arms, waiting for Darien to speak.

Darien put his hands up. "Before you go off on me, I

think you are absolutely right."

Ali's mouth gaped for a moment. She had expected a lecture, not his surrender. That was new.

"Explain," she said, eyeing him suspiciously.

"Colin's moping around the office and refusing to do jack shit." Darien settled himself in the chair across from hers.

Ali nodded slowly.

"So, what are you planning to do about it?" asked Orin from his place next to Ali.

"Excuse me, who are you?" said Darien sharply.

"The owner of this club, and a friend of Ali's," he sniffed, glancing over at her. "Also, a concerned Supernatural."

"Right…" said Darien.

"Orin," said Ali. "Could you give us a couple of minutes?"

"Of course."

He went to check in at the bar, leaving Ali and Darien alone.

"Look," said Darien. "I want to keep the peace in the office, but we'll get nowhere if we sit around waiting for Colin to make a move."

"Good," said Ali, "then we're on the same page."

Darien nodded.

Of course, there was a part of Ali that had known this already, but she needed to hear him say it. Ali needed the reassurance that she was not alone in her frustration with Colin.

"So, where do we begin?" she asked. "Do we go back to the place where she was abducted?"

"That was my thought." Darien cracked his fingers absentmindedly. "I know we've already searched the area, but it's worth another look. Are you up to it tonight?"

Ali nodded. "The sooner we get answers, the better."

Ali and Darien approached the entrance of the alley. It was dark and foreboding to Ali. She pulled out a flashlight and switched it on, but Darien didn't bother with a light. One of the perks of being a Vampire that was he had excellent night vision.

"Okay," said Ali, "you tracked Laila back down the alley the other night. Can you show me where?"

"Sure, this way."

Darien led the way down the alley and to where it opened up onto a small street. It was mainly used for parking and storage since most of the storefronts were located on the opposite side of the block. A large rat scurried away from the beam of Ali's light, making her cringe. Darien ignored it and continued down the cracked asphalt, then turned down a smaller alley on the opposite side of the road.

They stopped in front of an old, two-story office building. The building was worn out and dilapidated. It had probably been abandoned since The Event.

"This is it." Darien jerked his thumb at the building.

Ali glanced around at the buildings surrounding them. There were no windows overlooking this part of the alley, and the chances of a pedestrian walking by in the middle of the night were slim. She doubted there would be any witnesses.

Darien frowned and took a step closer to the building.

"Something's wrong," he said. "I smell blood and decay."

That was never a good combination.

Approaching the door, Ali knocked, but there was no answer. Not surprising given the condition of the building. Ali tried the doorknob. It wasn't locked. She glanced over her shoulder at Darien and removed her gun from its holster before pushing the door open.

"Hello?" she called, but there was no answer. A putrid smell assailed her nose.

"There's no one home," said Darien. "Well, no one that's alive, anyway."

"Right," said Ali, but she did not holster her firearm yet. She cautiously stepped over the threshold and into the room, wishing she had something to use to cover her nose.

By the light of her flashlight, she could see the layers of dust that had been recently disturbed by multiple sets of footprints. There was a gaping hole in one wall. It appeared to have been recently made.

As she neared that wall, the smell became worse. Peering through the hole, she discovered the source of the smell.

"Shit." She looked over her shoulder at Darien. "We better call HQ for backup. We're going to need an investigative team."

Darien stepped up beside her and examined the rotting corpse.

"Well," he said, "it looks like we found our lead."

"That's morbid." Ali left the building to call the office and escape the smell.

The IRSA investigative team of specially trained humans was on hand to help with the crime scenes. They helped to relieve the pressure on the field agents by handling crime scene investigation, aiding in research, and doing other grunt work, while the Supernatural field agents dealt with the potentially hazardous situations.

Technically they were a part of the same team that Colin oversaw, but over time the two units had become separated. The humans preferred to keep to themselves. So instead, the investigative team acted as a filter, sorting through calls and cases and passing on information requiring the field team's attention.

"They'll be here in twenty minutes," said Ali as Darien joined her.

"He was killed the night Laila was abducted."

"Wouldn't you have smelled him?" Ali asked.

"Normally, yes." He shoved his hands into his pockets. "But I was so focused on Laila's scent, I must've missed it."

"But there's no sign of her inside though, right?"

Darien shook his head. "No, no sign of her in there. They must have loaded her into a vehicle, because her scent had vanished by the time I arrived."

"So, they would've parked the car somewhere around here?" Ali indicated the area where they were standing.

"Yes, there were tire tracks heading that way." Darien pointed towards a road on the opposite side of the alley.

Ali walked past the building in the direction he indicated, searching the walls of the buildings as she went.

"If you're looking for a security camera, there's one down there." Darien motioned to an old apartment complex.

"Has anyone contacted them to ask for the recording from the other night?" she asked, a thought occurring to her.

"Yes," said Darien. "They were going to bring it by today. But it won't do us much good. I doubt they are driving around the streets. They probably disappeared into the Old City."

"That's what I'm counting on," said Ali, feeling hopeful for the first time in days.

CHAPTER 26

Laila spent the next few days observing the guards. She noted how often they passed her, when they were in groups, what their weaknesses could be, and most importantly, where they kept the charms to unlock the cuffs. She figured that one of them would slip up eventually, and she could seize the opportunity to steal the charm. However, she knew that even with her powers, the chances of escape would be slim.

Still, she watched and waited.

One day, as a guard was shoving a tray of food into her cell, she requested new clothing that was suitable for fighting. She didn't really care about the clothes. She was fine in the ones she wore, even if they were in tatters. But maybe the guard would come close enough for her to swipe his keys.

The guard gave her a suspicious look but returned later with a small bag of clothing. Much to Laila's annoyance, he never got close enough for her to reach his charm. Instead he tossed the bag in her direction.

So much for that idea, she thought. She dug through the bag, hoping for a tag or forgotten receipt, and instead pulled out a black bra studded with spikes.

"Really?" She rolled her eyes. Some of the men snickered.

"You were the one who asked *Demons* for clothing," Jerrik snorted. "What did you expect they'd give you?"

"I believe this one is for you." She flung a strappy thong at his face, which he swatted away. Mato, who occupied the cell across from hers howled with laughter, while one of the others whistled.

"If I make it out of here alive, I'll wear anything you want me to," Jerrik said, tossing the lingerie back into her cell.

Torsten was rummaging through the bag. He held up a black leather corset.

"I think you should wear this one." He held it out for her.

Laila raised an eyebrow at him, and he blushed.

"No, it's not like that," he said hastily. "I mean, it offers the most protection, look…"

He showed her the inside.

"It's not much, but the leather and the plastic bones are much stronger than your cotton shirt."

She took a closer look at it. He was right—it would be better than what she had on, so long as it didn't hinder her movement.

"Okay, turn around," she told the men while undoing the hooks of the corset.

"Really?" Jerrik asked.

"You heard her," Torsten replied.

The corset wasn't nearly as comfortable as her shirt, but at least it fit. Torsten helped to lace up the back so it wouldn't shift around too much.

She tore the remainder of her shirt into strips and used them to tie her hair back into a low ponytail that would keep it out of her face when she was fighting that night.

"At least you have the eye candy thing going for you," Mato yawned. "It makes it less likely they'll want to kill you."

As much as the comments and the looks she received from

the Demons left her unsettled, she had to admit that Mato had a point.

"Are you a Shifter, Mato?" She figured he was, but it was hard to tell.

He nodded, "Yes, a bear Shifter." He indicated a tattoo on his arm of a snarling bear.

There were two others occupying cells in the concrete room. Henrik occupied the cell across from Jerrik. He was a type of ice creature called a Mörkö. Klaive occupied the cell across from Torsten, but never told anyone what he was. Since it was the only common language amongst them, they all spoke in English.

She still had time to kill before she was dragged back to the arena, so she decided to warm up before the fight.

As usual, the guards showed up to lead her to the ring.

Jerrik watched as the guards led the other Elf away. He was surprised she had actually chosen to wear that corset, but he wasn't going to complain. She looked good enough to eat.

He noted that her body was relatively free of scars, save the curious markings from her miraculously healed wound. It was unlikely that she would have seen battle, although she was clearly trained very well. Whatever her story was, he knew that it would only bring him trouble. His top priority after getting out of here would be to ensure that he maintained a low profile.

Another guard came to take him up to the ring. He was grateful for the chance to get out of the little cell. He waited with his escort in the entranceway and saw that the Elf was still fighting her opponent, a scrappy Fae. The Fae was a decent fighter. He was unpredictable but untrained, so he wouldn't be much of a match for the Light Elf. He breathed a little easier.

Jerrik watched the Elf closely, examining her every movement. She easily evaded her opponent's attacks but held back, making no move to return the attack. She was quick, intelligent, and, he would admit, beautiful to watch.

He reminded himself that even if they weren't locked away, this Light Elf was definitely not someone that a rogue swordsman like himself should be tempted by. He still had his suspicions about her anyway. But still he watched her.

Laila ducked and recovered, stepping back out of range of her opponent's attacks. They circled each other, knives at the ready. She had avoided attacking the Fae and hoped that if he tired enough, she could disarm him and get rid of the knives altogether. Her opponent didn't seem to be tiring, though, and she knew she needed to change tactics.

He rushed her suddenly, and she tripped him. He went down, but as he fell, he grabbed hold of her long auburn hair. Laila managed to keep standing but had brief seconds before he would have his knife in her back. In one swift movement she severed her hair at the nape of her neck, freeing herself from the Fae's grasp.

She spun around in time to see his attack.

It felt as if time slowed, and she counterattacked, cleanly slicing the underside of his wrist.

Her opponent screamed, dropping his knife. The cut was deep, and the hand would be useless now. She kicked him in the jaw, and he went down.

She stood there for a moment to make sure that her opponent was truly unconscious, then slowly backed away, running a hand through her now short hair. She wasn't particularly vain but had always loved her long hair. At least this way it would be harder for another opponent to grab it.

She received a handful of compliments from the men when she returned to her cell. Despite the circumstances, a sense of camaraderie had formed among the six of them who shared the makeshift cellblock. It reminded her that they were all trapped together and only had each other in these cells— even if the reality of the situation was that they would likely have to kill each other out in that arena.

She started to realize that the Goddess was right, if she was going to get out of there, she would have to trust the others, and ask for their help.

The next day Laila and Jerrik were both pulled from their cells. It was hours until the first match. She exchanged glances with Jerrik, who was apparently just as confused as she was. Whatever was going on, she just hoped that she could get a good look at any possible escape routes.

They were taken to a higher floor of the complex. Here the guards were better dressed, and people hurried about their business preparing for the night.

They stopped at a heavily guarded door. The room inside was lavish, housing expensive décor and large, soft leather armchairs. At the back of the room was an opening to a balcony that overlooked the arena. Behind a desk sat a familiar face.

The Master of the Games.

He leaned back in his chair looking them over, his ever-present smirk settling on his face.

"I've called you both here for a reason. You two are my most popular fighters among the fans right now. Congratulations."

Laila didn't feel particularly honored. When it was clear that she and Jerrik weren't going to speak, the Demon continued.

"In any case, tonight we are expecting a particularly large crowd with particularly wealthy guests. Tonight, you two will fight each other, but let me be crystal-clear. You will fight, and the Dark Elf will win. However, if one of you kills the other, know that you will die the slowest, most painful death I can imagine. Believe me, two centuries in Hell have made me exceptionally creative."

His words dripped with venom, and the hair on Laila's neck stood up. She forced herself to keep a neutral expression.

"The same goes if the Light Elf wins," he added.

She didn't doubt him. He was obviously a despicable creature if he had been sent to Hell, and she didn't want to know the kinds of atrocities he had committed to be sent there.

He appeared to be waiting for an answer, so Laila nodded. Jerrik just stood there staring at the Demon.

"You may go," he said, and returned his interest to the laptop computer on his desk.

They were quickly returned to their cells to await the match that night. Neither of them spoke to the other. It occurred to her that the Demon had probably rigged the outcome of the match the last time he had spoken to her, when he had asked her not to kill her opponent. After all, when you were running illegal gladiatorial competitions, it wasn't as if you were opposed to cheating.

A couple of hours later, the fights started. The two waited the entire night until finally, at the end, they were called.

Laila was nervous. She knew that Jerrik was an excellent fighter. She was obviously going to get her ass kicked. Even if the outcome hadn't been planned, she wasn't entirely sure she could beat him. But at the same time, she was excited to see what it would be like to fight him.

They were led to opposite sides of the ring and were armed with hand-and-half swords. Laila was very familiar with the weapon. They were still used in the other worlds, and she had lots of experience with the weapon. So, she guessed, did Jerrik.

They climbed into the ring, and the announcer took his cue.

"Ladies and gentlemen! I'm sad to say that this is the final match of the night. By popular demand we have the Dark Elf facing the Warrior Princess!"

Laila and Jerrik took their positions, and the crowd went silent. Then the gong sounded, and the match began.

Ali waited next to Darien's SUV in the garage below IRSA while she flipped through a series of photos on her phone from a surveillance camera in an alley. It was the far end of the same alley where Laila had been abducted. One photo showed a van that exited the alley just after Laila had been taken.

The quality of the photo was poor, but one of their techs had been able to zoom in on the faces of the men visible in the vehicle. One of the men was unremarkable. He wore a dark hoodie and a hat that hid the majority of his face. The other wore a business suit. His black hair had been slicked back, and his expression was cool and confident. Even in the low-resolution photo there was something unsettling about him.

The clack of footsteps on concrete caught her attention as Darien approached.

"How was the morgue?" asked Ali. "Did they finish the autopsy?"

"Yep," said Darien, unlocking the vehicle. "Nothing too interesting though. The cause of death was a broken neck, probably from when he was thrown through the wall. There was a scale found underneath one of his fingernails. It looked serpentine but smelled human."

"So, there's a Shifter involved?" Ali climbed into the SUV. "Well, I ran the victim's name through LAPD's pre-Event database. Looks like he was convicted of some misdemeanors, but there's nothing on him after The Event. Not even a social media account online."

Darien pulled out onto the main road, where they were joined by the rest of Los Angeles' inhabitants in the late rush-hour traffic.

"Now," said Darien, glancing in his review mirror, "the question is whether he was an innocent bystander, or if he was involved with the Demons."

"He was definitely one of them. Colin recognized him from the bar."

It was a pain in the ass to question Colin about the inci-

dent. She worried that he would want to be included in their investigation, but he appeared more disinterested than anything.
She was relieved that he wasn't slowing down the investigation,
but at the same time she wondered if Colin was still fit for his
position.

"I still say we report him to D.C.," muttered Ali, "he's a
liability."

"Easy," said Darien. "D.C.'s never taken an interest in us
before. What makes you think they'll care now?"

It was true. The politicians in D.C. had created the Inter-Realm Security Agency so that the government could help
keep the delicate peace between humans and SNPs. But the
truth was, IRSA as a whole was disorganized at best. Offices
throughout the country were understaffed. Field agents were
left to fend for themselves, following their own judgment more
often than protocol. But the same was true with most government agencies these days. While the local politicians liked
to tell themselves otherwise, Los Angeles had reverted back
to the Wild West. Sure, they had all the modern amenities and
comforts, but when it came to law and order, local branches of
law enforcement were pretty much on their own.

On one hand, this made it difficult to get help and equipment they needed. But it also meant that no one was breathing
down their necks, ensuring every protocol was followed.

"You're probably right," she said. "But if you don't come
up with a better idea soon, I'll report him anyway."

"Back to the problem at hand," said Darien, as he turned
off the highway and into the Old City. "Do you really think
this contact of yours will know anything about these guys? It
seems like a long shot to me."

"It might be a long shot, but Carlos has a lot of connections. He's come through on this sort of thing before."

Ali had never meant for Carlos to become an informant.
They had met one night when she was exploring the Old City.
She had recently moved to the city and was feeling lonely, and

the relationship she formed with Carlos was easy. No strings attached, and she liked it that way.

But as time passed, Ali began to realize that Carlos's connections in the Old City ran deep. It started with a case that led back to the Old City, so she asked Carlos a couple of questions. Then there was another case, and another.

It never offended him, but he always swore that she would owe him a favor for all this help. That's why Ali felt a little suspicious when Carlos tried to cancel their meeting. He'd been quite insistent, but so was Ali. They needed the information he had.

CHAPTER 27

The Elves circled each other carefully, watching and waiting for an opportunity as the tension built. The crowd faded from their minds as their entire focus was drawn to each other.

Jerrik attacked first with an overhead cut. Laila stepped to the side, angling the point of her sword down to parry the attack. In a flash, she counterattacked to his side.

He parried, and so their dance began—for that's what it was, a dance. They moved together in a whirl of steel. For each attack the other responded with perfect timing and counter-timing. Gradually they tried different tactics in an attempt to break through the other's defense, but to no avail.

Laila felt so alive. Her senses were alert to his every subtle movement. She had never felt so in tune with any opponent before. Everything was perfectly clear, and she could anticipate his every move. Together they worked like clockwork.

Perhaps it was because he wasn't trying to kill her, and so he wasn't trying to conceal his actions, but she felt that his patterns of movement were familiar to her, as if they had been training together for years.

The swords were most effective when there was a bit of distance between the two opponents. In order to end the fight without getting cut by the razor-sharp blade, she would have to get closer to him, where the blade would be useless.

With his next attack, a diagonal cut aimed for her left shoulder, she parried and stepped in toward him, forcing their hilts together.

For a moment they stood there, gazes locked. Laila kneed him in the groin, catching him off guard. She took the opportunity to force his sword down while striking him across the face with her elbow. She purposefully pulled the blow.

Recovering, he flipped the sword around and used the hilt to hook around her ankle. He pulled her leg out from under her, and she tumbled to the ground.

She started to get up but hesitated on her knees, knowing that Jerrik's attack was already coming. She could have evaded it but instead braced herself for the impact.

Jerrik saw her hesitate. He used the pommel of his sword to strike her in the back of the head, and Laila crumpled to the ground.

She was unconscious, but he knew he hadn't hit her hard enough to leave any lasting damage. Still, the crunch of the pommel connecting with her skull made him sick.

He kicked her sword out of the way. The crowd was on its feet cheering.

"An interesting fight, wouldn't you agree?" The Master of the Games prowled to the edge of his balcony. He observed the crowd for a moment before looking directly at Jerrik with a dark grin.

"Now kill her."

Ali and Darien pulled into an old parking lot filled with empty cars in various states of decay. Without streetlamps, the night in the Old City was dark as pitch. The headlights of Darien's SUV revealed a lone figure standing next to a motorcycle.

The two agents got out of the SUV, and Carlos approached them.

"You need to leave." His voice was low and shaky. He glanced around to see if they had been followed. "This isn't safe, not for any of us!"

"Whoa, slow down." She reached out to touch his arm, but he swatted her away.

"You don't get it," he hissed. "They know about us! They'll kill me if they can. I have to get out of town and lie low for a while."

"Hold on," said Darien firmly. "Who are 'they'?"

"No one you should mess with," said Carlos, cramming his helmet onto his head.

"Carlos, are these men involved?" asked Ali, showing him the picture of the men who had abducted Laila.

The color drained from the human's face. "Where did you get this?"

"You remember my friend, Laila?" she asked. "She was abducted last week, and we believe these were the men that took her."

"Look," said Carlos hastily. "I'm sorry about your friend, but if those guys took her, she's not coming back."

He swung a leg over his motorcycle and started the engine.

"Wait!" said Ali, grabbing his arm. "What aren't you telling us?"

He shook her off, but Darien grabbed the front of the bike, preventing Carlos from taking off.

"Let go!" shouted Carlos frantically.

"Not until you give us some answers," hissed Darien.

Gunshots rang out in the night. Darien shoved Ali between two abandoned cars next to them before vanishing in the gloom.

"Carlos!" screamed Ali as she saw his still, bleeding form lying on the asphalt. She started to move towards him, but the roar of an automatic gun forced her to take cover again.

She grabbed her gun and searched her surroundings for the source of the gunfire, but it was so dark that it was impossible to see their attackers. Darien was nowhere in sight, but she knew he would be dealing with the assassins.

Watching her surroundings, she whipped out her phone and called for help.

CHAPTER 28

The Master of the Games' words hit Jerrik like a punch to the stomach. What kind of game was he playing here? The Demon had made it very clear to him that he was not to kill Laila, but now he was ordering him to execute her in front of the crowd.

No matter what he did, he realized that they would probably kill him. It was a trap.

He saw her still, slender form lying on the bloodstained ground at his feet. So vulnerable. He could easily kill her. One clean cut, and it would be done.

He had killed countless men in the time he had been here. He wasn't even sure how long it had been since he had arrived. The weeks and months had passed him by in a blur of blood and gore. Gone was the man he had once been, reduced to a hollow shell of a man.

That was, until Laila had arrived. Something had changed in the air within the last weeks, and he could sense the disruption she had caused. Only she had found a way around the cuffs to heal herself, and she still had the determination to escape. She was keeping secrets, and he was not sure that she could be trusted. But if Laila had a snowball's chance in hell to save any of the others here...

The audience shifted and waited for him to make his move.

"No."

Some of the guards moved to grab him, but the Demon waved them off.

"It appears that the ruthless Dark Elf is growing soft," he taunted over the speakers. "Is it because she's a woman? Or is it because you have feelings for her? She is alluring—I wouldn't blame you for falling for such a captivating woman."

Jerrik didn't react. The audience watched attentively. This was all a part of the Demon's plan. They never planned to kill Laila, or him for that matter. They were worth too much.

"I suppose I was a little hasty in my decision," the Demon continued. "I'll let you both live. This time, that is."

Jerrik waited a moment, then scooped Laila up and carried her out of the arena. She would probably kill him later for treating her like a damsel in distress. But at the moment she was unconscious and better off in his hands than in the hands of the Demons.

"Carlos!" screamed Ali as she cautiously left the cover of the old cars.

Blood stained his shirt from multiple wounds on his chest. Ali wadded up her jacket and applied pressure to the wounds, but there was so much blood. It soaked the ground around them.

"I'm so sorry," she sobbed. "I shouldn't have made you come! I should have been more careful! I'm sorry, Carlos."

"Ali," said a gentle voice beside her. It was Darien.

"Don't just stand there! You're a Vampire, do something!"

He shook his head. "I can't. I'm sorry, Ali, he's gone."

"No. No!" She struggled to apply more pressure to the wounds, but Darien carefully pulled her away.

"Ali," he said softly, pulling her into an embrace.

She shook as burning hot tears spilled down her cheeks.

"They're gone," said Darien as he held her. "They ran."

"Fucking cowards!" she spat. "Won't even show their faces."

She pulled herself away from Darien as the police and ambulances arrived. One of the paramedics gave her a blanket, which covered her blood-soaked clothes.

Darien dealt with the cops while she silently watched the emergency workers cover Carlos's body with a sheet.

What had she done? This was all her fault.

The first thing Laila noticed when she drifted back to consciousness was the massive headache. She lifted her hand up to gingerly touch the tender lump on the back of her head. At least the pain meant that she was still alive.

Slowly she opened her eyes, allowing them to adjust to the dim light of the cells, and sat up.

"Careful," a concerned voice cautioned her.

"Ugh, I know you had to be convincing, but damn, that hurts!" She turned to look at Jerrik, who had assumed his typical position lounging in the back of his cell with his arms crossed.

"What happened?" She cautiously felt her head. "After the fight, I mean."

"Lover boy here just revealed his weakness for beautiful women and showed his heroic side in front of the largest audience we've ever had," Henrik called from his cell.

Right, she thought, because Jerrik was about as heroic and charming as a Troll's ass.

She clearly was missing something. The others informed her of what had taken place after she lost consciousness. By forbidding them from killing each other, the Master of the Games was able to create a story for the audience that would draw them back. She just hoped that a larger crowd would get the attention of the authorities.

Jerrik had been unusually quiet. That also wasn't like him. Of course, she was grateful that he hadn't killed her. Perhaps he wasn't as much of an arrogant ass as she had suspected.

She'd been lucky this time but she needed to come up with a plan soon. Laila sat awake thinking as the men slowly drifted off to sleep one by one, until she too succumbed to a restless slumber filled with long concrete corridors and sneering Demons.

CHAPTER 29

"Hey, you awake?" a voice whispered in Elvish from nearby.

Laila wearily sat up and looked over at Jerrik. "I am now."

"Sorry."

"It's okay, I wasn't sleeping well anyway."

They sat there for a while in companionable silence while the men in the surrounding cells snored on. It was probably still the middle of the night, and they were the only ones awake.

"You were pretty good out there today," he said somewhat awkwardly.

"You too," Laila said, barely whispering, "but it won't matter for long. We're all disposable, and once the Demons get bored they'll have us killed."

She paused, unsure of how much she could trust him. He could be a spy for the Demons—hell, any of the men in the room could be spies—but she knew that she would have little chance of making it out of there on her own. And if she didn't find a way out, there would be no one to rescue those wretched souls who were trapped along with her.

"The only way to stop this," she whispered as loud as she dared, "is if we can get out of here and find help. I've got an idea of how we could do it, but I can't do it alone."

Laila paused, waiting for a reaction. Jerrik nodded in agreement. "Go on," he whispered.

"If I can get a charm off of one of the guards, I could deactivate my cuffs and use my magic to deactivate yours as well. There must be entrances to this building on the floor where we were taken today. We could find the nearest phone and alert the authorities."

Before he could say a word, another voice answered in the darkness.

"I can help."

Laila turned to see Torsten watching them gravely.

"I can help," he said again, switching to English.

"You speak Elvish?" Laila asked, surprised.

"Only a little. Someone will have to cover for you while you are escaping. I can organize a distraction in the workshop where I repair the weapons. That will help keep the guards occupied."

Laila nodded. The more people involved, the more likely they were to be caught and killed, but at the same time they would need every advantage they could get.

"We should leave during the fights," Jerrik said. "The guards are always more occupied then, and there will be more chaos and vehicles that we could use to escape."

"The only issue is that Torsten doesn't normally work during the matches," Laila reminded him.

Rather than fighting, Torsten worked in the forge to repair weapons. It was one of the reasons he had been able to survive there so long.

"Leave it to me," the Dwarf winked. "I can ensure that a distraction will occur. I have my ways. I've been stuck in this hole for too long. I would do anything for the chance to see my daughters again."

Laila's heart ached to think that somewhere his family was grieving for him, assuming he was dead. Or worse, thinking he had abandoned them. How many men were in his situation? How many children were left fatherless, or wives left to raise their children alone? She made a promise to herself that she would do whatever it took to free as many men as possible.

They talked a while longer until they had created a plan. It wasn't foolproof, but Laila hoped that she and Jerrik could handle whatever threats they encountered.

By the time she went to sleep, though, Laila still hadn't figured out how she would get the charm to unlock her cuffs.

She had no time to ponder the question that morning because she was shaken awake by a guard.

"Get up!" He roughly dragged her to her feet. "You're coming with me."

Fear clawed at her stomach. Had someone overheard their conversation and ratted her out? She glanced at Jerrik, who sat watching helplessly from his cell as the guard pulled her down the hall.

Great. Now she was probably headed to her execution. She tried to remain calm and sent out a silent prayer.

"No, no, NO!" Jerrik shook the bars of the door as if he could rip the door off its hinges.

"What the hell, man? We're trying to sleep!" growled Henrik, the ice creature, in the cell across from him. The others grumbled and scowled as well.

Jerrik ignored them, kicking the lock on the door, succeeding only in making more noise.

"Jerrik, calm down," Torsten warned.

"How the hell am I supposed to calm down!?!" he growled back. But he regretted it the moment he saw the pained look in the Dwarf's eyes.

Jerrik slid to the floor, knowing that there was nothing he

could say or do that would make any difference.

"How did they know?" he said softly.

"Now we don't know what this is about. For all we know, everything's fine," Torsten reminded him.

"What the hell is going on?" asked Klaive.

"That woman was the best chance we had of getting out of here, and it appears someone discovered that," Jerrik snapped.

The men exchanged glances.

"Not only was she planning to get herself out of here, but to save every one of us as well. And if my theory is right, she has sacrificed a whole lot more than she's said."

"What do you mean?" Torsten asked him.

"I mean, I don't think it's a coincidence that she ended up in this place. She clearly has had training and was not nearly as surprised as I expected. I think she willingly came here to rescue someone."

He didn't tell them that he thought his family might have sent her. They didn't need to know about his family. He had run from them and their political games a long time ago, but he wouldn't be surprised if they had been watching him all along.

The men around him exchanged glances.

"It's not just that," Mato said. "You care about her."

He said it as if it was a fact, not a question. Jerrik was ready to make a sharp comment back to him but stopped. Mato was right—he had feelings for her. Despite his intention to avoid connecting to others, that strong, determined woman had captured something inside him.

Every time she stepped into that arena, he couldn't take his eyes off her. He kept replaying those brief moments when they fought together, where nothing else mattered. He carried her back to her cell because he would rather be beaten by guards than watch them touch her. There was something familiar about her that he couldn't explain, and yet there was something about her that was different from any woman he had met.

To admit his feelings would be giving others leverage against him. After all, she might even be working for his parents, and they would certainly use that against him.

But a small flame of hope had burned within him last night, when she had confided in him her plans to escape. Although now it seemed that hope was likely lost forever.

He didn't answer Mato, but the others in the room seemed to understand.

"Your secret is safe with us," Klaive told him, the others nodding in agreement.

"Not that it will matter at this point."

"Do not give up hope. There are a thousand reasons she was taken," Henrik said.

At that moment the door opened down the hall and the guard reappeared.

CHAPTER 30

The guard led her down the hallway, along the same path she had been taken the day before with Jerrik. Laila's heart beat so loudly she was sure the guard could hear it.

When they reached the door to the Demon's office, one of the guards keeping watch knocked on the door.

"The girl is here."

Laila couldn't hear the response on the other side of the door, but the guard shoved her into the room.

The Master of the Games on an overstuffed armchair. He motioned for her to sit in the chair opposite him and waved her guard out of the room, leaving the two of them alone.

Laila cautiously watched the Demon. This didn't seem like an execution, unless he was trying to get her to drop her defenses. She took a seat but sat on the edge, never taking her eyes off him. Even if she was doomed to die, she wanted a chance to take him down with her.

The Greater Demon sensed her unease and laughed.

"My dear, I did not bring you here to harm you." His voice was smooth and his manner careless, but Laila could feel him using some of his magic charm on her.

"Cute parlor trick. Now cut to the chase. I'm assuming you didn't have your thug drag me up here to exchange pleasantries."

The Demon laughed, again grating on her nerves. She really hated the self-satisfied look that permanently resided on his face. It would make it all the more worth it to watch that expression change when she brought his entire operation crumbling to the ground.

"You're right. I had so looked forward to playing out a little tale of romance and strife between you and the Dark Elf. No doubt it would have breathed new life into these games. And who doesn't love a bit of drama? But it seems that someone has thrown a wrench into my plans."

He gestured to an open letter sitting on the side table next to him.

"This was sent to me by one of my patrons. They seem rather... *fascinated* by your performance and are offering me an object of great personal value in exchange for you."

"What?" she blurted out. Whatever Laila had expected, this was not it.

"Now, I'm not sure what they plan to do with you, and I really don't care. I simply cannot refuse such a great offer. A Charon's Obol is hard to find, particularly one blessed by Hades himself, and this patron is a man of great power and importance, so it is best to stay on his good side."

Shit. This guy who intended to purchase her must be a higher-ranking member of the Greater Demons. No matter how bad things were here, she was sure that whatever future awaited her would be much worse.

He watched her with mild interest as his words sank in.

"When?" she asked.

"Tonight. They will be attending the games to watch your final match, and once that is over, you will leave with them."

Laila nodded mutely. What could she say? She was about

to be sold like livestock to the highest bidder.

Jerrik breathed a sigh of relief as the guard thrust Laila into her cell. She didn't even glance at him when the guard left, just paced back and forth scowling.

"So, what happened?" he asked.

She stopped and turned to him as if she wanted to say something, but just shook her head.

"It's okay, they know," he told her, nodding at the others. He ignored the venomous look she shot him and continued.

"I thought they were going to kill you."

Her expression was unreadable, but finally she spoke.

"We have to go. Tonight."

She quietly explained to the others what she had been told and took them through her new plan.

Once Laila and Jerrik had removed their cuffs, they would be able to use magic in order to free the others of their cuffs as well. There were few with any magical ability, but it would make it easier for them to try to fight their way out if something went wrong. Mato pointed out that the guards would notice if the stones on the cuffs weren't glowing, but Laila told him they could use a spell that would make them glow as if they were active.

Next, Klaive would cover for them by projecting images of them in their cells. Apparently, he had some ability to trick the minds of others. The images would vanish when touched, but it would buy them a little more time.

Torsten assured them there would be an explosion of sorts in the room with the forge to help cover their exit as well. He was scheduled to work that afternoon, so he would prepare it then.

The only thing left at that point was for Laila and Jerrik to make it out of there alive.

She knew that they were all taking a great risk. She thanked them and promised to do whatever it took to get them out of there.

"If we are going to go down, we might as well go down fighting for the chance we'll make it out of here." Henrik grinned and rolled his shoulders.

"But how are we going to get one of those charms to deactivate the cuffs?" Jerrik asked.

"Leave that to me," she winked.

CHAPTER 31

"Hey! HEY! Is anybody out there?" Laila yelled, rattling the bars of her cell. Finally, a guard came trudging around the hall.

"Shut the hell up!" he said, slamming a metal pipe against the bars. If her fingers had still been there, they would have been broken.

"What kind of a pig-sty operation are you running here? I'm about to be sent home with one of your boss' supporters, and do you think he wants me stinking like one of them?" she said, gesturing to the men in the surrounding cells.

She leaned close to him, revealing a little more of her cleavage that was already bursting out of her tightened corset.

"Please, you look like a reasonable man. What would the harm be in a quick shower? Especially if I'm supervised?" she reasoned.

The guard swallowed hard and took a step back.

"I-I'll see what I can d-do," he stammered.

She winked at him, and he hurried off down the hall.

"Well, that certainly would not have worked if I had tried

it," Mato commented. "Are you sure this is a good idea?"

"It's worth a shot." She adjusted the corset so she could breathe again.

Moments later the guard returned and unlocked her door.

"Follow me," he said, and quickly led her through the building until he stopped at a plain door.

He waved her in, and she entered an old bathroom with cracked tiles. It housed two shower stalls at the far end of a row of old urinals and toilet stalls.

She turned as she heard the door shut behind her to see the guard standing there. She walked over to him and pressed against him. He grabbed for her ass. While he was occupied, she discreetly locked the door behind him.

She forced herself not to cringe as he groaned.

"Try anything funny," he said, "and I'll electrocute your ass straight to the realm of the dead."

She let out a short laugh and ran her fingers through his hair.

"I like a man who plays rough."

She gripped his hair, pulling him closer for a kiss. Just before his searching lips met hers, she slammed his head back against the door. He crumpled unconscious at her feet.

She breathed a sigh of relief and swallowed the bile rising in the back of her throat. So far everything was going according to plan.

She searched the keys on his belt until she found the charm for the cuffs. With one swipe they deactivated, and she quickly removed them. She rubbed her wrists where the cuffs had chafed her skin.

Needing a test subject, she locked the cuffs onto the wrists of the unconscious guard. This time she used magic to unlock them. All it took was one simple spell to deactivate them.

It appeared that the purpose of the charms was to enable the guards without magic to lock and unlock them.

Laila replaced the cuffs on her wrists and illuminated the

stones. To anyone examining them, they would appear to be fully functioning.

She replaced the charm on the guard's key ring and grunted as she dragged the unconscious guard to the showers at the back of the room and left him in one of the stalls.

Since he hadn't woken yet, she decided to chance a quick shower anyway. He was still unconscious by the time she had finished, so she turned on the showerhead in his stall, spraying him enough to rouse him.

"Oh my!" she said, fastening the top hooks of her corset. "Are you okay!?!"

"What?" he said, rubbing his head.

"I think you got a little distracted when I asked you to help me with my corset. You slipped on the tile and hit your head. Don't you remember?" She hoped that he would believe her. Unfortunately, elemental magic was basically useless to confuse or trick the mind.

"You've been out for nearly ten minutes."

"Right…" he said, confused. "Well, maybe we can pick-up where we left off?"

He grabbed for her, but she stepped out of the way. She tried to come up with a valid excuse when a commotion from the hall caught their attention.

The guard swore, and Laila wondered if someone noticed she was missing. He grabbed her roughly by the arm and dragged her back to her cell. He thrust her into the cell and slammed the door before he returned to whatever task he'd been neglecting, shaking his head and muttering to himself in a confused manner as he went.

Laila noted that Torsten was still missing from his cell, likely at the forge working on whatever distraction he had planned.

"What the hell did you do to that guy?" Henrik watched the door, where the guard had left.

Laila shrugged. "I think he has a concussion. He's a little confused at the moment."

"Then it worked?" Jerrik said. She smiled and unlocked his cuffs. After a few minutes, they had deactivated all of the cuffs in the room. Now they would wait until night fell.

CHAPTER 32

Laila waited restlessly all afternoon. She could have sworn years had passed by the time they heard the echoing noise of the spectators filtering into the stadium-style seats.

Torsten was back in his cell by then and assured them that some sort of an explosion would occur, but he couldn't predict when exactly. Something about pressure having to build. That being the case, they would likely have to start their escape whether or not they had the extra diversion.

They couldn't leave too soon—there were sure to be late arrivals—so they would wait until the first few fights had played out. There were usually a dozen fights or more each night, so that would hopefully give them a bit of a head start.

After the third match, they made their move.

Laila and Jerrik unlocked their cell doors, taking care to shut and relock the doors behind them. Klaive cast a spell, and identical copies of the two of them appeared in the cells. Jerrik's copy was sleeping in the far side of his cell, but Laila's was restlessly moving around. She was quite impressed.

"You are quite good at this," Laila told the man. He

shrugged but couldn't quite cover a grin.

"I can only hold it for so long, so you better move fast," Klaive explained.

Laila nodded and cautiously moved down the hallway, Jerrik following her. They didn't know who would be fighting, so there was the chance that they would encounter guards on their way.

They moved as quickly as possible, taking the same route Laila had followed that morning. They passed other prisoners in cells, but the others paid them little attention. Those who did notice them either assumed that they were supposed to be there, or knew better than to draw attention.

They had almost made it to the door of the last room of cells when an angry Ghoul let out a cry, startling them. While often mistaken for living creatures like Goblins, Ghouls are undead creatures created from corpses—but unlike Zombies, they have a small capacity to think. The magic also mutates their bodies to preserve them, giving their leathery skin a mummified appearance. They can't speak, but they can growl and scream. Ghouls are rare, very difficult to kill, and can only be created by Necromancers.

"Shit!" Jerrik said. He gestured, and the screams stopped, silenced by whatever spell he had cast.

They listened at the door to the hallway but couldn't hear any footsteps, so Laila silently opened the door.

She hadn't seen the Ghoul before, so it was likely that he had just arrived. In any case, it meant that there was a Necromancer on the loose somewhere, and she would bet that the Demons here were working with him.

They hurried down the long hallway to a stairwell. There were no doors down that hall, but they made it without incident.

Jerrik cautiously opened the stairwell door, and they stepped inside. Laila had just shut the door when they heard footsteps on the landing above them. Jerrik dragged her under the stairs where they crouched silently as the two guards began to speak.

"I hate that damn creature! It's been screaming the entire afternoon! I don't know what the boss thinks he's going to do with it."

Their feet came into view on the floorboards above the Elves' heads.

"I mean, you can't kill it, and who wants to try to drag his ass back and forth from the fights?"

"Shhh!" the second hissed suddenly.

Laila stiffened. Had he seen them? She started to weave a spell.

"Talk like that will get you killed pretty quickly here, new-bie. Now get a move on."

Laila relaxed and let her spell fade away.

The guards trudged on into the hallway, leaving Laila and Jerrik alone in the stairwell. Breathing a sigh of relief, they climbed the steps of the stairwell and eased the door open.

As they expected, there were few people up in this part of the building. They were probably all in the arena, save whatever guards were left to patrol the doors.

They snuck along the hallway that led to an open entry hall. It was the lobby of the factory or whatever the building had once been. They could see guards up ahead who were armed with guns of various types.

The Elves crouched in a dark doorway, trying to get a closer look at the room. There was a stone counter between the hallway and the doors, with another hallway to the left side of the room. Laila could see two guards on their side of the counter and five guards on the other side, but she couldn't determine if there were more waiting around the corner and out of sight.

Jerrik leaned close and whispered, "I don't suppose you know a spell to make us invisible?"

She shook her head. Elves in general were bad with

illusion. Fae and other SNPs were much more talented in that area. She searched for anything that could help and noticed that their hallway was dimly lit in comparison to the lobby.

While Laila's power dealt mainly with the elements and space, she also had some control over light. She concentrated and very slowly dimmed the lights as much as she could without drawing attention. It would give them a little cover to get closer to the end of the hall without being seen.

Keeping low to the ground, they crept forward. There were two guards behind the counter sitting in office chairs. On the right side of the room there was a wall of windows where they could see the orange glow of old halogen lights.

There was a loud boom, and the walls shook.

"What the hell was that?" one of the guards said.

"Fire! Quick! There's been an explosion in one of the workshops," someone shouted from the other hallway. The guards exchanged glances, and the five on the other side of the counter rushed towards the hall. That left the two guards sitting in front of them.

They waited a moment, then glanced at each other. The less attention they attracted, the better, so they silently crept up behind the guards.

Jerrik hooked his arm around one guard's neck, squeezing until the guard went limp, while Laila cast a spell drawing the air out of the other guard's lungs until he lost consciousness. He quickly collapsed as well. They rolled the guards under the counter, hoping no one would notice them right away.

Outside was a concrete courtyard. No guards appeared to be waiting, so they stepped out into the night.

CHAPTER 33

Across the courtyard was another building about two hundred yards from where they stood. It had been a storage building at one point. Now it had been converted into a parking structure. Other than that, they appeared to be in the middle of nowhere. There was nothing in sight but oak trees swaying in the cool night air.

If they were able to get to one of the cars, they would have a better chance of finding help. But separating the two of them from the cars were a number of guards patrolling the area.

"Think we can make it?" she asked Jerrik.

He just scowled, observing the guards.

They needed to move soon. Someone would eventually enter the lobby and spot them. She glanced around, but there was nothing they could use for cover.

Suddenly headlights came into view, and an old Jeep slowly rounded the corner.

"Come on!" She bolted for the Jeep as it passed.

The Jeep was topless apart from the roll bar, and it was

moving slowly enough for them to climb in.

Laila launched herself over the door to the cargo space and into the back, holding onto the roll bar for balance. The guard in the passenger seat whipped his head around.

"What the—"

She elbowed him in the face and grabbed his gun, pointing it at the driver.

"Keep driving," she growled in his ear.

The guard did as he was told while Jerrik climbed into the Jeep behind her and knocked the Demon in the passenger seat unconscious. They drove around the building until they reached the far side of it, out of sight and away from the other guards in the area.

She didn't take her eyes off the driver.

"Slowly come to a stop," she commanded. "Here's what you're going to do. You will put the car in park and get out of the vehicle. You will keep your hands visible at all times, or I'll kill you before you can try anything. My friend here is going to tie you up, and we will leave you here. Understand?"

He nodded.

"Good, now move. *Slowly.*"

He parked the car and stepped out. Jerrik was about to get out and tie him up when—

"PRISONERS HAVE ESCAPED!" the guard screamed.

"Shit!" She knocked him out with the butt of the gun. It was too late though, the other guards had been alerted. She clambered into the front seat, shoving the unconscious man out of the vehicle.

"Hang on!" she warned Jerrik, and floored it.

Guards fired at them, and Laila crouched low in the driver's seat as bullets whizzed past. There was a gate up ahead made of old chain link fence. It was closed, but that would have to be their way out.

"Hold on," she yelled back.

She floored it straight towards the gate. Guards in front

of them scrambled out of the way as the Jeep hurtled towards them.

Just before the impact, a shield appeared around the Jeep. It protected them and the vehicle as they burst through the gate.

"Thanks!" she called over her shoulder.

"Don't mention it," the Dark Elf said.

Laila slowed her speed just enough to keep control of the vehicle and headed down the cracked asphalt road leading away from their prison.

She could see headlights in the rearview mirror behind them, so she kept driving as fast as she dared. Laila had no idea where they were. They were on a long country road with no signs and no cross streets. There was no choice but to keep driving straight.

Jerrik reached around to unbuckle the remaining unconscious guard from the passenger seat. There was nowhere to keep him, and he could attack them when he woke. Laila slowed the vehicle as much as she dared. Jerrik picked up the guard and tossed him into some plants on the side of the road.

"Now what?" he said, buckling himself in.

"We need to find a phone—a working one, that is—to call for help. We can't be too far from a city. Not with the number of people watching the fights."

It would be easier said than done, of course. After The Event, large areas of land were left abandoned as people flocked to bigger cities. So, even if they came across a house, if the phone lines weren't working they would have to keep searching.

Laila kept an eye on the headlights following them.

"Eventually we are going to have to stop, and I don't see any way of losing them on this road. Can you do something to impede them?"

"I can try," he said. After a few moments there was a loud clap of thunder, and a bolt of lightning stuck a large tree behind them, splitting it. The fallen half landed in the road, leaving tangled branches and splintered tree trunk to obstruct their pursuers' path. It would help slow them down, but only until they could move it.

"What about those rocks?" she said, pointing to boulders on a hill up ahead.

She couldn't see what he did, but he managed to start a rockslide that covered the road just after they passed. Now the Demons would have to shift the rock and dirt off the road before pursuing them. Even so, Laila didn't slow their pace. She simply followed the road, guessing at turns and hoping she was headed in the right direction.

Jerrik searched the Jeep as she drove. He found a couple of guns, some ammunition, a large flashlight and a tire pump. But unfortunately, there was no phone, not even a radio.

"Well," said Jerrik, "at least we have weapons in case they catch up to us."

"We're going to need more than two guns and a couple rounds of ammo if that happens."

Laila was half certain that Loki, the God of Chaos, must have been watching over them. That they had managed to get this far was nothing short of a miracle, but now they were faced with a new problem. How would they find their way back to civilization?

They were following a road in the middle of nowhere on a pitch-black night. For once Laila found herself wishing she were a Vampire. At least then she could see the road. Fallen branches and other debris littered their path, creating another set of hazards to avoid.

Something darted in front of the car. Laila slammed on the brakes as a lone coyote scampered into the brushes next to the road while the Jeep came to a screeching halt.

"Okay," said Jerrik shakily beside her. "I think we should stop for the night."

Laila nodded and cautiously drove off. It would be easier

to navigate during the day, and they both needed the rest.

"There's a building up ahead." She pointed to an old wooden structure. "At least it'll provide some shelter."

She pulled off the road and drove up to a gate. Jerrik climbed out of the Jeep and forced the rusty hinges open far enough for Laila to drive through. He stepped up onto the back bumper of the Jeep as Laila slowly drove up the dirt path.

The old building was a barn. The wood was rotting, but it seemed sturdy enough for one night.

"Let's park the Jeep inside," said Laila as she glanced back at Jerrik. "Just in case the Demons drive by."

He nodded and opened one of the large sliding doors for her.

The barn was large, and there was plenty of room for the vehicle. Laila cut the engine and conjured a ball of light so she could examine the interior of the barn.

It was filled with cobwebs and dust. Old stalls stood empty along the walls, and riding tack rested on hooks and shelves. The horses that once inhabited the stalls were nowhere to be seen.

Jerrik slid the barn door shut and joined Laila as she searched the back of the barn.

"Are you looking for anything in particular?" he asked.

"Gasoline," she said. "The Jeep is running low on fuel, and I would think a ranch like this should have extra gasoline canisters."

"I'll check out back," said Jerrik, conjuring his own light. "I think I see a truck through that doorway."

He stepped through a back door and into the night.

Laila tried a light switch, but as she had expected, there was no electricity.

She wandered over to a workbench that held a variety of tools. There was also a bookshelf with a collection of books on horse care. There was no sign of gasoline, but she did find some old candles. She lit a few and placed them in jars to protect the flames.

"Hey!" called Jerrik from the doorway. "Look what I found!"

He held up a large, clear container of brownish liquid.

"It's sort of dirty," said Laila, examining the contents. "But it'll have to do."

"Catch," he said, tossing her an apple. "There's a tree outside, and it's full of them. We should stock up. Who knows when we'll find more food?"

He grabbed a wooden crate and headed to the door.

"Good thinking," said Laila, spotting an old pile of letters on the bookshelf. "I'll help you in a minute…"

It occurred to Laila that electricity was not the only way she could send a message. She would just have to get a little creative with the resources at hand.

Laila searched for a blank sheet of paper. There wasn't a notepad on the bookshelf, so she tore a blank page from a horse-training guide. She also found a carpentry pencil in the drawer of the workbench.

In the light of the candles, she wrote a letter. It was brief, explaining that she had escaped the Demons and would find a way to contact IRSA with her location as soon as she could.

When she was finished, Laila placed her hand on the paper and reached for her magic. When she lifted her hand, the paper folded itself into a delicate origami bird. It ruffled its feathers and chirped at her as she carefully scooped it up and carried it outside.

"What's that?" asked Jerrik as Laila stepped out into the night.

"A message," she said, starting to weave her magic. "So the others know that we're alive and free."

She finished a spell to call up a breeze that would guide and protect the small paper bird on its journey, and then released it into the night.

"What others?" asked Jerrik as the bird vanished into the

dark sky.

"My teammates," said Laila. "They'll help us."

She turned toward the door, but Jerrik grabbed her arm, stopping her.

"What are you hiding?" he growled dangerously low. His face was inches away from hers. "Who are you working for?"

Should she tell him? If the demons caught up to them, he could sell her out. She wanted to believe that he was a better person than that, but in all honesty, she hardly knew him.

Laila kept her gaze level. Her face revealed nothing. She could fight back, but that wouldn't help her gain his trust.

"Nothing that affects you," she said honestly.

He didn't budge.

"If we get caught, it's safer if you don't know." She paused. "All you need to know is that help will be ready when we need it."

"Are you a mercenary?"

"No," she said incredulously. "Why? Are you on the run from one?"

It was subtle, but she felt his body tense. She'd hit a nerve.

She reached up, gently placing her hand on Jerrik's shoulder. "We both have our secrets and our pasts. My secrets pose no threat to you or your well-being. You've trusted me this far, so can't you trust me on this?"

Laila saw the hesitation in his eyes before he stepped back.

"My apologies," he said, grabbing the carton of apples and disappearing into the barn.

Shaking her head, Laila wondered what haunted Jerrik's past. She sensed fear and pain. But if they were going to survive long enough to reach help, he would have to trust her.

CHAPTER 34

"We should take shifts," said Laila, placing some candles she'd found on an empty crate.

Jerrik found a stack of pads and blankets in the corner of the barn. They were covered in dust and dirt, but it was better than sleeping on the hard dirt floor, or in a concrete cell.

"I'll take the first watch," said Jerrik. He shook out a dusty blanket and wrapped it around his shoulders before retreating to the other side of the barn.

Laila found a blanket for herself. It smelled dusty and slightly moldy, but it would keep her warm. She curled up on the stack of saddle pads and shut her eyes.

It was so quiet out there in the countryside. After the nights of sleeping surrounded by so many other people and noises, it was a bit unsettling. Eventually, though, she drifted off to sleep.

It seemed as though only moments had passed before Jerrik's voice stirred her from her sleep. She wished she could lie there longer and rest, but with the Demons nearby, sleeping without a watch was a risk they couldn't take.

She rolled off the pads and curled up with her back against a stall. As Jerrik drifted off to sleep, Laila listened to the sounds of the countryside surrounding them. It was close to dawn already, even though she had probably only slept an hour or two at the most. The creatures that inhabited the area were silent. Even the nocturnal ones had settled in for the night. The silence would help alert Laila to any signs of pursuit, but for now they were alone.

Laila's thoughts drifted to her family. Had anyone told them she was missing? Hopefully not. That was a mess she would rather avoid. Her mother was all too likely to create a political scene out of it. She would probably try to convince the Elves to withdraw their support of the Earthly governments, and Midgard would lose magical backing that it needed.

No, it had become abundantly clear that organizations like IRSA needed all the help they could get. The balance in Midgard was delicate at best, and the humans were still trying to understand magic in general. More than ever, Midgard needed Supernaturals like her to protect its people from these growing threats.

Time passed, and Laila watched as a faint light appeared on the horizon. Dawn was approaching, and it was time for them to move on. She woke Jerrik, and together they loaded the apples, gasoline, blankets, and other useful supplies into the Jeep.

As the first rays of sunlight reached across the land, they were already driving down the road.

"Any idea where we are?" asked Jerrik.

"No," said Laila. "Probably in California somewhere. If we can get out to a main freeway, we should be able to determine our location."

"And the nearest inhabited city," added Jerrik.

As they continued down the same road, they found no evidence of other life, aside from the occasional squirrel.

After about a half hour, the road narrowed. Laila frowned. That wasn't an encouraging sign. A few miles further and the road ended at the border of a large property. It was a dead end.

Laila turned the car around. "Shit, it looks like we'll have to backtrack and look for another road."

"Great," grumbled Jerrik.

"Do you have a better idea?"

Jerrik didn't answer.

Laila took a deep breath and tried to remain calm. They'd wasted precious time by taking this route. They retraced their steps. A few miles past the barn where they had spent the night, they reached a crossroads. There was no street sign, but it looked promising. Hopefully this time they would be heading towards civilization, and not away. They just needed to choose a direction.

"If you happen to know a spell to help us find our way, now would be a good time to use it," muttered Laila, staring up and down the crossroads.

"Let's go left," said Jerrik, selecting an apple from the box.

"Why left?"

He shrugged, "Why not?" He bit into the apple with a crunch.

Laila rolled her eyes but followed his suggestion. After all, they needed to pick a direction.

In the daylight it was much easier for Laila to navigate the abandoned roads that wound through the hills. She could actually see the debris that littered the road and was able to increase their speed. But it was also easier for the Demons to spot them. By mid-morning they had backtracked and found another road that wove through the hills.

She slowed just enough to round a blind turn but slammed on the brakes when she saw what waited just around the corner.

A barricade of fallen trees stood three feet tall, with gun-toting Demons on either side. Nearly a dozen Demons waited for them. They'd driven right into a trap. The Demons fired at them, but there was not enough room for them to turn and retreat.

"Hold on!" she yelled, cranking the steering wheel to the right. Three Demons dove out of the way as she veered towards the hillside that sloped down and away from the road.

Laila realized that it was probably a suicidal move. Then again, when faced with a choice between death and Demons, a swift death would be preferable to the torture that inevitably came with recapture.

She threw up a magical shield to protect herself and Jerrik as the vehicle went crashing through the brush. The front of the Jeep clipped a tree and sent them spinning sideways down the hill. Laila thanked the Gods for the roll bars that protected them from the crushing weight of the vehicle.

Finally, the Jeep slammed into a tree, bringing them to an abrupt halt.

"Are you trying to kill us!?!" moaned Jerrik from the seat next to her. He unbuckled his seatbelt and crawled away from the wreckage.

"Are you hurt?" she asked, extracting herself from the car as well.

"No. Are you?"

"I don't think so." She glanced up the hill where the Demons were scrambling down towards them. "We need to move though."

Gunshots rang out as they sprinted through the forest, weaving through the trees as the Demons followed. Jerrik looked over his shoulder and threw a ball of flame back towards the Jeep.

"What are you doing?" shouted Laila.

"It's a distraction. Keep running."

Ahead she saw a river that curved between the hills. The current was strong, but she could make it across with the aid of magic.

As they reached the edge, an explosion rang out behind them. The fire that Jerrik had set to the Jeep had reached the gas canister. A box of ammunition got caught in the blaze as well. The Demons scattered for cover as the bullets discharged at random.

"Let's go!" she said, wading into the water. Laila didn't wait to see if Jerrik was following. Instead she pushed onward, fighting the current. Despite the warmth of the day, the water was frigid. It sapped the heat from her body and left her gasping for breath.

She pushed herself forward, using magic to propel her against the current. The shore was ahead, and she pulled herself up onto the rocks.

Spinning around, she searched for Jerrik, but he wasn't behind her. Further downstream she spotted him struggling to get a grip on the slippery, algae-covered rocks.

Gunshots rang out, and she ducked behind a boulder. Peering around it, she saw the Demons aiming towards Jerrik.

"Over here!" she screamed, waving her arms. She wove a spell, causing the water in the river to rise in a thick fog that obscured them from the Demons' view.

On the other side of the river she could hear the confused Demons calling out to each other to fall back. She took the opportunity to hurry downstream and offered Jerrik a hand. He crawled onto the rocky shoreline and took a moment to catch his breath. Then Laila pulled him into the cover of the dense brush.

"Still okay?" she asked.

"Well enough to stand." He grimaced, though, and Laila was not entirely convinced he was unharmed.

"Let's put some distance between us and the Demons, and then we can tend to injuries."

He nodded, and together they fought their way through the underbrush. They climbed up the hill, then turned and hiked parallel to the river. The footing was treacherous with slippery layers of dried leaves giving way beneath them.

Sounds of pursuit faded behind them, and they found a

game trail worn into the hillside by deer. They followed it for a time around the side of one hill, and then another. Eventually the ground leveled out into gently rolling landscape covered in dense copses of oak trees.

It was under the arching canopy of an ancient oak where Laila dared to pause and take stock of their injuries.

"You're bleeding," said Laila, noticing a trail of blood dripping down the side of his leg. Looking closer she saw a dark, blood-soaked patch on his black T-shirt.

Jerrik removed his shirt, exposing his muscular torso. His skin was pale silver that contrasted with his long obsidian hair. There were many scars along his body, most of which were recent, but none as long as the deep abrasion running across his side.

"How did this happen?" she asked, examining the wound.

"I hit a sharp rock in the river when I was crossing." He flinched as Laila pulled a patch of fabric away from the wound.

"You should've said something sooner."

That would explain why he had had so much difficulty pulling himself out of the river.

"I'm going to heal this," she said, preparing for a spell. "You've lost a lot of blood already, and who knows when we'll find clean bandages to dress it."

"I don't want you to expend your energy," he frowned.

She laughed, "I'll manage."

Reaching out to the magical fibers that wound their way through Jerrik's body, she wove a spell to mend and heal the tissues. There was a shimmer of magic in the air around the wound as it started to knit itself back together.

As the spell ran its course, she felt another source of pain calling to her. It was another gash on his thigh. So she continued the spell, working downward to heal his leg as well.

By the time she finished, Laila was exhausted. The use of magic combined with the lack of food and sleep was taking its toll. She sat down on a patch of fallen leaves to keep from toppling over.

"See," said Jerrik, sitting next to her. "This was what I was worried about."

"I'll be fine, I just need a minute."

Laila could tell by the lines of concern etched on Jerrik's face that he did not believe her.

They sat there in silence for a moment before he spoke again.

"Thank you for healing me. And for saving me back there. I'd probably be dead by now if you hadn't distracted the De-mons."

He looked over at her before continuing. "I also want to apologize for the way I behaved last night. It was completely unwarranted. I—"

"It's fine, Jerrik," she said, cutting him off. "We're on the run. Tensions are high right now, and we're trying our best to get out of this alive."

Jerrik shook his head. "I still shouldn't have treated you like that. You haven't given me any reason to mistrust you. It doesn't matter who you work for, you got us out of there."

While she had understood Jerrik's reaction the previous night, it still stung. She knew it didn't matter what Jerrik's opin-ion of her was, so long as they could work together. So why did it affect her so much?

"We should get moving," she said abruptly. She tried to stand and wavered slightly, causing Jerrik to grab her arm to steady her.

"Not so fast," he said, still holding onto her. "There's a creek over there. We both need water, and I should wash away this blood."

Laila nodded and allowed him to escort her over to the creek. She knelt by the running water as he waded in and scrubbed off the blood that was caked onto his side. She couldn't help but notice his lean form. He was toned from years of training.

She pulled her eyes away, as she realized she was staring, and turned her attention to the water instead. It was cool and clear, but she knew it could easily make them sick.

Laila closed her eyes and reached out into the space around them, searching for stray strands of magic. There were far fewer here than in Alfheim. But the few strands of floating magic helped to revive her a little.

Cupping her hands, she directed a small stream of the purest water up and into her hands. She drank her fill and realized that Jerrik was watching her.

"It's just a small spell," she said, rolling her eyes at his disapproving look.

He shook his head but followed suit, using magic to draw out the clean water.

CHAPTER 35

The water helped, and Laila felt well enough to continue. When Jerrik finished washing the blood out of his shirt, they followed the creek through the rolling hills.

"Well," said Laila, scanning the landscape around them, "now we're definitely lost."

"I vote we *don't* go back the way we came." Jerrik paused to stretch a muscle in his leg. "That didn't work so well the last time."

Laila ignored the comment. "If we climb to higher ground, we might be able to see a town, or at least a road."

Jerrik nodded. "We should be able to make it to the top of these foothills before nightfall. That'll give us time to make camp for the night."

So, they left the creek and made their way to the tallest of the peaks. They clung to trees and tall bushes wherever possible and tried to stay out of sight. The trees also helped shelter them from the intense afternoon sunlight.

She noticed blotchy red patches spreading on her skin. At first, she thought it was from the sunlight, but the patches were raised and itched badly. It had to be some sort of a reaction. She noticed Jerrik was scratching at his arms as well. She couldn't risk using magic to heal the rash—she was already overexerted—so she ignored it and focused on the climb.

Neither of them spoke as they ascended the hill. Instead they conserved their energy for the hike. The brush was thick, and tree branches hung low. Squirrels and birds rustled in the foliage, nearly giving Laila a heart attack for fear it was a Demon crony. It made her feel ridiculous to jump at every noise, but she noticed that Jerrik was equally on edge.

Fortunately, they did not encounter any snakes. Laila knew there were a variety of venomous snakes living in the United States, but she never had a reason to study them. Now she regretted it. If she ever made it back to Los Angeles, she would find the time to study the flora and fauna native to North America.

Laila's legs buckled as they climbed the hill. Her muscles protested the day's exertion. But the sun was starting to sink in the sky, and they were running out of time. She pushed herself onward as she imagined how amazing it would be to take a nice, hot shower and curl up in bed.

Finally, they made it to the top. Her corset top and jeans were soaked through with sweat. Her feet ached as well, and she didn't want to know how many blisters she'd accumulated throughout the day.

"This seems like as good a place as any," said Jerrik, walking beneath the massive canopy of yet another oak tree. "I'll ward the camp, so we'll know if anyone or anything approaches. Why don't you see if you can locate any sign of civilization from up there?" he indicated the tree's branches.

"Sure," said Laila.

She pulled herself up onto a lower branch and reached for the next. With its gnarled, twisted branches, the tree was easy to climb.

It occurred to her that this was the first chance she'd had

to explore Midgard's natural landscape. The energy of the earth and life here was wild. Despite the pollution and destruction that humans had wrought upon the land, it always fought back. She had the distinct feeling that no matter how hard the humans tried to dominate the planet, nature would always follow its own rules.

Back in Alfheim, the forests were also known to be wild, but her people had learned to coexist with nature long ago. They respected the land, and so the land had come to accept and protect the Elves. Even the creatures that lived in Alfheim's forests had grown bold enough to communicate with her kind. There her magic resonated on an intimate level with the forests of her homeland. But here the magic was barely perceivable. It was just the faintest traces that wove themselves into her surroundings.

Laila climbed as high as she dared, then carefully stood and surveyed the countryside through the foliage.

To the west a road wound away through the hills where it vanished into the distance. She guessed that it was the same road they had taken before they encountered the barricade. It probably led to a town or city, but it was also the first place the Demons would expect them to go.

To the south there were a few roofs that poked up through the trees on a distant hill. Laila couldn't see a road leading that way, and there were a number of smaller hills separating them, so the houses were the only sign of civilization in that direction.

As the sun sank below the horizon, she turned and looked back the way they had come. In the distance glowed the orange lights of the Demons' complex.

She found it odd that so many people would come there to watch the fights, especially since it was so far out into the countryside. But as darkness fell, a faint glow on the horizon revealed the presence of a city somewhere beyond the complex.

Carefully, she lowered herself down, climbing through the tree until she reached the lower branches. She dropped down, landing softly like a cat.

While she had been up in the tree, Jerrik had cleared away the layer of dry leaves and collected enough wood for a small fire.

"Do you really think that's a good idea?" she asked.

"Relax," he said, stacking wood into a pile. "I warded the area to hold in the light. It should prevent us from being detected. And as far as the fire hazard goes, I think it'll be worth it. Especially since we left the blankets in the Jeep."

Ugh, she thought. He was right. They really had no protection from the elements, and now that the sun was gone, a chill crept into the air.

"So, what could you see?" he asked.

"Let's get that fire started first and see if there's any food around."

On the hike they had found little in the way of food. There were small, smooth acorns from the oak trees. The paste from inside the nut had looked promising at first. Upon tasting it, though, Laila quickly spat it out, gagging on the awful, bitter taste. Jerrik tried cooking some acorn paste on a stick and had a slightly better result, but they decided against eating it since there was no way to know if it was poisonous or not. Jerrik had suggested they hunt, but aside from the occasional sparrow or crow, wildlife had been scarce.

Jerrik sighed as they sat by the fire. "If only we had those apples."

"Don't do that," said Laila, smacking his arm gently.

"Do what?"

"Talk about the food we could be eating."

"Why not?"

"It'll only make it worse."

He raised an eyebrow. "I sort of get the impression you're speaking from experience."

"Sort of," she said, shifting. "It was back when I was training for the Royal Guard. There was an entire section of our training that prepared us to deal with different kinds of stressors: starvation, torture, etc."

"What!?!" cried Jerrik. "They *starved you* as a part of your training?"

Laila shrugged.

"That's ridiculous!" Jerrik shook his head. "Master Kyvik used to tell me these crazy stories about the Royal Guard of the Light Elves. I always thought he made up those stories to intimidate me!," he laughed.

"Master Kyvik? Was that your Sword Master?" asked Laila, her curiosity overwhelming her.

"How did you—?"

"You're one of them, aren't you?"

"No," he shook his head, "I'm not, but I was trained by one."

The fire crackled and snapped, sending sparks into the air as Laila watched to make sure they didn't land on the dry leaves around them. Laila reflected on the new information. Sword Masters were not only the most elite fighters in Svartalfheim, they were considered to be a part of a holy order as well. They dedicated their lives to the preservation of peace and balance in the name of a variety of Gods. It was Laila's understanding that when the level of Sword Master was achieved, they chose which God or Goddess they would dedicate their life to. They were free to marry or have families, but with the understanding that their calling as a Sword Master always came first.

"So," said Laila, "you spent years training, but never tested to become a Sword Master?" It seemed a shame that he would work so hard for so many years just to abandon the effort.

"There was an incident..." he started. "My father didn't approve. He ordered me to stop, but I continued training in secret. I was just preparing for the exam when he found out."

He stared into the flames.

"What happened?" asked Laila when he did not continue.

"My father killed Master Kyvik as punishment for my disobedience."

There was a sorrow in his voice that made her heart ache. Laila glanced over at him. His pained expression told her that the wound was still fresh.

She felt the sudden urge to reach out and touch his arm, but hesitated.

"I-I'm sorry," she said instead.

He just sat there watching the fire and reliving a distant memory.

Laila realized this was the reason why he had come to Midgard. But as much as her curiosity urged her to dig further, she changed the subject.

"The training I went through was difficult. It is one of the most physically and mentally challenging things I've done. But being rejected by the Royal Guard... that was worse."

"Why did they reject you?" asked Jerrik, tearing his eyes away from the fire.

"They said I wasn't experienced enough." She tossed a stick into the fire. "Honestly, it's not unusual for trainees to take the time to gain experience. Usually they work as a guard for a prominent family, or join the army, or something. I really shouldn't have been so shocked."

"If it's normal, then why were you so disappointed?"

"It's ridiculous, really," she blushed. "I thought I was good enough to make it in. Well, that's what the instructors told me."

A smile pulled at the corners of his mouth.

Laila rolled her eyes at him. "I told you it was ridiculous. But they said I should apply, even though they knew I didn't meet age and experience requirements. They told me over and over that I was good enough, and that they would let me in."

"But they didn't?"

"No, of course not. They'd rather choke to death on their fancy Elven wine than break tradition."

There was silence for a moment before Jerrik burst into laughter.

"What's so funny?" cried Laila, glaring at him. She had to wait until Jerrik could compose himself enough to speak.

"I'm sorry," he said, wiping tears from his eyes. "I just never thought I'd hear a Light Elf complain about rules and tradition. Your people are so obsessed with it."

"Well," said Laila, fidgeting, "now you've heard it. And keep your voice down. There are Demons looking for us!"

Jerrik took a deep breath and shook his head. "Well, if it's any consolation, you would scare our guards shitless if they'd seen the way you fought back there," he nodded towards the buildings in the distance.

"We didn't even have magic back there," she pointed out.

Jerrik sighed, "It feels good to use it again. I never realized how much I depended on it."

Laila nodded in agreement.

She examined her boots, which were starting to fall apart. They were not intended for hiking, and her feet ached. She was not looking forward to tomorrow's hike.

"Oh," she said. "I didn't tell you what I saw from the canopy."

"Any sign of a city?" he asked.

"No, not one we can get to from here. We'd have to go back past the Demons to get there. It looks like we have two choices. We can find our way back to that same road we were on when the Demons found us, or we can make our way to some houses in the distance and hope to find our way from there."

"Well," said Jerrik, tossing another handful of branches and bark into the fire, "we need something in the way of supplies and food. If we make it to the houses, we should be able to find what we need."

"I agree, and I think we'll be less likely to encounter any Demons that way too."

She glanced around the clearing. "We should probably take watches."

Jerrik shook his head. "The wards are strong. We both need to rest and conserve our energy for tomorrow."

Laila didn't have the strength to argue with him. She nodded and curled up facing towards the fire on the layer of leaves that blanketed the ground. They were crunchy and bowl-shaped with prickly little edges that dug into her skin, but they were softer than the bare earth.

Jerrik checked the fire once more to be sure it wouldn't blaze out of control. The night was cold, and she welcomed the extra warmth. As Jerrik added more fuel to the fire, she drifted off to sleep.

Despite her relative discomfort, Laila slept deeply through the night until the first rays of sunlight pierced through the trees, causing her to stir. In the night she had burrowed down into the leaves in an attempt to stay warm after the fire had died.

As she opened her eyes, she realized she was snuggled up to another source of heat. It was Jerrik.

CHAPTER 36

Ali sat with her eyes fixed to the wooden coffin. It rested on a plain bier and was surrounded by candles and flowers. The lid was shut, and a portrait of Carlos rested beside his casket on a stand. The picture was old, most likely taken before The Event. In it he was smiling and standing on a pier in a white button-up. He looked so different from the man she knew, so relaxed and easygoing.

Only a small group of mourners had gathered there in the early morning sun. Some were friends of Carlos's that she recognized from the Old City. There were also a couple of cousins in attendance as well as his sister.

It was his sister who stood at the podium telling a story from their childhood. The story was sweet and sentimental, and it did nothing to help the guilt that was eating Ali alive.

She wished the ground would open up and swallow her. She was the reason they were there. If only she had listened to Carlos, he would still be alive. He had known someone was following him. That was why he had been so reluctant to meet with her.

The guilt was unbearable, and all she wanted to do was leave. But for the sake of Carlos and the people gathered there, she stayed. Some of them cast her dark glances. They'd probably heard about her by now. They didn't appear to be hostile, but she memorized their faces nonetheless. She didn't blame them for being angry, though, and a part of her even welcomed it. She knew she deserved it.

Carlos's sister finished her speech, and tears shone in her eyes. A priest took her place and said another prayer before inviting the mourners to say their final farewells.

Ali stood with the other mourners to approach the coffin. In her hands she carried a single purple flower, the same shade of violet as her eyes. It had been difficult to find, since it was native to Alfheim, but a friend from back home had managed to send her a small potted plant.

The flower looked similar to the lilies of Earth, but its pollen shimmered with magic in moonlight. To the Fae it was sacred and was said to guide the dead to the afterlife with its magic.

She placed the purple flower on the casket and whispered a prayer to the Goddess Morrigan to watch over Carlos and to prepare her team for the struggles ahead.

Turning, she walked back down the aisle. One of the passing men shouldered her out of the way as she passed. Ali stumbled but regained her balance. Another man shoved her, and she crashed into a row of chairs.

"Freak!" he spat. "Get out of our city!"

Ali ignored him, brushing grass from her black slacks. She turned and walked away from the ceremony. Having said her goodbye to Carlos, she had no reason to stay.

As she stepped onto the path, someone grabbed her arm. Ali spun around, expecting an attack. But instead of the men, she found herself face to face with Carlos's sister.

"Sorry," the woman said, "I didn't mean to scare you."

"Oh, that's okay," said Ali, embarrassed. She paused a moment before adding, "I'm so sorry about Carlos. I—"

The young woman held up her hand. "Please don't. I know you feel like this is your fault, but I know it isn't."

Ali took a step back in surprise. She had not expected this.

"I know," she said though a teary half-smile, "that's not a typical reaction from a mourning sister. But he used to tell me about you, the Fae woman who worked for the government."

She sat down on a bench and motioned to Ali to join her before continuing.

"Carlos knew what he was doing was dangerous, but he was really proud that he could make a difference. That he could help people in some way. You see, we had a rough time after The Event. It was hard for us to go back to living like nothing had happened. We had no jobs, no money, and most of our family had died. We did a lot of stuff that we aren't proud of to survive."

She turned and looked at Ali. "Did he tell you our father was a cop?"

Ali shook her head.

"Yeah," she smiled to herself, "he was. He was kind of a hard-ass sometimes when we were growing up. He didn't make it through The Event, but Carlos used to hate to imagine what his father would think of him if he had survived.

"But you gave him an opportunity to redeem himself in his eyes. Probably in God's eyes too, and for that I thank you." She squeezed Ali's hand.

"Even so," said Ali, "I wish I could go back and change things."

The woman nodded.

"If…" began Ali. "If you ever need anything, please give me a call." Ali took out her wallet and handed the woman one of her cards.

She accepted it with a little nod and another half-smile before returning to the other mourners.

Ali stood and walked away through the graveyard, trying to

wrap her head around the situation. The knowledge that Carlos had been proud of his work lifted her spirits ever so slightly.

She passed along a bend in the path when a flutter of movement caught her eye. It was an origami bird perched on a headstone. More complex than any origami bird she had ever seen, it must have been an offering that someone had left at the grave.

But when she stepped away, it followed her, fluttering to the next headstone.

"What—"

Ali reached out to touch the bird. Immediately it hopped onto her hand and unfolded itself. It was a letter.

> Ali,
>
> I am free and safe for now, but I have no idea where I am. Hopefully I will find a way to contact you with my location before the others catch up to me. When I do, I hope the team will be ready.
>
> Laila

"She did it!" said Ali. "Oh, my Gods, she did it!"

A passing couple gave her strange looks and hurried away as Ali danced a jig on the graveyard path.

Ali laughed as she clutched the letter and hurried back towards the car. Of course Laila had managed to escape! She wished that they were able to talk to Laila somehow. But at least they knew she was alive and free.

She pulled out her phone and called Darien.

"Ugh, you know it's 8 o'clock in the morning," said Darien wearily. "If you—"

"Darien, Laila's contacted me."

"What? How?"

"I'll show you tonight. Meet me at headquarters just after dusk. We've got a rescue to plan."

CHAPTER 37

Well, this is awkward, thought Laila as she carefully inched away from Jerrik. She reasoned that sharing their body heat was the most logical reaction to the cold night air. So why did she feel so ridiculous, then?

Laila quietly rose to her feet, but the sound of leaves crunching underfoot stirred him from his sleep.

"Huh?" he mumbled, sitting up and looking around. "Is everything okay?"

"We should go." Laila smothered the last of the coals in the fire pit with dirt. "We've got a long way to hike today."

Jerrik rubbed his face and got to his feet. Leaves poked out of his dark hair, which was starting to escape from the elastic band he used to keep it pulled back. Laila patted her own short hair and discovered that it was a tangled mess filled with twigs and leaves. She attempted to shake the worst of them out, but their little prickly edges clung to her.

"Don't worry," said Jerrik, chuckling, "it'll help you blend into the forest."

She gave up and started walking south, with Jerrik following behind her.

It was not long before dehydration forced them to stop. There were no streams nearby, but Laila drew the moisture from the morning dew into her cupped hands. As they drank their fill, Laila wished they had bottles to keep the water in. Hopefully they would find some in one of the houses.

As they descended the hill, Laila watched for any sign of edible plants. Surely there had to be something around here they could eat. There were native peoples who had once lived off the land here, but to Laila the plants were strange and new. There was nothing that resembled the edible plants of her home world, and nothing that resembled the Earthly plants she saw in grocery stores.

Finally, as they reached the base of the hill, she spotted some sort of berries. They looked and tasted like blackberries, even if they were a little under-ripe. She and Jerrik ate as many as they could, being careful to avoid the thorny stems. There were not many left—the birds and other animals had already picked the bushes over—but it was enough to take the edge off their hunger and to give them a little energy for the day of hiking.

They wound down through the valleys, sticking to the cover of the trees and keeping watch for any sign they were being followed. Somewhere on a distant road they heard the rumble of an engine, but nothing closer to them.

In the evening, they paused by a stream to take a break. Laila's feet were aching, so she pulled off her boots and socks to soak her feet in the stream. They were covered in more blisters than she cared to count. After some consideration she used a spell to heal her feet. The relief was immediate.

"Feeling better?" asked Jerrik.

"Much better," she sighed as she flexed her feet, stretching the muscles.

"Good, then you should put your shoes back on before the smell attracts too much attention," he smirked.

She threw a piece of bark at the Dark Elf. "As if yours smell any better after being crammed in those boots for over a month."

"But you don't see me taking them off now, do you?"

Laila rolled her eyes and pulled her boots back on. "Better?" she asked as she stood.

"Yes, but you might want to burn those shoes when we get back to civilization."

"I'm burning this entire outfit. Particularly this damned corset!"

"What!?!" said Jerrik with no small amount of drama. "You can't burn the corset! It completes your warrior princess look!"

Laila shook her head and turned to leave when he caught her wrist.

"Honestly, though," he said, "it looks very good on you."

For a moment she stood there inches away from him as a whirlwind of emotions passed through her.

"We've stayed here long enough," said Laila, taking a step away from him. "We should go."

She turned and continued south without waiting to see if he followed. But after only a couple of paces, Laila froze. Her blood ran cold as she heard voices on the hillside above them.

"This is ridiculous!" shouted Ali. "Of course Laila wrote this. Who else would have sent it?"

Once again, she was seated in the conference room with Darien and Colin. She had just shown them the letter, which sat on the table before them.

"It could be a forgery," said Colin. "Someone's probably trying to throw you off their trail by getting your hopes up."

"I don't know, Colin." Darien picked up the letter. "This looks like her handwriting to me."

"Seriously!?!" said Ali. "It found me in the form of a magical, flying, origami bird, for Danu's sake! If that doesn't scream

Elf, I don't know what does!"

"You know how ridiculous that sounds, right?" Colin shook his head.

Ali started at him incredulously.

"Why can't you just admit that this could be the good news we've been hoping for?" demanded Ali. "Why are you so damned pessimistic?"

Ali knew her temper was getting the best of her again. But it was hard to stay calm when Colin was so unenthusiastic. It made her want to scream.

"Look," said Colin coolly, spreading his hands on the table before him. "Even if she did write this, I don't know what you expect us to do. We have no information."

Colin rose from his chair and left the conference room.

Ali fumed as Darien shut the door.

"He has a point," said Darien, sinking into a chair. "The letter is pretty vague. We don't even know what to prepare for, or where we'll be needed. We'll have to wait for more information."

Ali knew he was right, but she was so sick of waiting.

Darien sighed. "I know you've had a rough day. Why don't you go home, spend some time with your sister, and try to get some rest? I'll call you if we hear anything."

"I'm fine."

"You've had a long day. The funeral…"

"So what?"

"Ali—"

"You think I can't handle this?"

"That's not what I—"

"I'm not made of glass," she spat. "So don't tell me what to do!"

The Vampire paused, unsure of what to say.

"Sorry," she muttered. "I didn't mean to snap at you."

"It's fine," said Darien. "I'm sorry too."

Ali folded her arms on the table and rested her head on

her forearms.

"Why is it that every time we take a step forward, it's like we're taking two steps back?"

Darien shrugged. "Probably because we are way outnumbered."

"Then why are we still fighting? Why are we still trying to keep up with this new Demonic threat?"

There was a pause, then Darien said, "Because we are the only ones standing between the Demons and the people of L.A."

He was right. She knew he was. But it was frustrating nonetheless. How was a ragtag group of government agents supposed to take on this threat?

"This is not what I expected when I signed my contract. I thought we would be dealing with the ordinary Supernatural conflict. Not an entire group of Demons, or whatever we're dealing with here. This stuff is supposed to be behind us!"

"But would you walk away?" asked Darien.

"What?" asked Ali, surprised.

"Would you leave and go back to Tír na nÓg?"

Ali thought for a moment. "No, I wouldn't. I couldn't do that to you guys. There aren't enough of us as it is. I couldn't leave you here to deal with this on your own."

"Good," said Darien, "because we can't afford to lose you. Now I want you to go home and rest so that you're ready. If Laila contacts us during the day tomorrow, I'll be stuck inside, and someone needs to be ready to go."

CHAPTER 38

Laila crouched, completely still, in the bushes next to Jerrik as the car drove slowly past them, scanning the area. Luckily, night had fallen, helping to hide them from view.

Their progress had been slow the entire afternoon, as they avoided more and more Demon patrols combing the area. They finally arrived on the edge of the neighborhood sometime after sunset, but a truck had been circling the area, preventing them from accessing the houses.

"They have to move on eventually," whispered Jerrik.

"Maybe, but they've been here over an hour," pointed out Laila.

"Then we should make a run for it. If we make it over the fence across the way, we should be safe enough."

Laila nodded. "Fine. Once he rounds the corner, we run."

They waited until the truck reached the end of the street where the road bent behind one of the houses, and then they slipped out of the bushes. As silently as they possibly could, Laila and Jerrik sprinted across the street, vaulted over the fence and into a yard.

They waited a moment with their backs to the picket fence

and listened. The truck looped back around, and the headlights flashed through the boards of the fence. Laila froze. Had they been discovered?

But the truck didn't stop. It continued down past the other houses, and Laila breathed a sigh of relief.

The neighborhood had been abandoned during The Event, and the plants in the yard around them had become overgrown like a jungle. They wove their way through rose bushes and shrubs until they reached the back door.

Laila used magic to unlock the sliding door. They hurried inside and latched the door behind them. Laila drew the curtains shut.

They were in a small kitchen that was covered in a thick layer of dust. As they walked through the room, they stirred up dust into the air, causing Laila to cough and sneeze.

"Okay," she whispered, wiping her eyes, "first things first. We need food."

"Everything here is going to be rotten."

Laila ignored him and conjured a dim blue light. She opened cupboards, but they were filled with dishes and cups— no food. Jerrik was about to open the refrigerator, but Laila caught him just in time.

"I wouldn't do that," she warned.

Jerrik gave her a questioning look but backed away from the refrigerator.

They kept searching the kitchen. Eventually Laila found a pantry around the corner. Most of the food was in various stages of decay or had been eaten by insects, but a few cans and packages were still intact.

"Here we go!" she said, passing two cans of beans to Jerrik.

"What's this?" asked Jerrik.

"Canned beans. They have a long shelf life and should be okay to eat."

She kept searching through the shelves and came up with

a couple of packets of instant noodle soup and some bottles of water. It was nothing special, and there was still a chance it would make them sick, but she thanked the Gods they had found something.

Of course, there was no power in the house, but it would have attracted too much attention anyway. She opened one can of beans and heated them with magic while Jerrik found spoons in a drawer.

They sat on the floor, out of sight from the windows, and split the can of beans. Within minutes it was empty, and they were left staring at the rest of the food.

Laila glanced at Jerrik. "We don't know if we'll find any-thing else, though."

"We could search the other houses."

"Not if the Demons are still patrolling the area." She shook her head. "But at least we have food now."

He nodded.

Laila opened one of the water bottles and took a drink before passing it to Jerrik. There was a stale, plastic taste to the water, but other than that it was fine.

"I wonder if it's safe to stay here tonight," said Laila as the set of headlights passed again.

"They are not searching the houses," replied Jerrik. "So long as we keep quiet and stay away from the windows, we should be fine."

Jerrik stood before continuing. "And I don't know about you, but I would rather sleep on a bed than on the ground again."

"Okay, then," she said. "You search the house and find the bedrooms. I'll look for any maps that might show us where we are."

Jerrik nodded and silently disappeared into the back half of the house while Laila searched an office next to the kitchen. On a desk there were stacks of bills showing the property's address, but a map was more difficult to find.

Laila opened file cabinets and sifted through files, hoping to find something useful. She found several maps from the previous homeowner's travels, but they were clearly from other locations around the country.

"How is it possible that these people didn't have a local map?" she muttered to herself as she tossed another file into a stack on the floor.

Crossing her arms, she looked around at the office. There was a bookshelf with some travel guides and an atlas. She removed the atlas from the bookshelf and flipped through the index, but the name of the town written on the old envelopes was not listed.

Frustrated, Laila replaced the atlas on the shelf. As she pulled her hand away, an old paperback book caught her eye. The spine of the book was so worn that she couldn't read the print. Out of curiosity she removed it from the shelf to examine it.

As she flipped through the pages, she saw maps of northern California. The corner of one page was folded, so she flipped to it and found a map of hiking trails. The name of one trail was circled in pencil.

"Did you find anything?" asked Jerrik, standing in the doorway.

"Actually, I think I did." She pointed to the trail on the map. "This trail begins somewhere on this street and leads to a town. We might be able to find help or some way to call from there."

"Wait," said Jerrik, flipping through the book. "Aren't we near Sacramento?"

"Yes, but it's back in the other direction. Those were the lights I saw in the distance beyond the Demons' complex last night."

"Okay," said Jerrik. "Well, I found the bedrooms, but one of them is currently occupied."

"What?"

Jerrik's expression was grim. "The remains of the previous owners are in the master bedroom. It's probably better if we let them rest in peace."

Laila shuddered. She didn't like the idea of sleeping in the abandoned house to begin with. Abandoned places like these creeped her out and reminded her of the horror stories from The Event. But knowing they would be sleeping in a house with the bodies of two victims?

She contemplated leaving, but it would be unreasonable to risk sneaking into another house with Demons in the area. Laila knew she was being ridiculous. The bodies were resting peacefully, and there were no Necromancers around to reanimate the bodies. There was no harm in staying in the house, but she found it disturbing nonetheless.

"We'll make it work," said Laila eventually. "It's just for one night. We can use the guest rooms."

She followed him down the hall and to a bedroom. The bed was dusty, but Jerrik had found a fresh set of sheets.

"You mean guest *room*," he corrected her.

"Oh," she said. There was only one available bed in the house. "You know what—I'm just going to take the sofa."

She turned towards the living room.

"You know," he called after her, "they don't have a sofa."

She stopped in her tracks. Great.

"Then I'll sleep in a chair."

"Seriously? We slept next to each other in our cells and in the woods. At least the bed is more comfortable."

When she hesitated, Jerrik added, "If it'll make you feel better, I'll take the floor."

He moved to grab a blanket from the bed.

"No, you're right," she said, stopping him. "We both need rest, and we'll sleep better on the bed."

He shrugged and proceeded to make the bed while Laila warded the house.

The bed was blissfully soft after so many nights on a

cement floor. She sighed as she sank into the mattress and was almost drifting off to sleep when Jerrik returned from the bathroom. Suddenly Laila was all too aware he was shirtless.

He caught her staring, and Laila was grateful for the darkness that hid her blush.

"Good night, then," she said, quickly looking away.

He slid into the bed beside her. Laila's heart skipped a beat when his arm brushed against her. She turned her back to him. But she could still feel the heat of his body.

"Careful," whispered Jerrik in the dark, "you'll fall off the bed."

"What?" said Laila. "I'm not, I mean—"

"All I'm saying is that you had no problem getting close to me this morning."

Laila's cheeks burned. Gods above, thought Laila, he *had* been awake. "I'm sorry, I didn't mean to…"

"Stop being such a Light Elf."

"Excuse me?"

"You are all so concerned about appearances and reputation." Jerrik snorted. "If it makes you so uncomfortable, I'll sleep in the living room."

"Wait!" said Laila, sitting up and stopping him as he tried to rise. "That's not what I meant."

He turned, and Laila was suddenly aware of how close his face was to her.

"Please stay," she said. "It's late."

"Are you sure?" he asked, his breath tickling her neck.

She hesitated, feeling drawn towards him. "Yes."

They sat there for a moment as if frozen in time. She turned away.

"Good night, Laila," he said softly.

She laid her head on the pillow as thoughts and emotions swarmed her head.

CHAPTER 39

A gentle arm wrapped around her waist, stirring Laila from her sleep. Eyes still shut, Laila savored the warmth of the body behind her and leaned closer. A nose nuzzled her ear, his breath caressing her. Slowly he kissed his way up her neck. She moaned as the slow intensity of his actions became overwhelming.

His lips found hers, kissing her deeply. He pulled away. She opened her eyes and saw Jerrik leaning over her…

Laila woke with a start, her heart pounding. She looked over at Jerrik who was sprawled on his side of the bed. She breathed a sigh of relief.

It was just a dream. Just a hot, intense…

"Time to get up," she muttered to herself.

Jerrik mumbled something and wearily sat up, but Laila was already out the bedroom door.

By the time she came out of the bathroom, he was dressed and searching the hallway cupboards.

"I found this," he said, handing her a backpack. "We can stock up on any supplies we might need."

"Good idea," she said, looking through another cupboard.

They found a small first aid kit, a blanket, and a lantern. They placed the items in the backpack with the ramen noodles, but Jerrik paused, holding the other can of beans.

"Breakfast?" he asked.

Laila nodded.

They quickly ate and took one more look around the house.

"Should we grab any clothing?" asked Laila.

"All the clothing's up in the master bedroom."

"Right," said Laila. "If we need anything, we should be able to find it in town."

They watched through the windows, but there was no sign of the Demons. Quickly they slipped out the front door this time and hid behind an overgrown hedge to scan the street.

Still there was no sign of any vehicles, so they cautiously walked down the street.

"Okay," whispered Laila as she looked at the map in the book. "The trail should be up ahead."

Jerrik shifted the backpack on his shoulder and watched for Demons. They found an old path marker for a dirt trail that vanished into the trees.

Laila glanced at Jerrik. "This must be it."

They left the street and followed the path silently, listening for any noise in the woods around them. They heard the sounds of birds and other small creatures rustling in the leaves, but other than that, they appeared to be alone.

It was an easy hike, especially since they had a trail to follow, overgrown as it was. The day was hot, but the trees sheltered them from the worst of the sun's heat. At any other time Laila would have enjoyed the walk, but the constant fear of discovery made it difficult to appreciate the scenery.

After a couple of miles the undergrowth became dense,

and they lost the path. They searched through the trees and shrubs, but there was no sign of the trail.

"We should probably backtrack and see if we can find it again," said Laila. She wiped away the beads of sweat that were running down her face. The heat was starting to get to her.

"Let's keep going," insisted Jerrik. "I think I see it up ahead."

He stood on the fallen trunk of a tree and pointed down the hill. He offered her a hand, and she stepped up next to him. Sure enough, she could make out a trail in the distance.

"Oh, good," she said, relieved. The last thing they needed was to get lost again. She hopped down from the tree trunk, but the second her feet hit the leaves, something stabbed into her calf.

"Ow!" she said. "What the—?"

There was a strange rattling noise coming from the leaves, and then a snake darted away under the log.

"What was that?" asked Jerrik, who still stood on the log.

"Some sort of snake, I think. I must have stepped on it." She took a step back, cringing. Her leg burned where the snake had bitten her.

"Are you okay?" asked Jerrik, stepping down next to her, being careful to watch for serpents.

"Yeah, I'm fine," she said, walking it off. "It surprised me more than anything. We should keep going."

They returned to the trail and followed it for another mile. By noon they reached the end of the trail where it opened to a park on the edge of town. They waited in the trees listening for the sounds of automobiles.

Laila leaned against a tree. She was starting to feel nauseous, but she chalked it up to the heat. They would have to find some shelter from the heat soon.

Jerrik nodded, indicating the coast was clear, so they made their way through the park and towards the main road.

"Now what?" asked Jerrik.

"Let's try that drugstore across the street. We can check the phone and Internet connections there. Hopefully something will work."

The doors were locked, and they had to break the doors down in order to get in. Water stains, cracks, and other damage covered the walls. Mold and decaying food on the shelves gave the building a rank odor. Laila hoped they could find what they were looking for quickly. Not just on account of the smell, but because they had no idea if the Demons were watching the area.

They searched the front counter for a phone, but the lines were dead, just as they had been at the house, and there was no power. She searched through some emergency equipment that she found in a first aid kit while Jerrik explored the aisles. She had no luck there either.

Laila sat on the floor for a minute and rested her head against the counter behind her. Exhaustion was creeping in, and all she wanted was a few moments to rest.

"I've got something," Jerrik called.

She sighed and followed his voice to find him examining a collection of cheap cell phones.

"Are any of these cell service providers still working?" he asked, waving his hand at the racks.

She checked and picked out two.

"These, I think."

"Is there any way to activate them?"

"We can try. Even if they aren't fully activated, we may still be able to call 911 from them."

Laila ripped open one of the boxes and pulled out the phone. She attempted to turn it on, but a warning sign flashed across the screen saying the battery was low. The screen went black.

"Great," she said. "No power."

Jerrik shoved the box into their backpack anyway.

"Just in case," he said, "I also found more cans of beans

and water."

"That's good," she said, wiping more sweat from her brow.

Jerrik frowned. "You don't look so good. I think you should rest a minute."

"I'm fine," she said. "I just need some water."

He passed her a bottle, and they left the drugstore. Back in the street, they noticed piles of sun-bleached bone littering the roads, victims of The Event. The townspeople had probably been killed, turned into Zombies, and left to shamble around decaying until their curse was broken. At least now they were left in peace, their bodies slowly being reclaimed by the earth.

There was no use in reporting the remains, even if they'd had a phone to call it in on. Rural areas like this were abandoned after The Event, leaving no one to dispose of the bodies, and it was too expensive to waste resources testing every decaying corpse that was found from that time to determine the cause of death. Eventually the population would expand back into these areas, at which time the remains would be buried and the ghost towns rebuilt. But at the moment there were more pressing issues for society.

Laila giggled, thinking how much she felt like a zombie. She was not sure why the morbid thought seemed so amusing.

Gods, her leg hurt. The whole thing felt as if it were on fire. She squinted, trying to read signs on the buildings around them, but everything felt blurry.

"I—" She stumbled, and Jerrik caught her.

"Whoa," he said, picking her up. "You are definitely *not* okay."

She tried to move, but her limbs felt like dead weight.

"I think it was the snake," she said, the words slurring as they left her mouth.

CHAPTER 40

Jerrik rushed down the street with Laila, half conscious, in his arms. There was a police station up ahead, and the door was unlocked. He shouldered his way inside, slowing so that he didn't hit Laila's head on the doorframe.

He took her around the corner and into an office. Gently he set her down before returning to lock the police station's door and shut the windows.

"Come on," he said, kneeling beside Laila. "Stay with me!"

Laila groaned and muttered something about her leg. He examined it and found two puncture wounds just above the cuff of her boots. He pulled the boots off and tried to roll her jeans up, but they were too tight.

"Can you hear me?" he asked. Laila nodded slightly.

"We have to remove your jeans," he said.

"Can't move," she said, her voice little more than a whisper.

"You're going to be fine," he said, pulling off the jeans. "You—"

He stopped mid-sentence as he saw the wound on her leg.

It was swollen and a sickly purple color with dark veins spreading from the puncture wounds. He was not sure what kind of snake had bitten her, but it was definitely venomous.

"Okay," he said, trying to calm himself. "Um, Laila, I need to draw the venom out of your body."

Healing was not his strong suit. Jerrik rarely had a reason to heal anything beyond bruises or broken bones. Never had he encountered something like this, but there had to be a way to save her. They hadn't come this far only to have Laila die from a snakebite.

He placed his hands on either side of the puncture wounds and reached out with his magic. He could feel the venom in her veins like a current of fire, burning its way through her body. He focused on the venom and pulled, drawing it back through her body and out of the wound. It was slow going, and her circulating blood fought him, pumping the venom through her body. Slowly, though, it seeped out of the wound and into the dusty carpet beneath them.

When the last of the venom was removed, Jerrik paused and drank some water before continuing. He glanced at Laila's face, but her eyes were shut, and her face was pale and covered in sweat. He placed one hand on her chest and reached out for any traces of the venom. While he had managed to remove all traces of the venom from her body, there was still a lot of tissue damage.

He allowed healing magic to flow from his body to hers, encouraging the cells to regrow and repair the damage. It took a lot of focus to make sure he didn't miss anything vital. Eventually the swelling in her leg went down, and the color of her skin returned to normal.

Healing was exhausting work, and he had repaired as much as he could for now. Laila was still unconscious, but she seemed to be in a resting sleep. He squeezed her hand before lying down and allowing the exhaustion to pull him into a deep sleep.

Laila groaned and opened her eyes. She was lying on the floor in the middle of an office. Her pants were lying next to her, as well as Jerrik, who was asleep. She shook her head, trying to remember how they had gotten there.

The last thing she remembered was walking down the street. There was something wrong with her leg. She remembered the snakebite, but when she examined her leg, it appeared normal. Even the pain was gone. All that remained was a smear of dried blood. She wiped it away and pulled her pants and boots back on.

Jerrik must've healed her, which explained why he was asleep next to her. Thank the Gods he had been there. She probably would have died otherwise.

She still felt weak from the venom, so she opened the backpack and pulled out another bottle of water and a can of beans. After drinking half the bottle, she opened the can and heated the beans with magic. She fished a spoon out of the bag and started eating.

Jerrik stirred and sat up.

"Beans?" asked Laila, offering him the can.

He nodded and sat next to her, leaning against the desk.

"Thank you," she said. "I owe you my life."

He chuckled. "I'd say we're about even. You healed me after the mishap in the river."

Laila shrugged and rested her head against the desk.

Sometime later Laila awoke, finding herself sitting in the same position but with her head resting on Jerrik's shoulder. He had fallen back asleep as well.

She carefully sat up, checking in with her body. Her strength was returning, and she was still ravenous, but her curiosity was getting the best of her. She stood and walked out of the office.

They were in an old police station. Laila walked through the desks, searching the building. They had to have some sort of radio that could be used to communicate. She found some equipment in the back, including an old dispatch console.

"Laila?" called Jerrik from the other side of the police station.

"Back here! I think I found something."

Jerrik found her and glanced at the machine. "What is that? A radio?"

Laila nodded. "It's a dispatch console. If we can find a way to power it, we could use it to call for help. They should have some sort of emergency power supply here."

Laila searched the building while Jerrik disappeared somewhere in the back. A machine rumbled to life. Laila jumped, expecting an attack, but instead the lights flickered on.

"There's a power generator in the garage." Jerrik reentered from a hallway. "Looks like we've finally had a bit of luck."

"It's about time."

Laila switched on the dispatch console. Luckily it was still working despite the years of disuse.

"So, who are we going to contact with that old thing?" Jerrik asked.

"There's supposed to be a military base somewhere…" Laila scanned a map of the area on the wall.

"What?" he said, watching her.

"Here!" She pointed. "If we can get a hold of someone at this base, they'll get me in touch with my office—"

"Really? You think the military will listen to some random Elf on a radio…?" He trailed off as he was hit with a realization.

"I can't explain right now." She quickly scanned through the radio's channels, searching for a signal.

"Thor's hammer," he swore. "When we get out of here you're going to owe me an explanation. And a drink."

She silenced him as she found an active channel. It sounded as if it was coming from the base.

"Hello? Is anyone there? Do you read me?"

There was a pause before a male voice responded.

"This is Captain Joseph Wagner from the U.S. Army. How did you access this channel of communication?"

"We are stranded in a small abandoned city south of Sacramento, with Demons hunting us down. I need to get in contact with Special Agent Colin Grayson at the Inter-Realm Security Agency office in Los Angeles."

She quickly gave the captain her identification information.

"Someone is calling him as we speak," the captain informed her. "I'll have them put Special Agent Grayson on the same channel."

"Thank you, Captain."

Jerrik stared at her as if she had grown a second head. Great.

"You work for the U.S. government?" he said in shock.

Laila took a deep breath. "I'm sure you understand why I didn't tell you."

He laughed. He laughed so hard that he cried. Laila wasn't sure what he found so funny, but eventually he calmed down enough to speak again.

"Well, that's better than what I thought," he said, wiping his eyes.

"What is that supposed to mean?"

"Nothing." He lounged on the desk next to the dispatch console.

At that moment the dispatch console crackled to life.

"Laila? Are you there?" came Colin's distorted voice on the radio.

It was all she could do not to sob with relief at the sound of his familiar voice.

"Colin! Thank the Gods! We escaped, but the Demons are still searching for us."

"Wait, where are you?"

"I'm not entirely sure—somewhere in northern California. I have a map…" She motioned for Jerrik to read off their coordinates. She repeated them into the mic.

"We have a group of Demons after us, but we're not sure where they went. We lost them yesterday, but we also stopped to rest, so there's no telling where they are."

"We?"

"I managed to escape with the help of one of the other prisoners, but there are so many more still trapped there. You were right—there is a huge operation going on, but if you don't get some help up here quick, we are going to lose everyone trapped there."

"I'll call in any reinforcements I can find to meet us up there. I'll have someone meet you at your current location in a few hours, and then you can give us the details of the place where you were held."

"Thank you!"

"Stay safe. We'll be there soon."

She hoped that Colin would be able to come up with enough help to rescue the others and catch the Demons. At the moment, though, there was nothing for her to do but wait.

CHAPTER 41

Laila leaned back in her chair and closed her eyes. Finally, help was on the way! A portion of the weight lifted from her shoulders, but she knew that with every minute that passed, their chance of catching the Demons diminished.

It would probably take a couple of hours for someone to arrive and pick them up. Exploring the town while they waited wasn't appealing. Lately she had seen enough destruction caused by the Demons. The thought of walking past the remains they had seen on the street disturbed her as well. Plus, they were both still recovering.

So instead, Laila sat by the dispatch console, waiting in case someone tried to contact them again. Jerrik retrieved the backpack, and they split another can of beans. After a while he wandered around the abandoned station and vanished into one of the back rooms.

"Well, *I* at least would like to take a nice hot shower while we wait," he called from one of the back rooms.

"What are you talking about?" she called back. The Dark Elf reentered the communications room.

"There is a locker room back here with working showers. They must have a working gas water heater, because the water is even hot!"

A shower did sound amazing.

"Fine," she said. "I'll wait with the radio while you go first."

He shrugged and headed back up the hallway. Laila could hear the water start running in the other room. She ignored it and studied the radio. A part of her wished she had gone with him…

Laila shook her head. She was in the middle of a mission with Demons in hot pursuit, and all she could think about was *him*.

The lights flickered out as the engine in the garage died. So much for that idea, she thought as she conjured a glittering light.

No power meant no communication. She hoped there was a way to get that generator working again. She swore and headed down the hall in search of the generator.

She found it tucked away in the garage and stood there staring at it. She didn't know a thing about generators. She cast a spell to try to clear away some debris. It appeared to help, because by some miracle it started again.

On her way back to the communications room she passed the locker room but didn't hear the Dark Elf.

"Jerrik, are you OK?" she called, but there was no response.

"Jerrik?" she called again, but still no answer. She hesitated, then entered the bathroom.

Jerrik swore as the lights flickered out. Of course, it was when he was just stepping into the shower that the power went out.

Sighing, he dried off with the old towel he found. Wrapping it around his waist, he stepped out of the stall and was searching for his clothes when the generator started again. He shrugged and turned back to the shower when Laila bumped into him.

"A little impatient, are we?" He gave her a wolfish grin.

"The generator—" she started.

Much to his amusement, her face grew bright red as she realized that all he wore was a threadbare towel. With amusement he remembered that she had turned a similar color last night when she saw him shirtless as he climbed into bed.

It had been maddening, lying so close to her. He had wanted to reach out and feel that gentle curve of her hip, and that deliciously soft skin. She was still wearing that corset...

Laila took a step back and bumped into the wall behind her. Her heart skipped a beat as he watched her curiously. She knew the smart thing to do would be to leave and return to the radio, but her body refused to move.

"I haven't thanked you for getting me out of there," he said, never breaking eye contact.

"It was nothing," she said as casually as she could.

He shook his head. "If you hadn't come along," he continued, "who knows what would have happened to me. To everyone in there."

She looked away. "I came looking for them, the Demons," she confessed. "There were kidnappings, but I had no idea where the men were being taken or who was in charge. I didn't plan on getting captured, but when they grabbed me, the only thing I could do was go with them to see where they were taking their victims. I was just doing my job to find them and free the men they had kidnapped."

"So, you volunteered yourself as bait to save a group of people you didn't even know."

"No, not exactly." Laila straightened and met his gaze. "I was just doing my job."

He was closer to her now. Close enough she could feel the

heat of his body.

"Laila, there is so much more to you than that. It's not your job to care about those men, for those of us stuck in that hellhole. Compassion was usually the first thing we lost. But you used your empathy for those strangers to drive you to find some way to escape. And the first thing you did when you contacted help was make sure that there would be people coming to help *them*."

He reached up to caress her face gently, eyes lingering on her lips.

"Despite all odds," he continued, "you were able to remain strong of spirit. That's not something you learn in training. Warriors with decent skills and training are easy to find in any corner of the worlds, but a warrior with the determination, courage, passion, beauty..." He trailed off.

Her heart pounded. The way he looked at her.

"I have never met anyone like you, Laila. From the moment I saw you I knew there was something about you that was different."

They were so close now it was maddening.

She wanted him. She wanted this so bad she could scream. She knew it was wrong, that she should be focused on the task ahead. But all she could think about was him.

He tilted her head up and kissed her.

It was slow and cautious at first but became intense and hungry. She wrapped her fingers in his hair and leaned into him. He slowly ran his hands down her sides, thumbs skimming her breasts through the fabric of the corset. The sensation sent shivers of desire rippling through her body.

"Do you want this?" He hesitated for a moment.

"If you can handle it." She gave him a wicked grin and unhooked the top of her corset. After all they'd been though in the last few days, she was done being proper.

Laila wrung out her hair while Jerrik watched her from

where he leaned half-dressed against the wall, looking twice as good as any human model. His muscular chest was marked with a handful of old scars, but in Laila's opinion they didn't detract from his appeal.

Chattering from the radio jerked them back to reality.

"Shit!" she swore.

"I'll get it. Take your time." He gave her a quick kiss before sprinting out of the locker room. She scrambled to get dressed and rushed after him.

"Hold on, here she is." He motioned her over to the radio.

"Hello? This is Special Agent Eyvindr," she said.

"Laila, this is Darien."

CHAPTER 42

"Darien, what's the status of our pickup?"

There was a pause. "I'm trying to coordinate things from back at Headquarters. I'm going to get help to you as soon as possible, but it won't arrive until morning. Can you hang tight until then?"

"Hopefully," she said. "The Demons are still searching for us. We'll stay here for the night, unless they find us."

"Okay, be safe. I'll contact you in the morning."

Laila turned to Jerrik and switched back to Elvish. "It looks like we'll be sleeping on the floor again."

Jerrik grabbed her hand and pulled her up out of the chair and into his arms.

"Somehow," he began, "I don't think that will be so bad."

"Unfortunately, the only beds are the ones in the holding cells, and I am not spending another night in a cage, even if this one isn't locked."

"Why don't we bring the mattresses out here?" suggested Jerrik. "That way we'll be close to the dispatch console."

It was certainly better than sleeping in a cell, so the two of them carried the mattresses out to the room in the back of the police station where the dispatch console was set up.

"I've got to eat something," said Jerrik, digging through the backpack. He found a package of noodle soup and left to find the break room. He returned with a large bowl.

"Why don't I do that?" Laila took the bowl and the package from him. "You've used enough magic today."

She opened the plastic package and emptied the dried, squiggly noodles into the bowl. She added water and heated the mixture until the noodles had cooked, then added the seasonings.

The soup tasted old and stale, but at least it was filling. Laila hoped that whoever came to their rescue thought to bring food with them, preferably food that was not over five years old.

"So, now you know why I'm here," said Laila. "But you still haven't told me what you're doing in Midgard."

Jerrik hesitated and set the empty bowl on a desk. They were sitting together on one of the mattresses, and Laila had the blanket they had brought from the house wrapped around her shoulders.

"There's not much to tell, really," he said. "After my father killed the Sword Master I was training with, I knew I had to get away. He's got a lot of power and influence though. If I had stayed back in Svartalfheim, he would've eventually found me."

He sighed heavily and continued, "So, that's why I came to Midgard. I didn't have much with me when I arrived. I learned English, and for about a year I took any job I could find, but none of them lasted. I was trying to find a new job when the Demons offered me one. I didn't realize what they were at the time, or what I was getting myself into, and I've been stuck in their prison ever since."

Laila was not sure what to say. Sure, she and her parents often disagreed, but she couldn't imagine how bad Jerrik's situation had to have been to force him to run away like that.

"The other night," she began, "when we were at the barn, you asked me if I was a mercenary. Did you think I had been sent by your father?"

There was a long pause before he answered.

"Yes, I did," he admitted as he cringed. "I was afraid you were going to take me back there. That's why it was difficult for me to trust you."

"I see."

"If there was any way I could take that night back, I would. I'm really sorry about that. You are one of the most incredible people I've ever met, and it tore me apart to think there was a possibility that you were just acting on my father's orders."

"It's okay," said Laila with a smile, "I understand."

He chuckled softly, "See, that's what I mean. I'm not used to people acting out of kindness, with no strings attached. Most of the women I met were looking for power and saw me as a means to an end. They would never turn around to save me from Demons or walk into a trap in order to save someone they've never met. The only people I've met like that are the Sword Masters."

"That's really awful," said Laila. "And I hope you don't mind me saying this, but your father sounds like an ass."

Jerrik laughed and leaned back onto the mattress. "Eventually I'll have to go back and face him. I'll have to right the wrongs he's done, but I need time to plan."

"What are you? Some sort of Svartálfr Lord?" asked Laila jokingly.

"No," said Jerrik. "But that's enough talk about my depressing past."

He wrapped his hands around Laila's waist and drew her closer to him. She let him and met his lips with a kiss. It was slow and playful, but after a moment, she pulled away.

"What are we doing?" she asked. "We live very different lives. My place is here, and your place is back in Svartalfheim.

This isn't fair for either of us."

Jerrik laughed. "Don't you understand? There isn't anyone else I would rather be with."

Laila shook her head, "But your father—"

"I'll deal with him when the time comes, but for now I would rather focus on you, and our freedom." He ran his fingers through her short hair and brought her mouth back to his.

Laila awoke curled up on the mattress. She lay there next to Jerrik, feeling the warmth of his body.

It had been a long time since she had been intimate, and it felt so good to surrender herself to him. She was used to keeping her feelings locked away, but now she felt so exposed and vulnerable. Whether this was a good thing or bad, she did not know.

"Good morning," he whispered, and ran his hand down to her thigh. He leaned in and kissed the point where her neck met her shoulder.

"We should probably get ready," she sighed.

"No one's contacted us yet," pointed out Jerrik.

The dispatch console crackled to life. And Jerrik groaned.

"Laila?" Darien's voice came from the radio.

Laila slid out of bed and stood before the dispatch console. "Yes?"

"A team is going to have to land in a nearby field. The street isn't wide enough for the helicopter." He explained where it was located. "They should be there in the next half hour."

"Okay, we'll head that way. See you soon, Darien," she said and switched off the radio.

Laila grabbed the backpack with their remaining supplies and slung it over her shoulder. There wasn't much left in it, but she decided to bring it just in case.

"Is there anything else we might need?" She glanced around the room.

"Wouldn't they have an armory here?" asked Jerrik.

"There should be one back there." She pointed back past the locker room.

"Great," said Jerrik, disappearing down the hall.

"Wait!" called Laila, but he didn't respond. She sighed and followed the Dark Elf down the hall.

Jerrik stood in the doorway of the room that had once been the armory. Racks and shelves stood empty. All that remained was a couple of empty ammo. boxes.

"Well, so much for that idea." Jerrik kicked a small cardboard box. It skittered across the room, stirring up a cloud of dust.

"They were probably taken during The Event. Or by the Demons. In any case, we should go."

She led the way back to the front door of the building. They paused, peering out the window and looking for any sign of the Demons before stepping out into the late-morning heat.

The pickup point was just outside the town, about a mile away from their current location. It was a straight shot via the main road, and this ordeal would finally be over.

But something felt wrong to her. The only sound was that of their footsteps on the concrete. There was no wind, and Laila couldn't hear a single bird or insect. The oppressing quietness made her uneasy, and she reached out with her magic to feel their surroundings.

"What's wrong?" asked Jerrik.

"I don't know." Laila frowned. She glanced back behind them, but didn't see anything unusual. Still, she couldn't shake the feeling that they were being watched.

Maybe the creepy ghost town vibes were getting to her. They passed more skeletons that were lying in the street, and she was reminded of the Ghost encounter she'd had in Los Angeles. It seemed reasonable to think that this town had its share of lingering Ghosts. Perhaps that was what she was feeling.

Silently they walked through the town. Buildings gave way to trees as they reached a bridge. The pickup point was just ahead.

Laila had expected a field, but the location was more of a grassy hilltop that protruded above the surrounding tree line. Laila stepped off the road and into the trees. She took a seat on a large rock to wait.

Jerrik joined her, and Laila couldn't help but wonder what would happen after they were rescued. Where would he go? She realized that she didn't want him to leave, not when she was just getting to know him.

Jerrik frowned.

"What is it?" Laila asked.

"Did he say they were arriving by helicopter?"

"Yes, why?"

Car engines roared in the distance, and they were headed their way. The Demons had caught up to them.

CHAPTER 43

They crouched down, obscured by lower branches of the oaks. The Demons hopped out of three cars and spread out. Tensing, Laila watched as a few of them headed in their direction.

They were outnumbered eight to two, and there was no time to run or hide. Their only chance was to fight. They had no weapons, only their magic, and that was exhausting to use.

"You ready?" she whispered to Jerrik.

"Cover me," he replied.

She called up a shield around them as he sent a bolt of lightning at the first. Immediately the man went down, but he drew the attention of the others who fired at them with their handguns. Laila's shield deflected their bullets, but with each attack it became harder and harder to hold the shield in place. Jerrik charged the men and tackled them to the ground. Laila turned in time to see another pair approaching her.

These were both Bubak, or boogeymen as the humans called them. They are humanlike in figure but totally hairless, with tan skin that is rough like bark and solid, black, sunken eyes. These two carried no weapons, but their black, talon-like nails were sharp as razors. And they were charging towards her.

She dropped her shield and searched for a weapon. There was nothing, not even a large fallen branch. Mud sucked at her boots as she took a step back.

She had an idea.

Pulling water up from the plants and earth below, she froze it into a handful of icicles with lethal points. She threw the first ice dagger at the Bubak on the left, sending it straight through one of his eyes. She grabbed another icicle and thrust it into the shoulder of the second, but it hit bone and shattered. He howled with pain and swiped at her face with his nails.

She dodged and slashed at his neck with her last ice dagger. It cut through flesh and severed a large artery. The creature clutched his neck frantically as he fell, bleeding out in seconds.

Laila stood there watching them die. What had she done? The logical voice in her mind told her that it was necessary, that he would have killed her and anyone else he was ordered to. But she was rooted to the spot, staring at the bloody carnage she had left.

What shocked her the most was how easy it had been.

Suddenly Jerrik was behind her, pulling her back to reality. He was casting a spell at the remaining four Demons that were approaching. They were a variety of creatures from the other worlds, but the one using magic to call up flames caught Laila's eye.

"They've got a Sorcerer," Laila warned Jerrik.

"Can you keep him distracted?" His voice shook and sweat beaded on his brow. She nodded. He was running out of energy.

Magic gave them control of the elements, but if the element wasn't present, it took a lot more energy to use. That was why Jerrik was quickly burning out, and why Laila had decided to take advantage of the water in the ground with her last opponents. The approaching Sorcerer, like Jerrik, would be expending a lot more energy while conjuring up fire.

She reached out with her magic, sensing the ground beneath their enemy's feet, creating a gap under the earth and pulling the other Sorcerer waist deep into the ground.

He was startled but recovered quickly and sent a blast of flames in her direction. She dodged to the side, but the grass of the hillside caught fire. It spread so quickly she assumed the Sorcerer was using magic to feed it. Through the flames she could barely make out Jerrik struggling against his three attackers. Fear gripped her, and she realized that they might not be able to make it out of this alive.

By now her opponent had pulled himself out of the rocks and was approaching her. He was casting a new spell, but she couldn't tell what it was. The smoke in the air was blinding. His spell struck her like a bus and threw her backwards into tree. The impact was jarring, but she picked herself up to face him.

Fighting for breath, Laila watched as the trees around her crackled and hissed, the wildfire consuming them. She would have to stop it soon before it was too large to contain, but the Sorcerer was bearing down on her once again.

She reached out to the spreading wildfire with her magic. Taking hold of its raging power, she harnessed the energy and concentrated it into one deadly blast that cooked the Sorcerer where he stood. He screamed as he was incinerated.

Laila was trembling. Another dead.

The sound of a helicopter came from the distance, growing gradually louder. Her first thought was that it was the Demons, but through the smoke she could make out the American flag on the side. Help had arrived.

With one last glance to where the Demon Sorcerer had once stood, she pushed her dark thoughts to the back of her mind. They wouldn't help her to save the others trapped at the warehouse. She put out the rest of the fire, smothering it with a layer of earth. Once that was done, the helicopter landed.

Two figures in black tactical gear jumped out of the helicopter. They rushed over to Jerrik, who was still struggling against two of the Demon henchmen.

A third climbed out of the helicopter, and Laila recognized her immediately. She grinned and waved at Ali as she approached.

"About time!" she yelled over the noise of the helicopter blades.

Ali hurried over and hugged her.

"How come you get to wear corsets on missions?" she said, eyeing Laila's clothing.

"I escape from Demons and the first thing you notice is my clothing?"

Ali grinned wickedly. "It's good to have you back. There's a rendezvous point closer to the warehouse you described. We were able to get a Joint Special Operations team from the military to back us up."

"Good," Jerrik said as he sauntered over, the remaining Demons now contained by Ali's backup, "because we'll need everyone we can get."

Ali raised her eyebrows at Laila. "A new friend?"

"I'll explain later," she winked and climbed into the helicopter.

The rendezvous point was an abandoned farm about four miles from the warehouse. Special ops soldiers rushed back and forth as Laila and the others were ushered into an old barn.

A group of people was huddled around a table, staring at a map of the warehouse. Someone must have found copies of the blueprints. Darien was nowhere to be seen since it was still daylight, but Colin stood there examining the map.

He looked up when they approached and gave her a silent nod. Ali didn't so much as glance in Colin's direction.

"Are you okay?" asked Colin, he seemed to have trouble looking Laila in the eyes.

"Relatively," said Laila, noting his odd behavior, "considering I've spent the last few weeks in a cage."

"I'm glad you're safe," Colin said awkwardly. He opened his mouth to say more, but then he noticed Jerrik standing behind her.

"Who's he?" Colin indicated Jerrik.

"The prisoner I escaped with," Laila said. "Believe me, we'll need his help."

Colin watched Jerrik skeptically for a moment before returning his attention to the map.

"What's up with you and Colin?" Laila asked Ali quietly.

Ali just rolled her eyes. She was definitely upset, but now was not the time to discuss it.

The next twenty minutes were spent finalizing plans for the ambush and raid. Since they didn't know who was still in the building, they approached the situation as if it were armed as heavily as the night she left, if not more. Once the team finished planning, they hurried off to their respective vehicles.

Laila quickly changed into her tactical gear that Ali had thought to bring. Despite how bone-weary she felt after using so much magic, Laila fell into line behind the team. She was determined to see this through, but Colin stopped her.

"I think it's better if you wait here," he said grimly. "I think you've been through enough lately."

"Colin…" Ali shot him a look. They stared each other down, and Laila could practically feel the tension between them.

"With all due respect," Laila cut in, "I have full intentions of finishing this tonight. Jerrik and I know this place better than any of you, and even with help from the military, we'll need all hands on deck."

"Him too?" he nodded at Jerrik.

"Yes, him too." She stood her ground, shoulders squared. She would not back down.

Colin started to reply, but seemed to think better of it.

He turned and climbed into a truck with Laila, Jerrik, and Ali behind him. Silently Laila wondered at Colin's behavior. She didn't know him well, but he was more distant and aloof than he'd been before her abduction. Something felt wrong, but now was not the time to bring it up.

CHAPTER 44

By the time they reached the factory, trucks and armored vehicles were swarming the place. The Demons were attempting to stand their ground, armed mostly with guns. They were running around and shouting orders at each other frantically, while some attempted to flee. There were half packed trucks waiting in the yard, and it appeared that they had caught the Demons preparing to leave.

Laila watched from the truck as the soldiers in the vehicles in the front line engaged the Demons in a firefight. The Demons had the advantage of cover, but the soldiers were trained for combat and quickly broke through the fence as the Demons fell back to the warehouse.

With every passing second, the knots in Laila's stomach tightened. While they waited for the soldiers to secure a path to the building, the Demons could be executing their prisoners. The thought chilled Laila to the bone. She attempted to focus on the task at hand.

One by one the soldiers took out the Demons. Some of the Demons attempted to flee, only to be caught by the soldiers lying in wait in the surrounding forest.

A massive Troll that was scarred and missing an eye charged one of the trucks, ramming it with enough force to tip it over. The other soldiers fired at him, but the bullets had little effect. They resorted to using a rocket launcher. The carnage from the blast left Troll gore splattered across the yard.

Finally, Colin gave the command to move in and search the building.

Their truck drove them up to the courtyard. Laila was the first to jump down from the truck, casting a protective shield around them as she did. The team cautiously approached the doors, which were barricaded from within.

One of the soldiers with them moved to get a battering ram from the truck, but Jerrik waved him off.

"I've got this." Jerrik stood before the door, working his magic, while the team prepared for the attack that would come. With a loud bang, the doors flew backwards, crushing several Demons who were unfortunate enough to be in the path.

The soldiers opened fire on the Demons who had quickly recovered.

"Do you know where the Demons in charge would be? If they're still here, that is," Colin shouted at her.

"There is an office through there," Laila said, pointing towards the hall to their left.

The Demons were beginning to surrender, and additional soldiers were pouring through the doors to arrest them. Meanwhile the team cautiously followed Laila down the hallway.

They hurried, pausing to check around corners and doorways, to deal with the fleeing Demons. One of them stopped in his tracks, appearing to surrender at the sight of their heavily armed company. His eyes met Laila's, and realization dawned on him.

"You!" He raised the shotgun he was holding, took aim, and fired directly at her head. The bullet bounced off her shield, and before the Demon could attempt a second shot, he collapsed with a bullet in his head. Someone lightly nudged Laila, and she continued down the hall.

Finally, they reached the door to the office.

It was unlocked. Dropping the shield, Laila armed herself with a spell and waited for Colin's signal to enter. He nodded his head, and Laila pushed the door open.

Nothing.

The office was empty. Laila reached out with her magic, but the room held no sign of the Master of the Games.

"Looks like they're gone," Colin said, and lowered the gun he had been holding.

Laila leaned against the doorframe. After everything that the Demon had put her through, she had managed to let him escape.

"No, no, NO!" She ran her fingers through her hair, trying to think. She went up to shelves searching for anything that might give her a clue as to where they had gone. Colin and Jerrik did the same, and it wasn't long before they had searched the entire room. Meanwhile, Ali and their entourage of soldiers stood guard outside.

Laila sank onto one of the armchairs in shock.

"Damn it!" Jerrik said, kicking the desk in frustration.

"I can't believe that after all this, they got away," Laila said, shaking her head. "I—"

She stopped. Lying on the floor under the desk was a letter that they hadn't seen before. She picked it up and looked over it.

"It must have fallen out from behind the desk drawers when Jerrik kicked it," she said, passing it to Colin.

He glanced at the envelope, frowning.

"There's no address. It was probably delivered in person. Just the name 'Marius.'"

He pulled out the folded letter and read:

Marius,

I've been generous in allowing you time for
your little side project, but you have yet to follow through with your end of our agreement.
You may have succeeded in gaining the trust of
many human supporters for your endeavor, but
don't forget your loyalty belongs to me. Bring the
Charon's Obol to Styx, or I will send someone to
retrieve you.

Regards,

Izel

"Marius must have been the one in charge," she said.
"And Izel?"

"I have no idea," she said, shaking her head.

Something nagged at her. Marius had mentioned he was
planning to trade her for a Charon's Obol, but she had no idea
what that was. Styx, however, was a river that flowed between
the worlds of the living and the dead, so perhaps it had something to do with the dead?

They tore the desk apart, but there was nothing else to
find. It was completely empty.

"We need to keep going." She headed to the door. "We
need to find the others."

The halls were empty as their group rushed back through
the building in the direction of the cells. They reached the level
where she had been held, when a hideous screech caught their
attention.

Stalking though a hall of empty cells was the Ghoul. Apparently, some idiot had let him out of his cage.

"Shit!" Colin swore.

The soldiers opened fire on the monster, but the bullets
barely affected it. It ran with inhuman speed towards the closest soldier and ripped a chunk of flesh out of his neck.

"What the fuck is that!?!" one of the others screamed.

"It's a Ghoul. It's like a Zombie, but worse," Ali told him.

Laila swore the man's pale face grew even paler as the memories of The Event were brought back before his eyes.

Jerrik kicked it in the chest, and it landed with a thud in one of the cells. Quickly he locked the door behind it.

"You," ordered Colin, pointing to the remaining soldiers. "Stay here and make sure no one opens that cell."

The soldiers nodded, eyeing the Ghoul warily.

The four of them continued onward down the hall past cellblock after cellblock, but they were all empty. They reached the door to the arena, and movement caught their attention.

CHAPTER 45

Three Lesser Demons stood in the center of the arena. The largest was holding Torsten with a knife to his neck. Laila's blood ran cold.

"Don't you move!" the Demon shouted, shaking Torsten. "If you want the Dwarf, then you let us out of here. Now!"

"Hold on a moment here," Colin said calmly.

"I said, now!"

"Colin, this guy is losing his shit," Ali muttered to him. "He's going to kill that Dwarf if we don't do something."

Colin took a step forward.

"Don't move!" the Demon screamed. His muscles twitched, and Laila knew his next move would kill Torsten.

Laila had to stop him.

Time slowed, as did the people surrounding her. Laila watched, stunned. It was as if she were in a dream. A surge of energy rushed through her body, and suddenly she knew exactly what to do. She reacted instinctively. Her fingers grasped the hilt of a dagger as she lifted her hand and took aim. She unleashed a cry of fury as she released the dagger. In a flash of blue light, the silver dagger lodged into the Demon's head, and he toppled backward.

That was odd. Laila didn't remember having a dagger.

There was a shift, and time resumed its normal speed.

The other two Demons stared in shock, but quickly recovered and charged. Again, she reacted through instinct. This time she cast a spell.

Both men were struck down in a massive and blinding flash of blue flames. When her eyes adjusted, there was nothing left of the Demons but a pile of settling dust. It was a terrifying and devastating display of magic, the likes of which she had never seen before, let alone attempted. She stared in shock.

"Laila?" a familiar gruff voice called.

Torsten untangled himself from the corpse of the first Demon. He smiled at her.

"I knew you would do it!" he cried. To the empty space he called, "It's okay, you can come out now."

Trap doors in the stage opened, and out climbed the prisoners. They had done it. They had saved them.

Laila took a step forward, and her legs gave out. Strong hands caught her. They were Jerrik's.

"Laila!" he yelled.

The words echoed in her ears. She wanted to respond, but she was helpless to do anything but look into his eyes as the world around her dissolved and she lost consciousness.

When she opened her eyes, she was lying on a stiff cot in a military tent. Jerrik sat in one corner on a stool.

"What happened?" she asked, carefully sitting up.

"You exhausted yourself with whatever trick that was back there. It was pretty impressive. I've never seen anyone move so quickly." He shook his head. "I have your dagger, by the way."

He sat next to her and gave her the most beautiful silver dagger she had ever seen. There were delicate runes etched into the blade, and a large moonstone embedded in the hilt.

She had never seen it before in her life.

"There must be a mistake. That's not my dagger. I didn't have this when I entered the compound."

"Maybe you picked it up and forgot about it," he shrugged. "In any case, it's yours."

Laila had no idea what the story behind the dagger was. She would have to look into it later.

"Well, we saved them." She set the dagger aside.

"But we were too late to catch the leaders," he said with a sigh. "Many of the Demons escaped or killed themselves after they were captured. The few that are still alive aren't talking."

"Great, now there's a Greater Demon running around Midgard," she groaned.

"What?" asked Jerrik sharply.

"You didn't know? The Master of the Games is a Greater Demon. One of the first days I was there, he touched me. I could feel his energy. It was like nothing I've ever felt before—so much hate and cruelty," she shivered at the memory.

Laila watched a range of emotions cross Jerrik's face as the information sank in.

The men behind this were still out there somewhere, and at the moment they had no leads. There was the letter they had found. She assumed that Marius was the Master of the Games. She had no idea who Izel could be, but perhaps having a name to look into would help.

They sat together in silence for a moment.

"I don't know what your plans are after this." She shifted on the cot. "But if you wanted to come to Los Angeles, I could probably help you find some work."

He raised an eyebrow with his usual sly expression. "Are you asking me to come with you?"

"After everything we've been through, I just want you to know that there are options for you here while you decide what to do about your father. We make a good team. Maybe Colin would find it useful to have you around."

"Is that all?" he asked, his expression unreadable.

She hesitated. Of course, that wasn't the only reason, but how was she supposed to tell him how her heart beat faster every time he was near. Or how he made her lose her breath with a single look.

Memories from the locker room were called to mind. The way he held her. The passion of his kiss… But how was she supposed to make him understand that need she had to be with him?

"*I* hope you decide to stay," she said finally.

His expression was unreadable, but then he leaned in and kissed her. Passionately, but gently, as if he were afraid he would hurt her. She didn't want it to end, but he pulled away.

"In that case, *princess*, maybe I'll stay." He gave her a wicked grin.

"Now don't you—!" She swatted at him, but he dodged out of the way. The movement made her dizzy, and she flopped down on the cot.

"Should I get someone?" Concerned, Jerrik watched her like a hawk.

She shook her head, "I'm fine."

His look told her he didn't believe her one bit.

"Really, I am."

"Fine, but you need to rest."

She nodded as a wave of overwhelming exhaustion washed over her. She closed her eyes and drifted off.

CHAPTER 46

Laila awoke to a peculiar antiseptic smell and in a bed much softer than anything she had imagined in the last month. She opened her eyes and found herself sitting in a familiar hospital room. She was back in L.A.

There was a chair next to her bed where Ali sat flipping through a file on her tablet and drinking a large iced coffee.

"Hey, how do you feel?" she said smiling when she noticed Laila was looking at her.

"I don't know," she replied, feeling groggy. She tried to sit up and realized that there was an I.V. in her arm, and immediately tried to think of something else. She hated needles. And hospitals.

"You passed out when they were wrapping up the scene. They determined that it was a combination of malnourishment, dehydration, and your body's reaction to the overuse of magic in your weakened state. The doctors here said that your body forced itself into a magically induced coma."

"How long have I been here?"

"Three days."

"What?" She would have missed so much in the past three days. "What happened with the factory? Did they catch the Demons behind it? What about Jerrik?"

Laila tried to sit up, but her head was spinning.

"Whoa! Calm down," said Ali setting her book on a side table. "You're supposed to take it easy. Don't you make me get the doctor!" She frowned disapprovingly and planted her fists on her hips.

"I thought that look was only reserved for Erin," said Laila with a grin.

"Hey," said Ali, "someone has to keep an eye on you! I swear you're more trouble than a preteen Dragon."

Laila laughed and leaned back against the pillows.

"We haven't been able to find out much about the Demons." Ali seated herself on the edge of the bed. "Nothing on the names Marius or Izel, but we are reaching out to the other worlds to see what information we can find about them.

"The SNP men that were rescued are trying to transition back to their lives. IRSA teams in their areas are monitoring and helping the victims track down any loved ones who have been searching for them. A lot of them had injuries that were treated. We also discovered the unmarked grave where they were burying the bodies," Ali sighed as she delivered the news.

"The nation is completely shocked by the whole thing. In a way it may help to bring tolerance. I think it is just the beginning, and the more disturbances there are, the more distracted we will be from the Demons."

"And Jerrik? Where is he?" Laila asked.

"I'm sorry Laila," said Ali frowning, "I really don't know. The Svartálfr came back here with you. Colin spoke to him for a while, but I haven't seen him since then. Colin's really been obnoxious since you were kidnapped. He blames himself, but it's as if he's upset by the fact *he* wasn't taken, and *you* were."

Ali threw her hands in the air and rolled her eyes.

"I feel like a lot's happened in the last month," said Laila, adjusting the pillows behind her back.

"Yeah," said Ali looking down, "Carlos was murdered last week."

"What?" asked Laila, shocked, "your informant?"

Ali nodded. "It was all my fault!"

The Fae broke down sobbing as the weight of the last few weeks came crashing down. She told Laila about how they were desperate to find a lead, and how Carlos didn't want to meet because someone was following him.

"I should've listened!" she said trying to pull herself together.

Laila leaned forward and embraced Ali. "I'm sorry."

"No, I'm sorry," she said shaking her head, "look at me, you wake up from a coma and this is what you have to put up with."

"Oh come on!" said Laila, "don't be so hard on yourself. It's been a rough month for both of us."

"I couldn't stop thinking about what would happen if I was kidnapped or even killed. What would happen to Erin?"

"Hey, don't talk like that. We've survived, at least for now, and there's so much more to do."

"What happened to your back?" asked Ali, pulling away.

"Oh," said Laila shifting the fabric of the hospital gown, "a Goddess of some sort healed me while I was trapped in there, just before I saw Arduinna on the Astral Plane."

"Did Arduinna know who it was?"

Laila shook her head. "No, and the Goddess left me with this ominous message, something about my fate being a long and dangerous road."

"Because that's totally reassuring." Ali frowned and shook her head. "So what are you going to do about it?"

"Nothing," said Laila, "you and Arduinna are the only ones that know about this. Hopefully if I just keep a low profile, this Goddess will forget about me and I can go about my business as usual."

Ali opened her mouth to say something, but was interrupted by a knock on the door. It was the doctor.

"Good afternoon Miss Eyvindr," said the Doctor as he entered, "I'm glad to see you are awake."

Laila breathed a sigh of relief, she didn't have anything against human doctors, in fact she admired how much they were able to achieve without magic. But Elven doctors could help speed up the healing process.

"I should go," said Ali standing, "but I'll stop by later. Erin wants to see you too, when you're ready."

"Okay," said Laila smiling, "do you think you could bring my computer?"

Ali rolled her eyes and glanced at the doctor.

"So long as Miss Eyvindr takes it easy, I don't see the problem will allowing her to work on the computer," he said simply.

"Okay," said Ali reluctantly, "but only because he said so."

Ali slipped out the door as the doctor bombarded Laila with questions.

CHAPTER 47

A few hours later Laila was typing up her report on her laptop, which Ali had brought by. She's also dropped off Laila's cellphone. At least she now felt somewhat useful, even if she was stuck in the hospital.

There was also a stack of empty plates sitting next to her. The doctors had warned her that her appetite would return as a backlash from the magical coma, so a nurse had plenty of food brought up from the cafeteria. It was the best meal she'd had in weeks, even if it was just hospital food. Now she could feel her strength returning quickly.

She pulled up a web browser on her computer and typed in "Charon's Obol" into the search bar. A list of results popped up. She skimmed through the first four results that discussed ancient human death rites, wherein payment in coin called a Charon's Obol was placed in the mouth of the deceased for the ferry that would carry them to the realm of the dead. But unless someone had died, what use would it be?

Laila picked up her phone and scrolled through her contacts and selected one of them. The phone rang a couple of times before it was answered.

"Hello?" said a voice on the other line.

"Hi Lyn, this is Special Agent Laila Eyvindr. I stopped by your shop about a month ago."

"Right! Is there anything I can help you with?"

"Actually yes," said Laila scrolling through another article. "Are you familiar with an object called a Charon's Obol?"

"Sure, its payment the dead take into the afterlife to the river Styx," said the Witch.

"Any idea why a Greater Demon would need a Charon's Obol blessed by Hades?" asked Laila.

There was silence on the other end of the line for a moment. Finally, Lyn spoke, "I'll have to do a bit of research into that. I imagine it would only be useful to someone who is dead, perhaps with their Ghost trapped in the mortal worlds, but I feel like I've read something about this somewhere…"

"I'd appreciate it if you could pass on any information you find to me. I'll pay you of course."

"No worries, I'll let you know what I find."

"Oh, one more thing," said Laila, "would you mind keeping this between us? It's for a case I'm investigating, and the fewer people who know about this the better."

"Of course. I'll be in touch soon."

The call ended, and Laila sat there wondering what Marius was up to, and who this Izel person could be.

There was a knock on her door, and Colin poked his head into the room. "Want some company?" he asked.

"Sure, I was just trying to get caught up on some work. The doctor said I'll be released tomorrow."

"Shouldn't you be resting?" Colin stepped into the room and shut the door behind him before taking a seat in a chair next to the door.

"I feel so restless. I should be out there doing something and tracking down those Demons."

"We can handle that. You need to take it easy. You've been

through a lot in the last few weeks."

She started to protest, but he held up a hand and gave her a stern look. "You will take a week off to make sure you have fully recovered. There are too few of us for me to risk losing you again. We're a team, and we need you, but we need to make sure that you are healthy enough to work."

She knew he was right, but she didn't like the idea of sitting around for a week. She had done enough of that lately.

"What happened to the Dark Elf? The one I escaped with."

Colin folded his arms across his chest. "He insisted on flying back here with you and stayed until the doctors were able to determine what was wrong. We didn't speak much aside from when I took his statement, but he told me he had to leave and to make sure that you were okay."

"Did he mention if he was coming back?"

Colin shook his head. "He just mentioned he had business to attend to elsewhere."

She kept her face neutral, but a storm of emotion raged within her. He wouldn't just leave, would he? Or did she really mean so little to him? Perhaps she was just another fling. She was seething, but remembered Colin was still in the room, so she pushed her feelings aside.

Laila spoke with Colin for quite a while trying to figure out the details of the investigation. He seemed hopeful that the Demons they did arrest would provide them with some leads. After ten minutes of awkward and somewhat forced conversation, he rose to leave but paused by the door.

"I just want you to know that I'm really proud of what you did," he said rather stiffly. "I don't like that you had to face it alone, but I'm amazed at how well you handled it."

She nodded.

"I know that this probably wasn't the job you dreamed of," he continued, "but I think this is where you are needed the most."

They paused, staring at each other. A silent understanding passed between them. They were the only ones that stood between the citizens of L.A., and those that sought to pervert this world for their own uses. They were the ones who had to take the risk, but they would stand together as a team.

Nevertheless, she felt he was more distant and closed off than he had been before she was captured. He started to open the door, but she shut it with magic. It took more energy than expected, but she was not finished talking.

"Colin," she said, "what's wrong? Did something happen while I was gone?"

"Nothing's wrong _I—"

"Stop it Colin, I know something's up," she said glaring at him, "you can't even look me in the eye.

"I…" Colin hesitated, "I'm sorry."

He took a seat once more, but as he sank into the chair, his shoulders sagged with the weight of his troubles.

"You know you can talk to me Colin," Laila added, "I won't tell the others."

He nodded and after a long pause, he finally asked, "do you think I'm the right person for this job?"

"Why wouldn't you be?" asked Laila, surprised. "You're the one who founded this team, and you've been with IRSA since its foundation."

He nodded, but still didn't look at her. "Sure, but lately I feel like I've been letting the team down. You wouldn't have been abducted if I hadn't insisted on going into that bar without backup, and I was useless in that fight against those Demons. How am I supposed to lead this team if I can't even handle two Lesser Demons?"

He stood up and started pacing back and forth across the hospital room. "I don't have magic, or superhuman strength, I'm just a guy who can turn into a wolf, damn it!"

It suddenly occurred to Laila that Colin was a wolf without a pack of his own kind. This team was the closest thing he had to a pack, and here he was having some sort of existential crisis about his role as alpha.

"Colin," she said gently, motioning for him to sit in the chair next to her bed, "stop being so hard on yourself. Being a good leader isn't about being the strongest member of your team, it's about knowing how to best use the resources you have. You know this world far better than Ali and I do. This gives you better insight into the potential dangers and challenges we face. Sure, Darien does as well, but he's not as good at working with people as you are."

He sat in the chair, and finally met her gaze. She could see the guilt, and self-loathing in his eyes that was slowly tearing him apart.

"If I've learned something from this whole ordeal," Laila continued, "it's that you need to let people in. We are a team, we are here to help each other face whatever challenges fate has in store for us. Trust the rest of us to help you deal with these challenges. Sure, you made a bad choice, but it's in the past. So, stop feeling guilty and move on."

"How?" he said throwing his hands in the air, "how am I supposed to trust myself now."

"Start by giving yourself time to rest. Stop overworking yourself and find some hobbies, or maybe spend time with friends. Just give yourself a break. I was a lot happier after I moved here and met Ali and Erin than I was working all the time in D.C. Why don't you give yourself the chance to be happy too?"

"Maybe," he said slowly as he stood again.

On an impulse Laila grabbed his hand and squeezed it encouragingly. He gave her a small, tired smile.

"Thank you," he said, "I'll see you tomorrow."

Laila nodded and released his hand. Colin gently shut the door behind him as he left.

EPILOGUE

A month later Laila found herself standing in front of the mirror in her bathroom preparing for a night out. Once Ali decided that Laila had sufficiently recovered from her burnout, the Fae insisted on another night of clubbing. Laila considered declining, but she realized a night out might do her good.

She hadn't heard from Jerrik since he had left without bothering to say goodbye. Laila was still miffed. That was exactly why she avoided any sort of romantic relationship. But Ali and Erin were determined to pull her out of her melancholy. Tonight, Ali was taking her out to meet a group of local Fae at a club. So, she would talk, and dance, and leave the past behind her.

Laila put down her makeup and pulled on the short, skin-tight dress that they had picked out one night earlier in the week. It was dark green satin with a plunging neckline. Even if it wasn't something she would normally wear, she loved the color.

She strapped on a pair of stilettos and headed downstairs. Ali waited in the kitchen, dressed to impress in a sexy red dress.

"Damn! Look at you!" she said, winking at Laila, who

snorted.

Much to Ali's surprise, Erin was dressed for the night as well.

Ali finished her coffee and set the mug in the sink.

"All right, ladies! The club awaits!" Ali made a grand gesture towards the garage.

"I'm glad you're back. Now we can suffer through this together." Erin rolled her eyes as she followed Ali to the car.

Laila grinned. She was back with her new friends and coworkers, relatively unscathed save for the curious scars from her miraculously healed wound. She had managed to find a major Demon group and helped to shut down their illegal business.

They were heading to the door when their newly acquired scrying glass rippled. The scrying glass was a gift from her parents shortly after she had escaped from the Demons. It was their way of ensuring they could directly contact Laila.

Now the image rippled like the surface of a pond. Laila sighed and waved her hand over the glass, activating the mirror's enchantment. When the image stilled, Laila found herself looking at her mother.

"I see you are preparing to leave," Ragna said, eyeing her daughter's clothing.

"Yes—" Laila started.

"I won't be long. I just wanted to inform you that progress is going well in the search for the Dragonling's parents."

Laila and Ali exchanged surprised glances.

"The Dragons I have spoken to have been very helpful," her mother continued, "and they appear to have found someone. They have assured me he will make contact soon. Other than that, I have no more information at this time."

"Thank you!" Ali said.

Ragna simply nodded before her image vanished.

"I can't believe it!" Ali said, hugging Laila. "Your mom did it!"

"I knew she could," Laila smiled.

Spirits lifted, the three women headed out into the night to celebrate.

While Laila may not have captured Marius, they had saved the lives of many men. To top that off, they could now expect to hear from the Dragons, in order to get Erin the help she needed.

There was still so much to do and so many questions left unanswered. She would find Marius and make sure that justice was served for the crimes he had committed. But in the meantime, she had enough on her plate adjusting to her life and job in the city, and she was planning to make the most of it.

The End

CHARACTERS

Laila Eyvindr – An Elf hired by the Inter-Realm Security Agency (IRSA). She is young for an Elf, appearing, to be in her mid-twenties by human standards, but is really eighty-three years old. Laila is a trained warrior in both physical and magical combat. She is determined, hard-working, caring, and passionate.

Colin Grayson – A Werewolf in his mid 30's with brown hair, short beard and grey eyes. He is a descendent of Shifters, who have lived amongst humans in hiding for generations. He is the supervisor of the IRSA team, and has been a part of the organization since its founding.

Alastrina Fiachra (Ali) – A Fae woman with long curly golden hair, and purple eyes. Like Laila, Ali is an IRSA agent, but she has been around for much longer and has adjusted to life in Midgard. Ali's parents died a few years ago, so she cares for her adopted little sister, Erin. Ali knows how to have a good time and loves the Los Angeles nightlife.

Darien Pavoni – A male Vampire with black spiky hair, pale
skin, and red eyes. Darien is another member of the
IRSA team, and Laila's partner in most investigations.
He is arrogant, and may not always make the most
professional decisions, but he genuinely cares about the
work he does. In 1724, he died in a duel and was turned
into a Vampire.

Erin Fiachra – A young Dragon who is trapped in her human
form. She is Ali's adopted sister, and appears to be about
thirteen, but is actually around sixty years old. She's had
difficulty contacting other Dragons to discover why she's
stopped ageing, is unable to use magic, and lacks the
ability to shift.

Einar – An Elven worker at the Alfheim Consulate in Los
Angeles.

Arduinna – The Celtic goddess of the Black Forest in Germany. She is a friend of Ali's, and is down to earth and wise.

Orin – The Fae man who owns the Club La Fae. He's cheeky,
but a reliable informant.

Carlos – A human, and one of Ali's informants in the Old City.

Ragna Eyvindr – Laila's mother who works in the court of the
Elves.

Lyn – A human Witch who lives in Los Angeles. She owns a
shop in Venice Beach called Lyn's Charms and Remedies.

Jerrik Torhild – A Svartálfr (plural: Svartalfar) or Dark Elf imprisoned in the same cellblock as Laila.

Torsten – A fatherly Dwarf, also imprisoned in the same cellblock as Laila. He works as a weapons smith.

Unknown Goddess – Appears to be watching Laila.

Marius – A.K.A. the Master of the Games. He's Fae and is the Greater Demon in charge of the illegal fight ring.

Mato – A Bear Shifter imprisoned with Laila.

Henrik – A Mörkö (ice creature) who is another prisoner.

Klaive – A mysterious creature with a human appearance, and psych magic. He was also imprisoned by the Demons.

Izel – Unknown. Connected to Marius and the Demons.

WORLDS

Asgard – World of the Gods.

Vanaheim – World of the Ancient Gods.

Alfheim (pronounced "ALF-hame;") – World of the Elves,
 Fae, Dragons and nature-related beings. Large cities of
 note include:
 Ingegard – Elven City
 Tír na nÓg – City of the Fae

Earth (or Midgard) – The world of the humans. For millennia it was off limits to the other worlds as humans and
 other creatures of this world were not gifted in magic or
 strength. Over time, the humans have become a force
 to reckon with as they created amazing technologies
 that rivaled the magic that others possess. The people
 of Alfheim were the ones who proposed the truce that
 would keep the human world safe from the other worlds.
 There are creatures like human Vampires, human Shifters, and a hand full of other creatures who have man-

aged to stay under the radar during the era before The
Event.

Svartalfheim (pronounced "SVART-alf-hame;") – The world
of Dark Elves or Svartalfar, Dwarves, and creatures of
the earth. They are known for their mines and craftsmanship.

Jotunheim – The world of brutish creatures like Trolls and
Giants. They are constantly at war with the races of
Alfheim or other worlds.

Muspelheim – The world of the Dammed, also known as Hell.
The inter-realm prison where the worst criminals are
banished. There is a political organization that has risen
to power within this world known as the Demons. They
have begun to gain connections in the other worlds,
particularly Earth, and have begun to plot their escape
and rise to power.

CAN'T WAIT FOR MORE?

Want monthly access to advance announcements, exclusive content and more? Check out Kathryn Blanche's Patreon page for more information!

patreon.com/kathrynblanche

ABOUT THE AUTHOR

Kathryn Blanche makes her debut as an author with Caught by Demons, the first book in her series Laila of Midgard. In addition to writing in cafes, Kathryn can also be found traveling around the world, working in the theatre, and indulging her love of martial arts and stage combat. She has trained with professionals from Los Angeles to New York, and even as far away as London, and Moscow.

FOLLOW KATHRYN BLANCHE FOR UPDATES ON NEW RELEAS-ES, EVENTS, AND MORE!

Website: www.kathrynblanche.com
Email: contact@kathrynblanche.com
Facebook: @LailaofMidgardSeries
Instagram: @kathryn_blanche
Twitter: @_kathrynblanche

THE ADVENTURE CONTINUES IN...

SUMMONED
BY
DEMONS

LAILA OF MIDGARD
❖ BOOK 2 ❖

BY

KATHRYN BLANCHE

CPSIA information can be obtained
at www.ICGtesting.com
Printed in the USA
BVHW070953051119
562314BV00012B/25/P

9 781732 665118